Control+ALT+Delete

Hashtag Magic

Blue Screen of Death

Control+Alt+Delete

Hashtag Magic

Control+ALT+Delete

J. Steven Young

Chapter One

A heavy mist still hugged the ground and shifted around the artificial tombstones and mausoleum staged in the side yard of the Stevens' home. Hours quickly passed since the last of the guests departed from the block-party style fundraising festival Colby and his club organized. Beyond the rows of houses and trees that obscured the view of Lake Shore Drive, the barely audible motors of few passing vehicles was the only noise breaking the stillness of the early morning darkness.

A strained squeak followed by a hushed click echoed around the yard. The noise was soon followed by a muffled padding in the grass. The mists began to swirl as the fur covered question mark cut through it, forcing the ground clinging fog to separate before folding back in its wake. Two glowing yellow eyes caught the moon's light as it floated down past its midpoint of travel across the star-filled sky.

The Russian blue cat leaped up to perch atop one to the tombstones and moaned deeply before releasing a single abrupt yowling call. He waited.

Minutes passed in silence, the only noise a slight buzz followed by a muted pop as Fizzlewink transformed into his blue-skinned small statured self. He twirled his favored eyebrow in time with his eyes that darted around, scanning the darkness.

"I have wondered how long it would be until I heard from you," a voice called as his shadowy outline stood out against the rising fog behind him.

Fizzlewink jumped at the sudden voice. He was surprised because he did not sense the man's approach.

A chuckle escaped the man's mouth. "You are slipping old friend."

Gathering himself in a feeble attempt to compose his dignity, Fizzlewink shifted around but remained seated. "We have never been friends."

"Regardless of our working relationship, you have failed to contact us as expected. Why now?"

"I have been rather occupied with the boy."

The man was not convinced. "I can see that. He has progressed dangerously fast."

Fizzlewink sat up defensively. "That is not my doing. He is more powerful than we calculated."

"A turbulent child with a temper is dangerous with a weapon of magic. You will teach him to control his emotions or he will be dealt with by others." The dark tone of the man's voice left little to interpret.

"He will be controlled and malleable as promised." Fizzlewink jumped down from his perch and started to walk away. His steps halted at the sound of the man clearing his throat. "Was there something more?"

"Are you certain you have the stomach for this Fizzlewink? You were quite vocal in your protests when the child was discovered."

"There are other variables at play that we did not account for," Fizzlewink protested. "There are Shizumu out of bounds and congregating everywhere in the area." Fizzlewink heard no response from the man, which meant he already knew. "Then there is the arrival of the Dreggs."

That got the man's attention. Fizzlewink, though he couldn't make out the features of the man from the way his shadow stiffened, could tell this was news to his late night visitor.

"When?"

"They were here last night," Fizzlewink paused as he watch the man's obscured head dart around, looking for signs of the beasts. "This was the third or fourth time they showed themselves to the boy."

"The boy has been working with them?"

"Heavens no, but they are drawn to him like a moth to the flame for some reason. And lucky since there was a seeker here tonight and it wasn't normal."

The man said nothing for several moments. When he did speak, there was a tightening to his tone and a hastening in his words. "You have a job to do, that hasn't changed. I will inform the others and they will deal with the Dreggs and discuss the seeker."

Fizzlewink stood, blinking. "I will do as I agreed."

"Then you are prepared to prove your worth?" the man asked.

Fizzlewink did not speak but nodded slowly.

"You will retrieve something for me. A small token to prove you will do as you are told."

Fizzlewink noticed the man said 'me' and not us. He wasn't sure what it meant but filed it away for later consideration.

"What would you ask of me beyond what part I have already conceded to play?" Fizzlewink attempted to conceal the worry, but his voice betrayed the sinking of his emotions.

"I have come to know that a certain object, a watch, has come into the boy's possession. Something once belonging to that traitor Jarrod." The man paused but only long enough to see the understanding in Fizzlewink's eyes. "Good, I see you know what I'm referring to. You will go and fetch it for me. Now."

Fizzlewink didn't like being in this situation, but he had little recourse. "Wait here."

He didn't bother changing form as he sullenly walked around the back of the house, shoulders sagging and head down. As quietly as he exited earlier he doubled his efforts at silencing his actions this time. Fizzlewink entered the house and with slow, stealthy, deliberate steps, making his way through the first floor to the stairs. He paused only long enough to make certain he hadn't disturbed the old witch sitting in the living room chair.

Nana sat with her head back and mouth wide open, taking in deep nasal breaths and exhaling with a vibrating rattle that would rival a buzzsaw.

Fizzlewink shook his head and proceeded to ascend the stairs, careful to avoid those that creaked. Once at the top of the first flight, he picked up his pace at the sound of a low howl outside. He took that to be a signal to hurry along.

The second door on the right, slightly ajar, was his destination. As he crept along and stayed in the shadow along the wall, Fizzlewink slinked into the room and scanned around for the watch. Colby had not been wearing it lately, but it wouldn't be far from him.

As he suspected, Fizzlewink spied the watch on the nightstand beside a radio alarm clock. In a silent burst of movement, Fizzlewink shifted position to stand before the watch, hand poised to snatch it up, but he hesitated. Another howl in the yard raised the hairs on his neck.

With a wave of his hand and a mumbled word, Fizzlewink dashed off and exited the room, shoving his hand in his front pocket. In his haste, he failed to notice the door just before the stairs open and a robed figure step out into his escape route.

"What are you doing, lurking around at nearly three in the morning?" Aria asked while yawning and rubbing her eyes.

"Off to see a man about a mouse," Fizzlewink said as he rushed past her and bound down the stairs.

"Don't mess in my garden!" Aria hissed. "Why can't he use a toilet like any normal person?"

Fizzlewink heard her but chose to ignore the comment. He had to get outside before his visitor made any more noise to draw attention.

Once outside, Fizzlewink found the man where he left him, only his hand escaped the shadow of the tree he stood beside.

"Excellent," the man said as Fizzlewink slowly handed over the prize. "We've searched for this a very long time."

"It's just an old watch," Fizzlewink said though he suspected differently. His eyes never left the timepiece as the man fondled and rotated it in his hand.

The man placed the watch in his pocket. "We'll be in touch." The man turned and disappeared into the darkness leaving Fizzlewink alone and glaring.

Once he felt it safe, Fizzlewink let out a long held breath and smiled.

He turned to head back to the house when he heard the muffled scream and sounds of struggle. He dashed below the closest bush as he transformed back into his cat façade.

The moments dragged on as he peered into the darkness and sniffed the air. There was no more noise, not even the buzz of cars on the drive nearby could be heard. Fizzlewink cautiously eased out from under the bushes when a rough hand took hold of the back of his neck and lifted him off the ground, dispelling his guise.

Feet dangling far from the ground, Fizzlewink felt the hot and foul breath of his assailant. The stench was unmistakable and only one thing could catch him by surprise when being right on top of him. He opened his eyes to stare directly into the cold, and depthless glare of the Dregg that Colby called Conrad.

"What have you done little man?" Conrad asked. He lifted his other hand to dangle the watch by its band as he held it between his fingers.

Before Fizzlewink could answer, steam began to rise from the place where Conrad held the watch. The face of the timepiece began to glow. As the intensity grew, both the Dregg and Shizumu tried to keep watching the item against the protest of their own eyes wanting nothing more than to retreat behind tightly closed lids.

In a flash, the watch was gone.

"That was unexpected," was all Fizzlewink could think to say.

"I think it past time we took a more active interest," Conrad said. "You will tell me what is happening."

Fizzlewink wiggled to get free, but it was no use. His skin burned where the Dregg held him. "I will tell you nothing."

The Dregg laughed, a deep and a low rumble. "You forget what the Dreggs were created to accomplish and what we can do. We shall see who has the cat's tongue before we are satisfied."

Conrad shoved Fizzlewink into a sack he pulled from his shoulder. Cinching it closed, he swung the sack around to his back then added a satisfied grin to his hard-featured face when he heard the grunt from inside the bag.

***

Colby woke suddenly and with a jerking start as he felt a pull on him. Not a physical pull, but one that reached into his being and yanked slight and quick as though plucking a stray hair. As his eyes opened, he thought he saw a flash or reflection, but couldn't find the source once his eyes adjusted to the light pouring in from the moon through the window.

He looked at the clock on his bedside table. Seeing it was not yet four in the morning, he grumbled but smiled slightly when he caught a glimpse of his father's watch next to the clock. The watch's crystal face reflected the blue-green light of the digital display of his alarm clock.

He fluffed his pillow and nestled back under the covers before closing his eyes and drifted back to sleep. He had a full few weeks at school ahead planning for Mexico and he needed his rest. Soon it would be Thanksgiving break which was the start of several holidays that ushered in winter, the last season before the upcoming spring trip.

Chapter Two

"Before we break for Thanksgiving, We should go over the results of the fundraising efforts," Rigel said. He stood before the members of the Archeology Club with the ledger for the club bank account. He opened the ledger and handed it to Colby.

Colby didn't notice the ledger held out in front of him. His eyes were transfixed on the red marks that appeared on Rigel's neck as he shifted and the collar of his shirt moved. Four diagonal marks slanted down the right side of Rigel's neck while a single, wider one angled back from the other side.

Rigel stiffened and pushed up his collar while shaking the ledger to shift Colby's attention. Once Colby took the book, Rigel moved back to his desk where the lighting was less revealing.

Colby scanned down to the total and grimaced, his eyes reflecting the defeat he felt within. "This isn't nearly enough. I thought we would have made more from the haunted house."

Taking the ledger back, Rigel closed it and set it back down. "There were some refunds issued to some attendees who were turned away from entering the yard at some point. Word of a disturbance spread and the line for tickets thinned a bit." Rigel narrowed his eyes at Colby and then Gary. "Did something happen because I don't recall hearing anything besides some pranksters in tall goblin-like costumes causing a stir in the yard."

Colby knew Rigel was referring to the Dreggs, but he shrugged his shoulders displaying his ignorance to what happened. "So we should have another fundraiser after the holidays?" he asked.

Rigel accepted the suggestion, but his eyes lingered on Colby. He held his stare until Colby sat down and looked at Gary. "I suppose we have no other business for now, so I will see you all just before the Christmas and New Year holidays break for a final meeting of the year."

The kids got up to leave, but Colby felt a firm hand on his shoulder.

"Colby, stay for a moment," Rigel said. "There is something I wish to discuss with you."

Colby looked at Gary, who shrugged and pointed at his phWatch. Colby knew his friend wanted to listen so without yet turning toward Rigel to respond, he initiated a call to Gary's device. When the connection was made, he caught Gary's 'thumbs up' as he left the room. Colby then turned to the professor.

"What can I do for you Rigel?"

Rigel laid his hand on the ledger and looked into Colby's eyes. He stood and walked around the desk to stand far too close for Colby's comfort. Rigel pointed to the ledger without taking his eyes off Colby.

"Who were those characters at the haunted house? Did you hire or recruit them to volunteer and scare off half the crowd?"

When Colby began to speak, he was cut off as Rigel continued.

"Not that I blame you for their antics, but I wish you would have introduced us so that we could have prevented the unfortunate turn in our fundraising." Rigel held his stare for a few more moments, almost daring Colby to say anything to explain. "Small matter under simpler circumstances, but we will have to work much harder if you wish this spring trip to happen."

Colby felt he was being scolded by Rigel, a man he barely knew and did not have reason to trust. His hands began to tingle. 'I have to get out of here,' he thought. When Rigel stepped back, Colby pushed past him and stopped only as he felt the shock when Rigel reached to intercept him.

"Ouch," Rigel said. "What the bloody hell was that?" Rigel pulled his hand back and looked at Colby with wide eyes.

"Static or something, is it dry in here?" Colby hoped his obvious lie would pass. When Rigel said nothing, Colby continued to the door.

"Colby…" Rigel said. "I see you no longer wear your father's watch in favor of that new gadget. My offer still stands."

Colby rolled his eyes and huffed before turning back to the professor. "I have no interest in parting with my father's watch." When Rigel opened his mouth to continue, Colby interrupted him. "And no, there are no journal's laying around either." Colby spun on his heels and walked out the door. "Good day Professor," he said in his best British accent then hurried off to find Gary outside waiting.

"What was that all about?" Gary said. He grabbed Colby's arm and they headed out of school for home.

As they walked to the bus stop, they talked about what transpired in the science lab with Rigel. Again he pressed about the journals, but Colby could not understand the man's fascination with the old watch. Gary mentioned that he was likely a persistent and avid collector that did not take no for an answer, but Colby felt different. There was something about the Professor's prodding that made Colby feel unsettled.

By the time the two reached the Stevens' home, Colby had replaced his worry with excitement. Tomorrow was Thanksgiving and Gary would be staying with the Stevens family while his parents were away on a business trip. It was also among the few times of the year his mother sobered up to spend the day in the kitchen cooking, a reprieve from Nana's culinary disasters.

As the two boys made their way up the stairs to the back porch, the smell of pumpkin pie and apple cider mingled as it wafted out the partially open kitchen window. The autumn breeze carried the delicious smells down to greet the ravenous teenage boys. The two of them looked at one another with wide grins before sprinting to the door.

The blend of spices and herbs that permitted the space within the kitchen was a symphony that propelled Colby and Gary into an olfactory induced bliss as they stumbled through the door and into the kitchen. They roamed from counter to stove then to the island and finally the table, gathering in the aromatic joy that each dish added to the air. Cinnamon, apple, and cardamom wafted from the one dish that was Colby's favorite.

Colby reached to pluck an edge from a dish of strudel only to retract said hand shaking the sting he received from the back of a wooden spoon.

"Keep your grubby little fingers off, this is all for tomorrow," Nana said. "Go wash up and change for dinner. Pizza will be here when Shelly and Bruce get back from the diner."

"Pizza? With all this just begging to be eaten?" Gary spread his hands wide gesturing at all the food around the kitchen. "If this is all for tomorrow, who else is coming to help eat it?"

Aria turned from the stove after dialing down a burner and setting aside her spoon. "Most of this food is for the local food pantry. I thought that this year we would help feed some less fortunate souls and you boys will be helping to serve these dishes." She held up her arms to stop the mounting arguments. "We will eat tomorrow evening after we deliver this food and help with the first sitting. There will be plenty to eat tomorrow so don't be greedy." She slid the strudel toward Colby and motioned for him to take a slice. "That, however, is for home since it's your favorite."

Colby swallowed hard, looking into his mother's face. He saw the light behind her eyes that was missing for as far back as he could remember. He was tempted to wait, wanting to wash his hands first, but he could see his mother's effort to make up for lost time. He held back and blinked the moisture collecting in his own eyes.

"Thank you," was all he could manage. Colby took a slice for himself and Gary before accepting a kiss on the forehead from his mother.

The boys retreated to Colby's room to wash up before heading down for pizza and food packing chores for the next day. In the meanwhile, Colby had some thinking to do about what to get his mother for Christmas. Every year he wracked his brain to find the perfect gift and each time since his early childhood, they went unopened or set aside unceremoniously. This year would be different, he could feel the change in his mother and that meant he had to outdo his past efforts and come up with something remarkable.

He jotted down some ideas, none really working for him. Gary offered suggestions, but Colby graciously declined. He wanted to come up with something on his own. Before long he had a pile of crumpled papers on the flow of all his failed ideas. He gave up only after being called down for dinner.

After they all had finished dinner, the Stevens and Gary began the work of transferring all the food to disposable containers they could take to the pantry. They were only staying for the first sitting of people and wouldn't be there later to take home any empty dishes. Nana preferred having everything cleaned up that same evening anyway so they wanted containers that could be left behind.

Soon the table and counters were stacked high with large foiled disposable pans filled with food and ready to be delivered. Bruce and Shelly had liberated most of the containers that they used from the diner. They were kept there for catering purposes, which it never seemed anyone wanted from the greasy spoon of an establishment. It was fine for takeout and a quick lunch or dinner, but when it came to catering a party it wasn't anything special to present to guests.

With that work completed and the cars loaded, Shelly and Bruce drove each of their cars uptown to the soup kitchen deliveries dock to drop off the food. That left Gary and Colby to finish helping clean the kitchen and then off to play some video games before bed.

"Rest up boys, tomorrow will be very busy and early," Aria said. She gave them each a peck on the cheek and sent them upstairs.

"You're in a good place today," Nana said. She poured herself a glass of wine and offered one to Aria.

Aria smiled and declined the drink.

Nana smiled back and swung her glass up to drink, keeping her eyes on Aria while doing so. Something was different about her daughter lately. Not bad, but different.

The often poorly named dregs of society gathered outside the food pantry on the North side where Colby entered with his family and friend. Lines formed of people anxiously awaiting to feast on the food inside that teased them as the wafts of fragrant air flowed out the door with every ingress of volunteers. Colby could not help but glance at the look of those awaiting the first sitting. Faces, smudged and dirty, carrying the life of the streets and the struggle to survive in their suspicious eyes and pursed lips. Though they watched with trepidation, the promise of the meal within combined with the flavor-rich scents that escaped the doors, elicited a steady flow of saliva and licking of lips in anticipation.

After Colby closed the door and entered the hall, Nana shoved an apron into his gut and pointed him and Gary toward the kitchen. He smiled when his eyes met Nana's and his gaze caught the slight twinge at the corners of her eyes causing her crow's feet to lengthen. She was in her element, Colby admitted to himself, serving food and watching people enjoy a good meal. Thank goodness she didn't cook any of it, he thought. He saw Nana's twinkling eyes narrow as she pointed again for the kitchen. Could she have read my mind just then, he wondered. Witches.

Colby grabbed Gary and pulled him along to the kitchen where he found his mother, Shelly, and Bruce already preparing plates.

"Put those on and shake a leg boys," Aria said.

Her eyes were bright and full of life, Colby noticed immediately. Warmth spread through his body as he absorbed the changes his mother was going through over the past months. Moisture fell over his eyes and began to blur his vision. Colby wiped his eyes then donned his apron and shoved Gary when he held a shaking fist to his own eyes.

"Cry me a river…" Colby had heard Gary croon before he introduced the back of his hand to the back of Gary's head.

"Let's get these plates out. The first of our guests are being seated." Colby grabbed two plates and shoved them toward Gary before retrieving two more and leading the way into the makeshift dining hall.

Colby eased out the door using his backside to push the door open. The plates he carried crashed to the floor and burst into pieces at his feet. His eyes remained fixed on the dilated pupils of the Dregg he came to identify as Conrad.

"Why are you here?" Colby watched Conrad's face tighten as he clenched his jaw. "People will see you."

"You need not worry young maker, like these cast-offs we Dreggs are looked over even by those with which we are associated." Conrad allowed a curl to form at the corner of his mouth. "Besides, only those with the active gift are able to catch a glimpse of our true form… if we wish it."

Colby held on to the last few words, searching for meaning. He wondered what that meant 'if we wish it', but he didn't feel Conrad would answer a direct question without a riddle. "That doesn't explain why you are here. I somehow doubt that my presence is just a coincidence."

Colby stepped back as Conrad lifted his arm. The sudden shudder that ran through his body surprised him. There was nothing menacing about Conrad beyond his true features that remained hidden from mundane eyes by the power of Emassa, but Colby still felt a deep trepidation about this creature and his ilk.

Conrad's arm extended out and away from Colby, pointing toward the television mounted on the far wall. "You must do something about this."

Colby squinted at the television and saw that there was a press conference of some type playing out on the screen. He was unsure what Conrad meant, but found the creature gone when he turned to question further. All he saw was the back of the Dregg as he exited the hall and the face of his sister twisted in disgust as she also watched the beast leave carrying a takeaway.

"What was that thing doing here?" she asked.

"A ghoul's gotta eat," Colby muttered then made his way through the crowded space, bumping and pushing through the throngs of homeless and less fortunate that feasted. He paid no attention to the complaints as he shoved his way toward the television, realizing who was standing behind the podium speaking to the press.

His eyes narrowed and he glared at Mr. Bodine, Jasper's father, and President of the software company that's software was causing the blue screen of death. Colby held up his finger to silence both Gary and Shelly as they arrived questioning what the matter was. He flicked his upright finger toward the screen and in an instant, the volume increased without Colby's direct touch.

"Did you-" Gary started.

"Quiet," Nana said holding the television remote. "I want to hear what the tool in the tweed suit is saying."

They all listened as Mr. Bodine spoke to the press about the growing cases of computer users experiencing blackouts and seizures in conjunction with the operating system fault display known as the blue screen of death. He droned on and on about endless testing and remediation of releases and patches. The corporate policy was plain in his words, they would take no responsibility for the odd behavior of computers running their software. "There are signs leading to a virus created by some malicious party to unknown ends."

When questioned about any hard evidence of a virus or malware, the President of MacroTECH declined to provide further information.

"Well isn't that something…claiming no responsibility," Gary said.

Colby squinted at the television until at last the screen changed to another story. "There is something odd about Jasper's dad, I just can't figure it out yet."

Nana grunted and turned the station to a holiday special program that provided a happier background to the festivities. "Can't smell nothing through television…yet, but I can certainly recognize an ass when I hear one and can almost smell the pile of bull."

Chapter Three

By the time the Stevens and Gary made it back to the house for their own Thanksgiving dinner, they were both exhausted and ravenous.

Colby and Gary dashed into the kitchen and were within striking distance of a bowl of candied nuts, when they were stopped in their tracks by a shrill and piercing scream.

"You two keep your filthy mitts off that food until you've cleaned up," Shelly shouted. "You both have the worst serving skills of any I've seen. More food ended up on your clothes and the floor than most patrons' bellies."

Though Shelly frightened Gary enough to stop, Colby wasn't so easily dissuaded. Ignoring her, Colby reached out for the nearest treat and was rewarded with a sharp pain on the back of his hand.

As the welt formed, Colby looked to his Nana. She shook her head and looked over at Shelly walking to the kitchen sink. He glared at her before noticing she wasn't wearing her phWatch. Thinking she used her smartphone version of the hashtag magic app, he scowled and followed Gary upstairs to wash up and change for dinner.

Aria smiled and stifled a giggle as she passed her mother, whose eyebrows were raised. "Something wrong mother?"

Glaring, Nana followed Aria and helped begin warming their dinner. "Jury's still out."

While the boys returned and began setting the table using the good china that Shelly retrieved from the cabinet, they all began discussing what Mr. Bodine said on the television. He spoke about the mysterious effects of the so-called malware spreading via his company's operating system.

"I don't believe a word of it myself," Aria said. "A computer program that causes people to seize and possibly spontaneously combust… that makes no sense at all." She looked at Colby as she finished her statement. A raised eyebrow inviting his thoughts on the matter.

Both surprised by his mother's interest and the fact she was paying attention, Colby stuttered before answering. "It is possible."

"How so?" Aria asked.

"A seizure can be triggered in many people under the right conditions. Strobe lights, repeating patterns, odd frequencies of sound, and perhaps many other things science and medicine have yet to discover. I think that the repeating symbols and flashes of light along with the pattern that accompanies the blue screen of death can trigger something within those people susceptible." Colby was being careful not to expand his theories to involve the mystical side of his new world. Though his mother was coming out of her liquor induced days of denial, he wanted to tread lightly.

"Oh is that all?" Aria asked. "And what of the reports of people burning up? There is something more magical involved in my opinion."

Everyone stopped what they were doing and stared at Aria. It was the first time she openly said the word magic and her strongest admission to what was happening.

"Oh, don't you all look at me like that. I may have been boozed up and in denial, but that doesn't mean I haven't been paying attention."

Nana stood at the stove stirring with one hand, the other propped on her protruding hip. "Well, look who decided to finally join the party."

Colby caught the tone of sarcasm but didn't understand the meaning of his grandmother's words.

Aria understood the baited statement but decided not to bite. "Colby has his magic. We all can see that. Now we just need to figure out why it happened now and where to go with it."

Shelly listened and watched the play between her mother and Nana, but held her tongue until now. "When did you know?"

"I knew as soon as that flea ridden cat started showing up again," Aria said and returned to whipping the sweet potatoes, pouring in a few extra fingers of bourbon. "Why your father ever trusted that old mouse chaser is beyond me."

"That isn't what I meant," Shelly said. "I meant, when did you know about our magic and what would happen?"

Aria ran her finger along the whisk and scooped off a booze-filled dollop of potatoes. Licking her finger clean and smiling at the taste, Aria laid the wiry utensil down and turned to Shelly, now standing near Colby and Nana.

"I've always known. There was just never a good time to talk about it. It was just me after your father left and I was too self-absorbed and grief-stricken. I succumbed to that grief and washed away my worries with spirits to avoid the ones that haunted me."

"Oy," Nana said. "Just you…If it weren't for me being here, these kids would have starved and gone off in dirty clothes."

Seeing that her statement wasn't fully addressing the question, Aria stiffened and ignored her mother's statement. "One day you will understand, but for now you will take what I say as truth. I have shirked at my duties in the past, but those days are behind us. I'm here now and we will face this together."

Silence followed for many minutes before Gary finally broke the stillness in the room. "What is it we are, dealing with? Do you know?"

Aria smiled at Gary and then looked at her son. "I have my suspicions. I think you do as well my son?"

"The Shizumu?" Colby said softly.

Aria nodded and smiled. "And what have they to do with this blue screen computer nonsense?"

"I don't know yet, but I plan to find out," Colby answered her questions with more conviction now.

Aria lifted the bowl of sweet potatoes and nodded for her mother and the others to help bring the food to the table. "I will do what I can to help, starting with the tool in tweed."

Confused, Colby looked at his mother wondering what she had in mind. "What are your powers?"

Aria laughed. "I was thinking something a little less direct and exposing. It just so happens my new temp job assignment is an administrative assistant position at MacroTECH."

"Since when?" Shelly asked, noticing her mother's circling around a direct answer to Colby's question.

"I start Monday," Aria said with a conspiratorial smile. "I'll work from within the belly of the beast gathering information."

"Using magic?" Shelly asked and looked at Colby.

He confirmed that he too noticed his mother's avoidance of answering what magic she possessed.

"Using my ears and eyes dear," Aria said as she watched her children glance at one another. "Now let's eat this well-deserved meal after we give thanks and…" Aria lifted a paper lunch bag from the table. "Everyone will pick a tool."

Colby wondered where the bag came from for only a moment, before realizing what it represented. A warm and genuine smile spread across his face as his eyes widened. It was an old family game. The name of a kitchen utensil would be written on pieces of paper within the bag. Each person would pick a piece and whatever they drew, they would have to use throughout the meal to eat with. There would be no forks or knives, regular spoons, or anything else easily used to scoop up food to eat normally.

Colby laughed.

Shelly hated this game, but she smiled despite herself. She drew her slip of paper to reveal the word 'egg beater'.

"Crap."

Everyone had their own implements for eating. Nana got the spatula. Aria held her tongs. Gary fumbled with a melon baller while Colby looked at his zester quizzically.

Nana dipped her spatula into the bowl in front of her, cursing as the liquid spilled over the sides. She licked the few drops that remained and grumbled. "This is gonna take all night."

Shelly was fairing poorer as she dipped and lifted her small whisk ended egg beater and frowned.

Gary and Aria were doing no better with their own devices, sharing glances and laughs that soon turned into grunts.

While the others grumbled and fussed over trying to start with the first course of squash soup, Colby held his zester out and pushed a hashtag spell in its direction, #PlugHolesAndCurve.

Aria watched with a smile as a shimmering film layered over Colby's new eating utensil, blocking off the many holes. Slowly the metal above the handle curved enough to allow Colby to dip the makeshift spoon into his bowl.

"Not fair!" Shelly said. "That's against the rules."

"Since when?" Colby said. "Nothing in the rules ever said you can't augment the tool with magic."

Shelly scowled at first but then grinned and decided to work her own spell. After a few moments, her construct became clear and she entered the hashtag into her phone, #MetalSpreadAndJoin.

Nana laughed. Though she couldn't yet use active magic, she decided to bend the rules herself and held her spatula over a candle until the plastic began to sag into a dip. "When in Rome."

Colby smiled at Nana's attempt to adjust her utensil by mundane means. "You know Nana I could figure out how to spark your powers and-"

"No," Nana and Aria cried in unison.

Trying her best to look affronted, Nana frowned at Aria then looked at Colby. "I don't think that is a good idea my boy. If you aren't sure how you did it before, I am not of the mind to be an experiment subject."

Aria laughed. "Beside that, your grandmother's spell craft was always about as safe as her driving on a good day.”

Grunting, Nana got up and poured a nip of whiskey into her coffee. “I’ll have you know, I was the best potion maker in my hay-day you snarky little sorceress.”

“Yes well, those days have gone the way of ‘Bell, Book, and Candle’. You aren’t in the same shape you were when you meddled with that old broom of yours.”

“Seriously?” Shelly said. “All this time I made comments about you and riding a broom, you actually did?”

Nana answered by placing her favorite finger below her right eye and pulling down on the lid giving Shelly the evil-eye.

“Careful mother,” Aria warned. “No need to teach them bad habits.”

They finished dinner and laughed while making jokes about Nana’s bad driving but with a broom instead of the car. With the meal enjoyed and dishes in the washer, everyone sat at the island for dessert and conversation.

While the boys drank milk and ate cake, Shelly poured coffee for Aria, Nana, and herself. Heavy on the pumpkin spice flavored creamer and they were ready to strategize over sweets and steaming cups of joe.

“There is something about Mr. Bodine that isn’t normal,” Colby said thinking back to the television coverage earlier in the day. “When I was watching the newscast, I could have sworn he was staring directly at me.”

Aria sniffed her coffee and set down her cup. “Not likely, but I wouldn’t rule anything out if he is in bed with the Shizumu.”

This single observation roused the groups curiosity. Everyone except Nana, who got up from the island and went to her favorite cupboard to root around in her things. She did her best to feign interest, but kept her level of noise-making down enough to hear what was being discussed.

"What do you know of the Shizumu," Colby asked his mother.

Aria lifted her cup for a long drink and time to choose her words. "Stories your father shared with me mostly," she finally answered. "They are not much different from people when you get down to it."

Aria explained how they are as united in achieving their own common goals as they are individually scheming and selfish as any humans can be. What they all want is power, but to what end has never been revealed. She once knew a Shizumu, who was kind and compassionate, but equally reserved and shared little in regard to her own desires.

"Did you see any demon like aura around Mr. Bodine like you did the guy at the DMV?" Shelly asked.

Colby shook his head. He hadn't seen the same shimmer of red and menacing presence below the surface as with the other Shizumu he encountered. There was something there, but he could not figure it out. He assumed it might be the fact that he was viewing the man through the television and that somehow obscured his vision. If many a truth is found in myth and vampires could be compared to the soul consuming effect some Shizumu had, then perhaps the not showing up on film or having reflections had some shred of truth as well.

"Fizzlewink could probably tell us more," Aria said. "If he ever shows his mangy self again."

Colby shook his head as though coming out of a daze. Only then had he realized that Fizzlewink had not been seen for weeks. "Where has he been anyway?"

"I haven't seen him since just after Halloween," Nana offered. "But he's been around based on the empty cans of tuna and cartons of milk I've found left in the recycling bin."

Colby shrugged and turned from Nana back to his mother. "Why don't you like Fizz?"

"It isn't that I don't like him," Aria started. "I have never understood why your father trusted him so implicitly. Fizzlewink always speaks half truths in my past dealings with him, and now he refuses to show his true face to me. When I saw him lurking around in the night a few weeks back, he snuck off into the darkness of the yard."

"What was he doing?" Shelly asked.

"I don't know, but I don't entirely trust him or the Nefslama for that matter. We should not plan on their help without duplicity."

"So how do we put the squeeze on that bastard Bodine?" Nana blurted out. She was eager to change the subject.

"I think something subtle would be for the best mother," Aria said. "I can snoop around and make some friends. I find small talk and water cooler gossip can be a useful means of gathering 'intel'."

Aria's process pun in regards to snooping around a technology company only garnered a few sneers and boos.

Colby and Gary would handle things from the electronic side of things, tracing the connectivity through the internet and attempting to isolate and decompile the code causing the BSOD.

Nana said she would look through all her old books to find anything useful and Shelly could push some power into them with the hashtag magic app.

Shelly wished she could do more, but while working in a public place where she could easily overhear conversations, it was not as though the likes of Mr. Bodine would venture into the diner. Unless she could somehow get some ghosts to go spy for her, there was little she felt she could do that might be helpful.

"What about the son, Jasper isn't it?" Aria asked. "Do you think he can be of any help?"

Gary snorted and Colby slugged him in the arm.

"Jasper is an idiot," Colby said. "He isn't a Shizumu."

Aria smiled but saw the hurt behind Colby's words. She remembered that they were once the best of friends him and Jasper. Colby never got over how his friend suddenly left and when he returned, completely disregarded their past relationship in favor of bullying and harassing.

"That isn't what I was implying," Aria said. "Can we get any information out of him?"

Gary decided to answer to spare his friend more aggravation. "Not likely. He doesn't speak to us anymore even just to tease since our little confutation earlier this year. Besides being a brilliant strategist and Runes player, he's less useful than a saddle on a cat."

Colby smiled before letting go of a well needed laugh.

"Well, we have a few weeks before Christmas break, anything can happen," Aria said.

The reminder of Christmas sent Colby off to continue thinking of his surprise for Aria. With only a few weeks left, he had less time than he hoped.

Chapter Four

Colby counted down the days remaining before classes let out for the winter holidays. He loved school, but this time of year was his favorite, not simply because of the holidays, but because it meant a lot of time out of school and away from Jasper. So as he passed him in the hall and dealt with the hushed words and obvious glares, Colby crossed off another day from his calendar.

Against his own feelings, he tried on a few occasions to engage Jasper in conversation to see if he could get any information. His attempts were fruitless and bordered on confrontational so he gave up. Gary suggested asking Darla to speak with Jasper, suspecting she had a gift for influence over people, but Colby decided not to bring anyone else in on their game of spy vs. spy unless absolutely necessary.

Today was the last meeting for the Archeology Club until after the holidays. Colby had not spoken much to Rigel since Thanksgiving, keeping to himself in the few meetings held before today. Rigel would often try to engage him, but Colby was getting a bit annoyed at the man's incessant questions about his watch and if he could talk about his father's work. Somehow, Colby sensed that Rigel saw through Colby's half truths.

Although there were no extensive journals in his father's things in the attic, Colby suspected that Rigel would want to know about anything belonging to his father. There was something there, but he wouldn't worry about it at present. The immediate issue was to deal with the Shizumu. The blue screen of death reports had waned, but Colby figured it was only a matter of time.

As he and Gary entered the science lab where Rigel already sat waiting for the small group of members, Colby avoided him by waving to Darla and Rhea.

"Hi guys," Darla said. "Ready for the holidays?"

Colby smiled as he sat across from the girls. "Can't wait. I have a great gift for my mom and we're gonna decorate for the first time in years."

"You usually have lights and stuff," Gary said.

Colby's eyes lit up and he moved his entire body as he explained. "That was nothing compared to what we used to do. We're going all out this year. Lights, holly, wreaths, the whole shebang. We already started, but I have something special planned."

Although Gary and the girls prodded for more details, Colby pantomimed zipping his lip and throwing away the key.

Rigel watched the exchange with interest and smiled before clearing his throat. "Now that we are all settled, I'd like to first talk about what we might do to extend our fundraising efforts for the spring trip."

The smiles slowly faded from the kids faces.

"Don't despair," Rigel said. "I'm sure we can manage something. I've been searching the internet and found some very good deals on ORBITZ.com, but we still need some more funding."

Colby raised his hand. "I have an idea."

When Rigel nodded, Colby stood and turned to address everyone.

"So with all the computer issues of late, you know the crashing and blue screening, I thought we could hold a PC tune-up like an anti-malware and virus check." Colby smiled until he looked at Darla's disappointed face. "What?"

"I guess, but I really know nothing about computers in that regard. I could do other things I guess."

"Well, that's the thing, all you would have to do is start up the computers with a special disk I already made, and it will do all the work." Colby tried giving Darla a reassuring look and it seemed to work based on the return of her smile.

When everyone agreed, all that remained was scheduling the event and advertising.

"Leave the advertising to me," Rhea said. "I can make up the flyers and make my little brothers put them up all over the area. My dad works at The Reader so he can get an ad put in the paper for us."

Rigel and the kids discussed their plans for the winter break during the remainder of the meeting. Before they finished and left, Rigel went to his desk and retrieved four wrapped boxes and set one in front of each archeologist in training.

"Just a little something to keep you interested in our club over the break. You'll need these when we go to Chichén Itzá." Rigel instructed them to wait until Christmas to open them and sent them on their way.

After exiting the science lab, Colby and Gary walked the girls to their lockers before saying their goodbyes for the break and then headed off themselves. On the way out they passed Jasper, who sat brooding on the stairs outside the school.

After they had moved far enough away, Gary turned to Colby. "So what is the deal with him anyway. He isn't hanging with his 'boyz' no more, and he's been all mercurial."

They exited the school grounds and began their walk home.

Colby didn't answer, so Gary persisted. "Are you sure you don't want the girls to try-"

"Gary, I told you I don't want them involved since we don't know if they are like us yet and it isn't as though we can just ask them. As far as Jasper goes, I'm not here for it. I don't know how I would possibly get anything out of him anyway."

"Perhaps you could start by accepting the Runes rematch," came Fizzlewink's voice from the bushes along their path home.

Both the boys jumped at the unexpected voice. Though they recognized the deliberate and vibrato sound of Fizz's purring voice, they were startled just the same. Before they could respond, a scrawny and more scraggly than usual Russian-blue cat leaped out in front of them and began circling their feet as they continued their walk home.

"Fizz," Colby hissed. "Where the hell have you been?"

Walking in front of the boys, Fizzlewink tilted his head and swung it back to look at Colby. "I'm not sure if that is genuine concern or anger in your tone."

Replaying the words in his head, Colby relaxed his jaw and decided it best to wait until they reached the house before continuing on in public talking to a cat.

The remaining distance Colby and Gary spoke little as they watched Fizzlewink with questioning glances. The cat looked as though he'd been in a fight with something but didn't seem too worse for wear. Though he had clumps of dried goo in his fur and what appeared to be scratches in a few places, he seemed well enough. Every now and again, however, Colby thought he saw a slight limp as Fizzlewink favored his back right leg. Once they arrived at the Stevens' back door, the questions came without reserve.

"What have you gotten up to Fizz," Colby asked as he held the door open for Gary and Fizzlewink to enter the house.

As was a habit, Colby used the back door that led to the small mud room and then the kitchen. After school, the boys enjoyed snacks immediately upon arriving home before doing homework or playing video games.

Fizz strode into the middle of the kitchen and leaped up onto a stool at the center island. He was careful not to put too much weight on his right leg as he landed and turned to morph into his little blue man self. He realized that Colby noticed something, but he wouldn't offer unrequested information.

"Well?" Gary said to Fizz. "You've been gone for some time."

Fizzlewink feigned interest as he picked at and preened his hair, loosening dried clumps of what looked like blood from his hair and dropping them on the floor. "You never seemed so concerned before."

"Before what?" Colby asked. "You've not been gone for more than a day or two before now."

Stopping mid-scratch, Fizzlewink looked at Colby. "Boy, I have come and gone from this house for spans measured in months and more over the years since you first learned to stop messing your own pants. Never in that time did anyone in this household show the slightest bit of worry over my whereabouts."

Fizzlewink's words stung a bit, but Colby wouldn't be berated by a cat. "You were just a cat that wandered from house to house as far as we knew."

"And a cranky, ill-mannered, vagabond at that," croaked Nana from the doorway to the dining room. She looked down at the floor beneath Fizzlewink where clumps of muck and hair lay in piles. "I hope you don't expect me to clean that up."

Fizzlewink waved his hand at the mess and in an instant it was gone. He painted on his most indignant face and looked at the refrigerator while twirling his eyebrow. "Many a cat has been searched for by its human. Psst- even mongrel's like the dog next door have been seen on missing flyers. Never old Fizzlewink."

"I could go upstairs and get my violin if you would like accompaniment," Nana said as she opened the fridge and laid out a plate of fish for the melodramatic cat-man. "Eat now, talk later."

Nana gave Fizz a look that welcomed no retort or complaint. She looked at the boys and pointed toward the door, then followed them out into the living room.

"I'll deal with Sir fuzzy-butt in there after he's eaten," Nana said. "You two can go finish the holiday decorating."

Colby and Gary went off after a bit more coaching from Nana to go and finish decorating the house for the holidays. Gary would be staying with the Stevens for the duration of the winter break as his parents have again gone off on some trip, leaving their son behind. Over the years, Gary became an extended member of the Stevens' household and family due to his parents constant travels, but his stays had been getting more frequent and longer of late. No one in the house minded, but there was more than enough hushed discussion about what the sudden changes were about.

While digging through decoration boxes in the attic, Gary and Colby continued to talk about how to get information on Mr. Bodine.

"Mom hasn't gotten much," Colby said. "She is on a lower floor and apparently intra-office fraternization is restricted to one's own floor."

"They have rules for that?" Gary asked.

"Mom says it's an unspoken rule, but she said she wouldn't let it stop her."

"I just hope she stays cute, as the girls would say. If she gets too above herself, she'll draw attention." Colby didn't sound as worried as he felt. His mother was only recently clearing the fog from her self-induced break from reality at the bottom of a bottle.

"I can't help but think Fizz may be on to something," Gary said.

Without breaking from his work sorting various tangles of lights and raggedy old garland, Colby replied. "What? You agree that nobody cares about where he goes?"

"No, not that. When he mentioned the Runes rematch." Gary watched Colby's face pucker into a frown. "You've put it off long enough."

Colby fussed over a knot in some lights and threw it to the side in frustration. "With the mood Jasper's been in lately, it's likely he'll go nuts and bust my face if I even look at him wrong." He pulled a picture out of his pocket that he found earlier in a trunk. He looked at the image of his mother and father playing in the snow and smiled.

"I disagree, besides if he makes a move on you, I think Shelly would be there to go all Solange on his ass." Gary laughed at his own joke even though it barely elicited a grunt from Colby. "I think Jasper is pissed off that he didn't have the chance to beat you at Runes and is stewing."

That got Colby's attention. He knew that Jasper wasn't stupid, in spite of his past bullying to get homework from Colby. That was just laziness and whatever made Jasper single Colby out. The one thing

Jasper excelled at was strategy in Runes and he was denied the championship this past summer over a technicality that required Colby to publicly concede or challenge him at a rematch.

"Maybe you're right," Colby admitted. "If we schedule and play the match to decide the title, maybe -just maybe- Jasper will relent."

Gary clapped Colby on the shoulder. "He may even respect you for it. People like Jasper Bodine respond better to those who don't back down. He could even start coming 'round to being more agreeable."

An unexpected snort escaped Colby's nose as he laughed. "Sure, he'd be more agreeable when cat's walk on the moon."

"So we agree then. I'll take care of rescheduling the match." Gary said. "Now let's get these decorations downstairs and put up. Then you can tell me what you have planned for your mother."

"Not a chance. You keep secrets as well as Nana cooks."

The boys gathered what they needed to finish making the house look festive and carried it down the four flights of stairs and outside to the front porch. They grouped the items according to a diagram Colby drew days earlier and began putting them up on the columns and bushes.

Colby glanced around at the other houses, taking in the gaudiness of the mishmash in colored light choices, inflatables, and candy cane lights. He inwardly laughed at how some people would throw everything they had out on the lawn and assume it looked good. Colby was far more organized in the way he was decorating. He had a theme.

Clear and red lights donned all the columns in spirals from the top to bottom like larger than life peppermint twists. At the top of each candy, column was an equally enormous red bow.

All the bushes got spreads of netted white lights that twinkled rather than flashed or chased in seizure inducing rhythm. Along the eaves hung large icicle lights that alternated between five lengths. Heavy bulbs the size of bowling balls hung from the fifteen foot evergreens that grew along the boundary of the yard while veins of green lights ran through the branches.

By the time the boys finished, the yard and house outshone the others on the block, but to Colby's approval, appeared elegant and opulent at the same time. He smiled and patted the pocket that held his parent's photo.

"Only thing that's missing is a blanket of snow," Gary said.

Colby grinned at his friend and followed him inside. "Let's get some hot cocoa and cookies."

"We never ate dinner, you think your Nana will allow our dessert first?"

"She was likely too busy chewing out Fizz to cook, hopefully. Maybe mom will pick up some take-out on her way home from MacroTech."

"I don't envy Fizz right now."

Chapter Five

"Spit it out fur-ball," Nana said.

Fizzlewink dropped the piece of fish from his mouth and turned from the counter to face an irate and frazzled old witch. His eyes widened at the sight of a bar of soap and wash bin.

Nana saw the look in his eyes and then remembered the items she held in her hand. Not wanting to lose Fizzlewink's attention, she decided against correcting his assumed use for the them.

"I didn't mean the fish. What have you been up to these past weeks? And why do you look like something that you yourself dragged in?

"Cat humor, how droll," Fizzlewink answered. "I was out working on something. I do have a life outside this house you realize?"

"Don't play cat and mouse with me little man. You're making me cranky and you won't like it if I get ticked." Nana narrowed her eyes and leaned in close, nearly nose to nose with Fizzlewink. "Now spill it, and I'll know if you're lying."

Fizzlewink huffed, but the widening of his eyes, slight as it was, let Nana know he understood she was serious. She stepped back and circled the counter, taking his dish of food away. She set it on the far counter.

Fizzlewink looked at the plate and frowned. He was hungry, but he knew he would get nothing more until he gave something to the old battle ax to satisfy her inquisition. He knew she had no active ability, not currently, but it was there. Waiting. Fizzlewink didn't want to risk spelling her and inadvertently activating her gift. She was already difficult, he shuddered at the thought of how worse she would get with magic as a tool instead of a rolling pin.

Nana narrowed her eyes at Fizzlewink, as though she could hear him thinking about her. She put the rolling pin down she held in her right hand but never took her eyes off the little cat-man. She pushed the plate of fish slowly, moving it along the counter until it teetered on the edge. One wrong word from the man and she would let her solitary finger off the plate's edge allowing it to free-fall into the awaiting trash bin below.

"So what is it that has required your attention for so long and returned you to us in such a mangled mess?" Nana asked.

Fizzlewink's eyes remained fixed on the fish. "I ran into one of Colby's new followers. I believe his name is Conrad."

"The Dreggs," Nana gasped and grabbed the sides of her head.

Fizzlewink sank at the sight of his plate of fish as it plummet into the trash. "Yes the Dreggs. It appears they are quite interested in what is happening under this roof. They hung around Halloween night and snatched me up from the garden while I was out... strolling." First half truth down, ready for more.

Nana was too busy pacing the kitchen now to pay close enough attention to Fizzlewink and catch his misdirections and holes in his story. "What did they do to you?"

Fizzlewink grunted. "After they manhandled me and threw me in a rancid smelling sack, I was bounced around and knocked senseless on the way to their lair." Sensing her sudden and unexpected concern, Fizzlewink laid it on thick. "It was just awful. I wouldn't treat a dog the way they treated me, and you know how I feel about dogs."

Nana nodded as she took a clean plate from the cupboard. "Stinky poop machines, oh and the drool, disgusting." She walked to the fridge and retrieved a fresh piece of cod. Placing the fish on the plate, she set it before Fizzlewink and sat down across from him. Her eyes wide awaiting more details.

"Well, that was the easy part," Fizzlewink whispered. He looked around as though checking for eavesdroppers ready to sneak a listen to his secret tale. "They started asking me questions. If they didn't like the answer, they would start the torture."

Another gasp from Nana.

Fizzlewink settled into his fish as easily as he did his tall tale. "It would appear that they have been waiting for someone like Colby for a long time. Someone who could harness enough power to meet their needs."

"What needs have those monstrosities?"

Fizzlewink had her hooked. "Who knows for certain. It has been many human generations since I last saw the Dreggs, and even then it was limited. They have been after power of one type or another for centuries. Perhaps they want to take over or topple the government."

"What else did you learn from your time with the Dreggs? You were gone for weeks."

"Like what, their mating habits and social structure?" Fizzlewink asked sarcastically before catching his tone. He didn't want to risk losing his upper hand. "They certainly know how to hit and in the right places." He rubbed his ribs and winced for good measure.

Nana tittered and took his empty plate. "More fish?"

"Please, if it isn't any trouble." Humans, regardless of how disagreeable they can act, are as pliable as clay, he thought. "As I was saying, they beat me whenever I did not provide pleasing answers to their questions. Like when they asked me how much Colby knew about his powers and what they were meant for." He frowned. He was getting too comfortable and that last statement slipped off his tongue before he could filter it properly.

"And what did you tell them to make them so angry?" Nana asked, handing him another plate of fish.

"The truth as we know it, we simply don't know for sure. Colby has a gift that was hobbled as a toddler by his father for unknown reasons. Now he has it back, but doesn't understand it and, therefore, can't control it."

"Seems vague and truthful enough to pass," Nana said. "I wonder why they didn't like your answer?"

Fizzlewink shrugged and reached for his dinner but did not reach it before it was snatched out from below his grasp.

"Because they must understand you well enough to know that if you are speaking, you are likely lying or speaking half truths."

Nana threw the fish in the trash and put the plate in the dishwasher along with the previous plate she let fall in the garbage. She laughed.

"Did you think I was buying your little fairytale? Honestly Fizzlewink, you forget who you are dealing with."

Trying his best to appear affronted, Fizzlewink puffed up in his seat. "I spoke the truth. Perhaps my retelling is a bit foggy from the strikes I received to my head."

Nana picked up the rolling pin. "Perhaps I should knock the 'foggy' out of you."

Hands up in mock surrender, Fizzlewink told a more accurate but not fully disclosed story of his time with the Dreggs.

"What is it you didn't tell them?" Nana asked, deciding on a different approach.

Fizzlewink reiterated the story of the Nibiru. He said how he 'thinks' it has some basis, in fact, at least as far as the foretelling of a child of power who would harness the ability to open the gateway.

"This gateway, you mean back to your world and that of the Shizumu?" Nana asked.

"And many others. It allows passage between many realms. The gateways to many plains of reality because it is the true Emassa."

According to Fizzlewink and the stories passed down through the ages, the gateway is how his forefathers traveled between worlds, only they used machines mixed with the power of the Emassa to pass through. When they passed through, they traversed a energy based universe where they encountered the Shizumu. That was as best he could spin the truth of their arrival and how the Shizumu came to exist.

Their encounter with the Shizumu was not pleasant. In their escape from their realm of reality that was falling apart they inadvertently dragged them along, affecting their traversing of the gateway, landing them in the realm where the Earth resides.

Fizzlewink was actually proud of his story telling. It changed each time he told it, but the truth was much harder to swallow.

When the Shizumu attacked, they destroyed the machines used to travel and those with the knowledge to repair or build new ones, were killed. With the knowledge to get home lost, the Nefslama remained in the Earthly realm. They worked to guide mankind to a point where one day, they might be able to recreate the means to travel back to their home.

"Muses," Nana grumbled. "And what do your muses say about my grandson? I mean beyond this Nibiru nonsense… he's just an ordinary boy."

"I think we both know that isn't the case. If there is one thing Colby is, it certainly isn't ordinary. He has a gift that I predict will be unlike anything ever known to those who practice transformational physics."

"Practice what?" Nana asked, her face twisted in confusion. She jumped at the sound of a loud bang as the back door closed.

"That's a fancy phrase for magic?" Aria said as she entered the kitchen and set two large bags down. The logo on the side reading Buena Diner.

Nana took the bags and moved them to the kitchen island. "Where did you get so smart?"

"I read it on a confidential email being sent to a distribution group at work. I normally wouldn't get such a communication, but when a new friend at work asked for assistance with a macro on her word processing program, I took the liberty of snooping."

Fizzlewink's ears perked up when Aria mentioned the memo. "To who was it distributed?" he asked.

Aria looked at Fizzlewink sideways without moving her head. "I don't know yet, but I'll find out. I'm getting friendly with some key employees. Next on my list is the email support guy."

Nana smiled and patted her daughter's hand. "You're pretty good at this."

"I watch Scandal." Aria turned her hand to grasp Nana's. "So what's going on here?" She tilted her head toward Fizzlewink.

"Fizzlewink was just telling me a tale concerning his latest exploits and adventures." Nana went back to taking the food out of the bags and setting them out on the counter.

Aria looked Fizzlewink up and down. "Looks like it was…a dirty job. Perhaps you can tell us more after you go clean up. You stink." She gave him a sour look.

Fizzlewink got down and headed out the kitchen door, passing the boys as they entered.

Nana began to speak but held her tongue when she saw Colby and Gary entering the kitchen. More talk on what Fizzlewink told her would wait until she could speak to Aria alone. He was lying to them.

Colby tried to get the little man's attention but was ignored. "What's his problem?" he asked Nana.

"You're mother sent him off to bathe. You know how much cat's like water." She snorted as she laughed to herself.

Aria smiled at the boys. "The outside looks wonderful boys, I'm sure it's even more beautiful at night." She looked off into the distance. "Only thing missing is a blanket of snow."

"There's still time, Christmas is a few days off yet." Colby could see how his mother gazed past him. He didn't bother looking behind to find the focus of her stare. He knew it was a memory of which she caught a glimpse.

Aria looked past Colby to see Gary looking at them. She saw the hurt in his eyes that Colby would be with his family for the holidays while his parents were off again on one of their unexplained trips. She motioned for Gary to come closer.

"Are you alright with spending the holidays here with us Gary? You know you are as much a part of our family-"

"I'm good," Gary interrupted. "I just wish they wouldn't go away so much. It seems their odd trips are happening more often lately."

Aria smiled and nodded. "I'm sure they have good reason." She looked at her mother as though to say 'never mind'. With a peck on his cheek, she guided him to a seat and began putting the plates out for dinner. She just finished laying out four plates when the back door opened and closed.

"Set a place for me would ya?" Shelly said. "I'm not excited about eating the same food I serve all day at that sad excuse for a restaurant, but it beats the hell outta eating anything the old battle ax would cook."

Nana threw a wet sponge from the sink at Shelly, who ducked as she passed. The sopping thing hit the wall instead and slid down to the floor. "Little witch," Nana hissed.

"Old hag," Shelly answered.

Aria cleared her throat but couldn't hide her amusement. "If you despise the place so much, why don't you find something else?"

Shelly sat down and dug into the containers of take-out. "I don't really have any other experience, so unless I go back to school, my options are limited."

"Sometimes you just need to get your foot in somewhere," Nana said. "Maybe your mother can get you in at MacroTECH. She seems to be getting to know a few folks there."

Shelly and Aria both made noises of disagreement. Neither thought it a good idea to be working at the same place.

"Wait," Gary said. "That would be perfect. You could both be spies in the place."

Colby agreed. "Don't they have their own building restaurant and cafe? No better place to listen to folk's conversations."

Shelly didn't like the idea of working at yet another food joint, but she smiled at the possibilities. "If I were to agree, and I haven't said yes, it could eventually lead to something better."

"Well then," Aria said. "I'll just have to see what I can find out in HR about openings, but I won't suggest getting your hopes up." Aria half smiled at Shelly.

Shelly was stung by the hint of doubt her mother held in her voice. She was feeling doubt for weeks since Colby discovered his power. He became the center of everything and she was taking a back seat. Shelly didn't begrudge her brother his gift or even being more important, she just wanted to feel a part in everything was meant for her.

Looking around at everyone's faces, they spoke to one another, making plans, scheming. Nobody looked at her. No one suggested she do or take part in anything. Shelly felt alone in a room full of people.

Chapter Six

Dots scattered across her vision, reducing visibility to only a few feet, causing Aria to sit back from the glass of the bay window in the living room. She sat back and widened her gaze to take in the limited view of scattered spits of snow as it floated upon the light breeze but was too scare to stick and cover landscape in a blanket of white. Colors of the red, green, and white lights glistened, brightening the otherwise dark and starless night. She only wished there would be a white Christmas this year. Aria loved the snow.

As she glanced around at the surrounding neighbors' homes, Aria's vision blurred further, remembering times past when she had not the heart to deck her own halls. How silly that was, she now felt, to have withheld the joy of decorating for the winter holidays and brightening up the doldrums of this time of year when outside activities were limited by the cold. The lack of sunlight was made up by the overabundance of Christmas lights that proliferated the neighborhood. Her smile widened as she wiped the tears that collected at the corners of her eyes.

She watched her children as they sorted out the gifts beneath the Christmas tree, with its twinkling lights reflecting off the myriad of colored metallic papers and elaborate bows. The ribbons were Aria's favorite. She spent hours wrapping and decorating each package, pouring her love for the season and her children into every fold and knot. Inside, her heart and mind battled over the agony of watching her hard work preparing each gift be ripped asunder in a blink of an eye. With the elation of seeing the joy on each recipients' faces when they revealed the treasure concealed beneath the beautiful wrappings she smiled anyway.

While her smile grew, her eyes glistened. It felt as only yesterday these young adults were, but toddlers, crawling from beneath the branches and shaking gifts. The frowns on their little faces signifying their frustration at not knowing who's gift was in their hand due to Aria's secret symbols used to label them. Over the years, Colby and Shelly learned what the symbols represented, but Aria still used them regardless of the secret being lost. There was, after all, a reason she chose to use the symbols, they were part of who she was then and now, who they all are.

At long last, each of her children and Gary, whose parents were yet again out of town, chose the one gift they would open. Tradition in the Stevens' family was that on the eve of Christmas, everyone would open only a single gift leaving the remaining for the next morning after breakfast.

Aria smiled at the looks of triumph on the childrens' faces when they pointed to each symbol representing their names on the gifts. She allowed their ignorance of the entire truth behind the scribblings, for they meant a great deal more than a simple mark to identify them as individuals. Tonight was for joy and revelry long overdue; tomorrow or the next days to come would test them beyond the limits of reality. The wrinkles at the corners of her eyes relaxed as the edges of her mouth lowered, her smile fading.

Nana nudged her. "Aria, what is bothering you?"

Aria reinforced her smile and wiped her eyes as she sniffled and sat up. "Nothing mother. I am happier at this moment than I have been in so very long."

She looked at her mother sideways, careful not to linger in her eyes. The old witch would see right through her rouse if given a moment too long. She watched as Nana's eyes began to narrow then relax as she nodded and looked back to the children.

Not a moment too late did Colby squat down before her with a grin spread across his face, distracting any further investigation from her mother. His eyes extended the smile inward and displayed the eagerness in his heart for her to open the package he now laid upon her lap.

"This is from me. I want you to open it first," he told her.

She looked down at the pristinely wrapped box and lifted it to examine his work. The folds were precisely creased and even overlapping the paper below so that the embezzled glitter snowflakes perfectly matched the pattern below, blending so well as to hide where they met. Each corner was crisp and taught to the point they seemed not to be a covering over a package within, but the actual box itself. Several ribbons cascaded down the sides of the parcel in a perfect synchronistic flow as though locked in a decorative dance. The streaming ribbon followed each bend in the box and proceeded around the next corner to meet back on top, colliding and twisting into an elaborate bow.

Aria taught him how to wrap gifts, it was one of the few things she continued to enjoy in the first years following her husband's departure. Seeing the effort of her son's presentation was more gift than she could have ever wanted. A soft breath escaped her lips as she exhaled past the slight tingle that began to overtake her sinuses. Her vision shimmered as the sheen of tears poured from her eyes without warning.

"It is exquisite. I hate to destroy such artistry. The pupil has surpassed the master," she admitted. "It would seem I have at least managed to teach you something in those troubled years."

As she dried her eyes on the tissue her son provided, she noticed the room was focused on her. "What?" she said and sniffed then set the box on her knees.

"Well, open the box already," Nana pushed it toward her where it lay on her lap. "If he spent so much time in wrapping the GD thing then it must be something special."

"You don't know what it is either then," Shelly said.

Aria stifled a giggle while she watched Nana's waddling skin below her chin while she shook her head. "No, the little snot wouldn't tell me a thing."

Gary also confirmed he knew nothing of the box's contents when Aria looked his direction. She smiled down at her son sitting anxiously at her feet staring at the treasure he presented her. Aria pulled the package close and gathered a deep breath.

The box looked as though it could hold something as large as a pair of shoes, but was light and felt as though it held nothing. Colby always had a way of wrapping small things in larger boxes, she remembered. He also had a knack for playing games and sending recipients of his gifts on scavenger hunts throughout the house. It would seem this year would provide no reprieve from his antics.

As Aria separated the tissue paper from the box, she found a small envelope with her name scrawled upon it in an elaborate hand. She gasped as the significance of what she saw enveloped her. What was written was not her English or human name, but the archaic symbol that signified who and what she was. She looked down at Colby, who held her gaze, expecting the surprise she wore like a mask.

"How?" was all she could manage past the lump in her throat.

"I have my ways," he told her wearing a devious grin. "Read the card inside."

Aria hesitated a moment while looking at the symbol of who she was, wondering how far she had come from being her true self. As she turned the envelope, she ran her finger along the flap and pulled out the card within. The corners of her mouth rose as she read the riddle.

"Where once I was bare save cone of the pine, take a tour of my arms and a clue shall be thine," she read aloud.

Without ceremony, Aria jumped from her seat and headed for the Christmas tree to begin searching for the next clue of her treasure hunt.

She stepped around gifts and gently moved around the tree and pushed at the decorated branches, looking for an envelope. Colby's shouts of 'you're getting cold' and 'you're getting warmer', only added to her excitement. How fondly she remembered these pranks, they played upon each other. Her joy took frustration for a mate as she stopped and stared at the spot where she was told was 'hot'. There was no envelope or obvious clue. She turned to Colby, who sat on his knees, restraining the urge to leap up and point out his brilliant clue. He raised an eyebrow and smiled with a devilish smirk as his eyes twinkled at her.

Aria turned back to the tree and scanned the area around where her next clue was alleged to reside until something caught her attention. Suspended from a branch was a wooden wind-up train. She took the train from the tree and turned it in her hand, finding the small card taped to the bottom side.

"Is this the train you lost all those years ago?" Aria said.

She was stunned to see Colby nodding his head and smiling. "I called it back days ago when I-"

"What he means is he found it when he recalled the memory of losing it," her mother interrupted. Aria watched the slight exchange between her mother and son but said nothing.

Why must they hold back what we all know to be true, Aria thought to herself. They had yet to fully discuss their family's magic and history to hear her own story. As she looked at her mother, Aria received a look that told her now was not the time, so she pulled the card free from the train.

"To get back on track of the game, you must abide. Visit my owners hiding place where you must set me to ride," Aria read from the card.

Colby always loved to play in the crawl space beneath the stairs leading to the second floor. Aria often found him there when he was nowhere to be found and the house eerily quiet. Unlike Shelly, who was always up to mischief when she went quiet, Colby would be found entertaining himself building something or drawing things with a skill well beyond his years. She ran to the closet and opened the door.

Aria found the next clue as the train rode the tracks set up in the small closet beneath the stairs. As the train passed through the covered bridge, it pushed out the next clue sitting atop a boxcar that was hidden within. Her next clue referenced her son's first word and his favorite blue monster puppet from children's television.

"Cookie," Aria laughed. She ran to the kitchen.

Inside the cookie jar, Aria found a small gift box. This box was not wrapped and only held closed by a simple ribbon tied in a double-looped bow. She carried the box back to the living room where the others waited. She assumed both from the weight of the box and the fact no one followed her into the kitchen, that this was the final piece and the box contained her gift.

Aria untied the ribbon as she sat back in her chair. She rolled her eyes up to glance at Colby without raising her head. His face beamed with excitement and impatience that filled Aria's heart to near bursting. She pushed back the delicate fabric that lined the box to find a golden pendant in the form of her personal rune. The dam burst and her tears flowed freely as she lifted the object from the box and held it to her chest.

"It's perfect. Your father had shown me this symbol before we married. Do you know what it is?" Aria wiped her eyes as dry as possible with the back of her hand.

"It is your name," Colby told her. "I found an old picture of you and pop in the attic when I was rummaging through old boxes. The symbol was etched below you and another was below dad."

"Yes it is as you say," she said, not wanting to explain further. Aria knew that Colby had begun to awaken to his powers, but she refused to acknowledge it aloud for fear of the questions that would most certainly be asked and the glares she received earlier from her mother. So she continued to play ignorant of what was transpiring beneath her roof.

"Well, that's just great," Shelly said. "Do you always have to outdo everyone when it comes to giving gifts?" She sat back and pushed her own present aside. Aria assumed Shelly opened it while she was hunting around the house for her own present.

The others began to open their 'one' Christmas Eve gift, but Aria stopped Colby from opening his own gift. "Wait, there is something I think past time you should receive, and tonight is as good a time as any. I will just go up to the attic to retrieve it." Aria began to get up but felt a hand on her arm.

Nana winked at her. "No need dearest daughter. I thought you might be coming around weeks ago," she said and mumbled, "at a snail's pace." Aria watched Nana pull a package out from behind the chair. "I took the liberty of wrapping it."

Aria took the package from her mother and transferred it over to Colby's waiting hands. Her mood was mixed. Aria was glad to give this gift to Colby, but she was mortified at the shoddy wrapping and cock-eyed placement of pre-fabricated bows that did not even match the gaudy paper. She smiled in spite of the train wreck of a job her mother did at wrapping the gift while she watched Colby tear the paper free without ceremony or reserve.

As she watched Colby peel back the layers of parchment that surrounded the old leather journal, her throat began to feel as though it might close up and choke her.

He lifted the thick leather bound tome and stroked the cover, feeling the supple and smooth texture that defied weathering and the years of neglect from being hidden away. His fingers paused as he reached the circular pit in the center of the front cover.

Colby's confused expression relaxed Aria somewhat as she felt the mystery and missing object from the cover would delay the inevitable. Adding to the mysterious cover was the multiple locks that adorned the side, sealing away prying eyes.

Frustration beamed from his eyes when he finally gazed back at his mother who held up her hands in mock surrender. "I have no answers other than you will find a way to open the book. Your father would not have meant you to have it if he felt it beyond your ability to open."

Colby hugged his mom and pulled her up and toward the window. "I have one more surprise." Colby entered a hashtag spell on his phWatch then waved his hand toward the window and sent a wave of Emassa out and up into the sky. After a brief and dim glow of light, white sparkles began to drift down and settle on every surface. It was snowing the kind of fall that sticks.

Aria pulled her son close and sniffled. "Thank you."

Chapter Seven

Colby sat in the middle of his bed, legs tucked lotus style as he stared at the large leather-bound journal before him. As he gazed at the supple hide that coated the tome. The otherwise unadorned cover was interrupted in the center by a circular indent. He had left off trying to open it for weeks now though he carried it everywhere in his backpack.

The indent was lined with a thin metallic thread only noticeable when gazed upon from certain angles. Colby learned from the first moment he touched the area, it held power. He just wasn't certain what the power was or what it might do.

He wasn't sure where to begin, so he sat and stared at the journal. Ideas of what may lay hidden in the pages within raced through Colby's mind. So many questions formed in his head that he hoped would be answered by reading his father's words. At the same time, he worried that there would be nothing inside but the scratchings of the archeologist rather than the expressions of his father.

When at long last, Colby worked up the courage to pick up the book, he reached out with his senses. Not the mundane senses. He wasn't interested in the tactile or olfactory givings or even the heft of the book. These thing he already knew. He wanted to become acquainted with the power signature that stirred just below the surface of the cover.

He knew the aged leather mixed with dust and must. The hint of Old Spice danced at the edge of his sense of smell and evoked an image of his father hunched over the tome, scribbling his notes. The crackled feel of the aged yet supple leather rippled below his stroking fingers as he slid them along the cover and spine. He examined and committed to memory, every intricate clasp and hinge that stepped down the outer edges, locking away its secrets from unwanted eyes. Colby knew all these things from the first night he received this gift. What he wanted now, was to bend the book to his will and release the secrets within.

Looking along the side of the journal, Colby looked at the seven locks dominating the side that would be where any other book would open easily and unhindered. One large main clasp was set in the center and was flanked both left and right by three locks, six total, each of different length. At first glance, Colby assumed these varied sized clasps, once unlocked, would release separate sections of the book. He only hoped what he had in mind would prove successful in releasing the locks and gaining him access to his father's words.

A gathering of Emassa spindled deep within Colby's chest. Not a forceful energy, but one of want and desire. Colby was unsure where the power was coming from, but he felt more than understood what it could accomplish. Without hesitation, he released the coalescence and shivered as it surfaced and traveled along his skin to take purchase upon the old journal.

The energy that flowed from Colby combined with the power of the book causing it to glow with a pure and sparkling radiance of every color imaginable, but not visible to the ordinary human eye. Colby saw the colors, but then again he was not an ordinary human. He inhaled sudden and deep as he both saw and began to feel the power coming from his father's journal. It felt somehow familiar. As his hands settled on the book, he felt a connection to his father. A memory of being held as a toddler. An image danced across his memory of sitting is his papa's lap and playing.

The feeling was both welcome and unsettling simultaneously. He jumped at a sudden change in the flow of energy. Before Colby had a chance to pull the book closer, the largest and center clasp made a barely audible click before falling open.

The glowing ceased and the book slept, or so it seemed. As the flow of energy dissipated, Colby moved his hand along the edges of the cover. He wanted nothing more at that moment than to open the old tome, revealing the secret he knew was meant for him. Understanding now the familiarity of the energy of the book was from his own father, Colby realized that only his own power could have unlocked the clasp. This book was for him and him alone.

Gathering his courage and tapping down his nerves, Colby slid his index finger under the cover and slowly lifted it open. There, on the inside cover was a list, words written in an unfamiliar lettering, some other language. Six lines, each as dissimilar from the next as they were from the first. Too excited to tarry long on those lines, he decided they could wait. His eyes shifted to the right and focused on the first page.

Waiting there on the page, for over a decade, a long hand written note from a father to son.

> *My dearest boy, my son, how I wish I could be there with you and our family now and you would not be facing what is happening to you alone. Though it was inevitable, you should one day come into your gifts, I had so much wished their burden could be taken from you. I should never have presumed to lay such a responsibility on my children.*

As Colby read the words, his own inner voice was replaced by his fathers. Light began to shine from the edges of the words and fill his vision. As the light spread, the room began to shift and Colby was no longer sitting in his own room, but inside the study his father once kept on the floor above. The room that remained locked.

Colby watched as the light and shadows grew and shifted into the outlines of furnishings and objects strewn around him. He looked down to see himself seated on a stool at the edge of a desk. A shadowy form began to coalesce and focus before him. The voice continued as his father's face became clear. Colby sat in awe while his father spoke to him from the dream spell.

We were never supposed to have children you see me and your mother. It was forbidden, but that is no longer important now. Once we had your sister and you, nothing else mattered.

There are those among our people who curse blended children, those of us who felt different came together and created the neighborhood, protecting it, shielding it, making it safe for our families. It is the last of many sanctuaries we have held over the eons.

As time went on, our kind drifted apart and we began to live separately and hid ourselves among the humans, never staying over long in any one place. It is a lonely existence.

When I met your mother, I could no longer bear to remain reclusive and decided it was time to live again. She took me in and accepted my differences, though I did not understand why until it no longer mattered. You and your sister were all that mattered so we moved past our issues and your mother and I tried the normal life. But then your gift surfaced.

You are a very powerful creature my boy and with that power will come not only much responsibility, but many who would seek to control or destroy you and everything you hold dear. Much you will learn as you grow into your abilities. I only wish I could tell you more about them or what is to come.

What I can share with you is thus; Keep your family and closest friends closer and rely on them. You will find people will begin to become drawn to you, you must be wary.

This tome contains all you will require in order to learn how to handle your gifts as best as I can wonder at as you are the first of your kind. It is yours alone this journal, and only you can open it. Only you can read it. Do not try to force the clasps as they will open when the time comes to reveal each section's secrets.

Your sister will be your best ally and defender, she always was even when jealousy and envy overruled her young mind. I suspect she has not much changed in that regard.

Your maternal grandmother, though cantankerous and rough around the edges, is wise and powerful in her own right. She may wish to remain weakened of the Emassa, but you must empower her before this is over.

You must tread carefully around your mother. Remember a mirror has two faces, and though both mouths move, only one speaks. She loves you dearly and fiercely. Make certain that does not form a barrier between you and your goals.

One day you will find me, you must, but not until you are strong enough to face what must be done. I love you, son and I look forward to the day I return to you. Until that day, keep this journal of Saiph.

Oh and I must mention Fizzlewink. He is my oldest companion, but I would…

The page faded and ink smeared at that point and the image of Colby's father sitting at the desk faded abruptly. Colby pushed his magic into the page, hoping to get his father's image to reappear, but it was not to be. The spell was spent, leaving Colby with more questions. The remaining page was blank, as though something interrupted his writing or erased it.

What was his father's cryptic warning regarding his mother about, and what was he supposed to know about Fizzlewink. His mother's moodiness was known to him, but somehow Colby didn't think that it was what his father meant. And was there a misspelling or weird translation in 'keep this journal of Saiph'?" Did his father mean he should keep his book safe?

Colby did not think long about these questions after he absently flipped to the next page in the journal. When his eyes scanned the notes and drawings, he saw a detailed account of an archeological study involving a place he knew mysteriously well, Chichén Itzá.

The drawings depicted various buildings, temples, and ceremonial places throughout the ruins compound. Next to each drawing was written copious notes in the now familiar hand of Jarrod Stevens. Though the notes were cryptic and likely in some sort of shorthand that Colby did not understand, he felt with more reading and examination he would figure it out.

A few of the drawings on the next page were easier to understand. He found pictures of what appeared to be the moon, one in darkness, the other eclipsing the sun. They were placed on either side of a rough drawing of the Earth. Below the Earth was written equinox 2015, and there were two red marks on the planet. One mark, on the left and darkened-moon side, was placed in the region of the Yucatan Peninsula. Colby took this to be Chichén Itzá. The second mark was over the North Atlantic near a small group of islands.

Colby continued to peruse the notes he now had access to. They were few compared to the rest of the journal remaining locked, but it was more than he dreamed to learn about his father. As he read, two thoughts came to him. First, he needed to share this information with the archeology club, only as much as it related to their trip. Second, he had to share the information without Rigel knowing he finally had something else the man coveted, one of his father's journals. It wasn't just any journal, it was meant for Colby. And it was magical.

Colby closed the journal and decided, though the book was meant for him, he could trust Shelly with the information for sure and he needed to talk to her. He needed to tell her that he saw dad and knew he was out there, somewhere.

Chapter Eight

Shelly could not grasp everything that was happening around her. She went to that damn school, she thought. Why hadn't something special happen to her when she attended. After all, she was the first born, wasn't there some rule about the first born child and prophesies or some fantasy story nonsense.

Since her earliest years of recall, Shelly could talk to the dead and sense bad things were going to happen. But she never had an active ability, at least not until Colby suddenly came into his power. She felt more ignored than when the little brat was born. Even now, she owed the active nature of her gift to Colby as the source of power and only with the assistance of his brilliant though annoying, hashtag magic app and a fancy gizmo smart-watch.

She didn't actually resent Colby. He was not to blame for what was happening, just the center of everything. And that was the rub. Colby was the center of attention as usual. She needed some answers, but she wouldn't get them from her mother or Nana. Shelly needed the insight of someone else. Someone who was able to see where others could not or would not look. Shelly would, for the first time, force a visit from her great grandmother's spirit.

Shelly stepped over a pair of discarded pants and kicked a solitary black high-top sneaker out of her way sending it sailing into a pile of clothes in the corner. As she sat down on the worn carpeted floor at the end of her bed, she pushed back against the frame and crossed her legs lotus style. Breathing deeply and closing her eyes, Shelly began to call out for her long dead relative.

With a final whispered call, Shelly slowed her breathing and waited.

Minutes passed, and Shelly slowly opened her right eye to check her surroundings for any indication her call was heard. Hearing and feeling nothing, she opened both eyes wide and scanned the room. Aside from the normal scattering of discarded clothes and garbage, nothing was out of place. Her room looked as it always had. Books, CDs, clunky big shoes, and takeout containers of half eaten food littered every available surface. Gothic rock posters spread across the walls covering what remained of the pink and yellow flowered paper that fought a losing battle against the days of her adolescence when she played with dolls and braided her long blond hair.

Wiping the images clear from her mind, Shelly huffed at the realization that her attempt wasn't working. She assumed she could actively initiate a 'ghost chat', as she called them. Her gift was now powered by Colby's connection to the Emassa, but she needed to figure out how to trigger the connection.

In the back of her closet, she dug through more piles of clothes and shoes. Articles flew through the air in every direction as she searched. Not finding what she was after, she focused on the upper shelf where boxes sat at odd angles teetering on collapse. She first glared at the avalanche waiting to cascade upon her head before deciding how to search without needing rescue.

Looking to her future buried beneath the countless boxes on her shelf, and the phWatch she wore on her wrist, the solution became frustratingly clear.

"Here goes nothin'," she mumbled as she typed in the hashtag. #StayInPlace.

The runes formed before her as the power of Emassa hummed and lifted from the device. The hashtag magic coalesced and with a wave of her hand, Shelly sent it into the boxes that promised a fast and loud shift in her direction should she dare disturb them in her search.

As the glowing energy dispersed amongst the boxes, they began to shift and vibrate slightly.

Shelly held her breath, watching as the boxes shimmied but then abruptly settled and then held firm. With a satisfied exhale, Shelly shifted the piles at her feet into a larger grouping and took a trepidatious step atop them. When they gave beneath her feet, she repeated her hashtag spell on them and used the bulking mound of soiled clothes and shoes as a stepladder.

Confident in the solidity of her footing, Shelly began to rummage around behind the boxes now held fast by her spell work. As she reached around, unable to directly see what lay beyond, Shelly grunted and stuck her tongue out the side of her mouth. Her expression shifted from determined to satisfied with a quick smile and widened eyes.

She pulled the dusty old box from its hiding place and leaped down. Wiping the collected layer of dirt and all things nasty in dust from the cover, she revealed the contents written on the cover. Ouija.

Tossing it to her previous spot on the floor, Shelly left the spirit board to gather a few of her candles that spread around the room. Black, of course. Once she was satisfied, she sat back down and lit the candles in a circle around her then took out the Ouija board to begin her summoning again.

Shelly knew growing up that the board was a game since it never worked, and the spirits that bothered her always came of their own accord. Somehow she felt that her active power would now enable her to use the board and planchette to call up whatever spirit she wanted. Shelly grinned deviously at the thought.

As she rested her fingers over the planchette, she took care not to touch the surface in an effort to not inadvertently influence its movements. Though her fingers hovered a hair's width from the tear-shaped plane, a buildup of energies across her skin tingled and danced across the planchette. Shelly closed her eyes and focused on the plain of the dead. She centered her thoughts on the spirits who have been close to her. Tingling in her fingers gave her indication that something was working. She focused more and the tingling grew.

A force of energy pushed from her palms into the planchette, sending it sailing around the room. Shelly ducked as the projectile zipped past her head. The lift of hair from the breeze produced by the missile surprised her. All she could do was huddle at the corner of her bed as the device soared around, breaking glasses and decorations, knocking clothes, cartons, and miscellaneous objects to the floor. When at last the planchette directed toward Shelly, shaking uncontrollably at the foot of her bed, all she could manage was to lift her hands. She put them before her and bury her head between her pulled up knees and chest.

Silence followed. Shelly looked up to find the Ouija planchette back on the center of the board, resting over the words, "Good Bye".

Shelly shook from the sound of cackling in her ear. A voice she knew all too well.

"Ma," Shelly shouted. "Did you have to cause all this? You couldn't just pop in and say hello?"

The laughing continued. "Oh heavens no child! What's the fun in that?"

Ma appeared from the ether next to Shelly's desk with an audible pop that caused Shelly to jump in surprise. She pushed a pile of cartons and papers off the edge of the desk and proceeded to try and sit down.

Shelly watched with a slight smirk as her great grandmother's ghost tried to lift all of her four feet tall and lithe frame up and onto the desk.

Frustrated at her inability to leap up onto the desk, Ma pulled over the chair and used it as a step. Turning in triumph, she plopped down and in all her fortune teller garbed glory.

"Just look at the mess you made." Shelly stood facing the apparition of her long dead great grandmother and pointed around the room.

Having lowered her laughter to a controlled giggle, the ghost of Ma looked around and shrugged. "Looks no different than your normal twister-wrecked mess of a bedroom to me."

Shelly shrugged and pursed her lips. "At least the Ouija board worked."

Another laugh erupted from Ma's wispy lips. "Don't be daft child. Those things are for parlor tricks and fraudsters." Ma floated down toward the board and stood in the center of it. "Though I would suggest next time ya not put so much zeal into the call. You don't know who might answer."

Shelly held a confused look, lips tightening and forehead pulled. "You mean I did that without the board?"

"Child I heard you the first time you called me. I just thought I'd stick around for the show," she laughed. "We don't get too much excitement in the other realm. Everything is so detached and everyone is stuck…Well, never mind that. Just be careful from now on."

"You said I called loudly? What do you mean?" Shelly was showing little on her face in the way of concern, but the shaken tone of her voice belied her fear.

"Well, you needn't shout. Your call was like a bullhorn at a pep-rally. You could draw anyone to you who has been close enough to rub your aura." Ma saw the concern settle across Shelly's face. "First-time mistake, nothing to fret about."

Moments passed in silence before Shelly finally looked up. "Ma? You seem less-"

"Off my rocker?" Ma laughed. "I'm not so disjointed any longer, thanks to your proximity. You've grown in your power my dear."

Shelly shook her head and sat back down. "It's not my power. I'm only channeling it from-"

"Colby!" Ma said in a breathy shout. "It has started then has it?"

Shelly looked around her room, seeing the mess for what seemed the first time, and began picking up. As she walked around putting things in a bin and throwing clothes in a large pile in the corner, she told her grandmother what had transpired after Colby turned sixteen.

It wasn't just that on his birthday, which happened to be on the vernal equinox, he gained some special magic. He became a source of power to others. At first it was only Colby who could tap into the Emassa, the secret flow of power used for magic. Those around him soon became able to use the power, if they were gifted from a bloodline of past practitioners and carried a device with Colby's #Magic app. Then there were the other creatures and odd things associated with the events that followed his birthday. These, among other things, had Ma concerned.

Ma pulled on her scarf that covered her head until it fell free of the tightly curled wig that shifted upon the scarf's release.

"Isn't this what you and Nana always talked about? The reason why Colby was so special?" Shelly asked as she sat in the now cleared off chair next to what would be a desk if it weren't covered in garbage.

"You always babbled on about Colby being special…Colby being the one…Honestly, you sounded like a half crazed gypsy."

"That's because I was," Ma said with a snort and toothless smile. "The times I visited you in the past…well I wasn't entirely here. Part of me was anchored to the other realm and that weakens the mind for a spirit that crosses back. You lose a bit of yourself when you pass beyond the boundaries of possession."

Shelly, confused, looked at her great-grandmother with new interest. "What did you mean by 'boundaries of possession'?"

Ma shifted her wig and adjusted her glasses on the edge of her pointed, wide nose. Eyebrow raised, she leaned forward to speak and then stopped as her mouth opened. Again she looked at Shelly ready to answer but found the words missing from here thoughts. "I'm not certain. Someone over there, I don't remember who, said something along those lines, but I don't know what it means."

They talked for several minutes while Shelly caught Ma up on the current events and what had transpired since last they spoke. Ma finally heard enough and moved to sit next to Shelly.

"What is it that has caused you to call your old crone of a great granny?" Ma asked, careful not to touch Shelly. "You never seemed too keen on my visits in the past, so why now?"

Shelly didn't look up from her folded hands held in her lap. It wasn't that she didn't like being visited by ghosts, she often found comfort in them. Though in the early days, she began to think herself crazy after repeatedly telling her stories about talking to dead people and losing friends out of disbelief or them thinking her a liar or nuts. Those days were gone and she told herself constantly that she didn't care what people thought, but the truth was she did. She wanted acceptance and belonging more than she would admit.

"This is about Colby isn't it?" Ma said.

"Yes," Shelly hesitantly answered. "No…I don't know."

Shelly stood up from the bed and paced before her disembodied relative, blurting out everything she was feeling.

"It's not as if I had a choice of powers. All of this was planned out long ago, right? Colby gets to be the special one, not me. Not the first born. I mean why does he get to be this power source, he can't even control it." Shelly went on and on with her tirade until at last she sat down at her desk and stifled a sob.

"Dear child," Ma said. "You have this in your head that you are not special when you are. As special as Colby, you both have a part to play I fear." She raised her hands to Shelly's pleading eyes. "I don't know what that is, but I have read it in the cards for years before my untimely demise."

Shelly looked back at the floor. "So I won't get any answers today?"

Ma laughed. "You haven't asked the right questions."

"What do you mean," Shelly asked, wiping the tears from her eyes.

"While you sulk and fester resentment behind this facade of gloom you paint on your face, you hide from what you can do to help Colby with whatever it is he must do. You both have a shroud of energy about you and share a common path, but at some point your goals will diverge before realigning." Ma held a stone-faced stare and began to flicker.

"My visit is coming to an end, someone has heard your call," Ma said as she snapped out of some sort of trance. A look of trepidation cascaded over her wrinkled old face. "I don't like the feel of this."

Shelly became worried and stood to approach her great grandmother.

"Do not touch me dear," Ma said, holding her hands up to ward Shelly off. "There is power in your touch."

"What am I supposed to do next?" Shelly pleaded.

Ma began to fade. "I can't say for certain my dear, but you should start by stepping out from behind your mask and embrace who you are."

Before Shelly could say more, Ma blinked out and the room recharged with a static buzz and things around the room began shifting from the force of a cold presence lingering on the edge of existence.

Shelly looked at her arm as the hairs began to stand on end. She moved her hand to place it on her other arm and smooth out the hairs when she saw her breath billow out as she exhaled. Something was in her room.

She turned around slowly while lifting her focus from her arm to the surrounding room. Shelly turned around, feeling the telltale tingle of eyes on her back. Something dead was there, and unlike Ma, this one was no relation. She could feel that.

Dead black eyes. Blistered and red skin covered with scorched wounds and festering sores. The stench of rot mixed with burnt hair and flesh assaulted her nose.

It reached out for her as the cropped skin cracked and fell from its fingers.

Shelly screamed.

Chapter Nine

"Help me," The monster said. Its raspy voice strained and hoarse.

Shelly, huddled in the corner, staring at the creature, confused at its request. She looked into its pleading eyes, seeing something familiar and human behind them. As her gaze traveled along its form, she began to realize that it wasn't a monster at all, but a man. He was covered in tattered and scorched remains of clothing. His skin, what was left of it, was either blistered and blackened by fire, or hanging loose from equally torched muscle and bone.

"What do you want?" she finally managed to mumble.

The man lurched forward, dragging his mangled feet as he floated. His pain showed through his charred features. "Help me," he repeated.

Shelly's heart sank. She felt horrified and sorrow beyond anything she ever felt before. Confusion surfaced as she registered his request. The man wanted her help, but she didn't know how he expected her to help him. She shook her head.

"I don't know how I can help." She looked closer at the man. "Who are you? I've seen you before."

The man sputtered and wheezed. "Help me!"

Shelly's shoulders tightened as her arms can down while she straightened her posture. She moved out of the corner and toward her desk, careful to avoid the man, getting more annoyed than frightened.

"Help you how?" Shelly said and her eyes widened as she realized who the man was. "You're that guy from the DMV aren't you?"

The man stopped moving and cocked his head. "Charlie."

"Charlie?" Shelly asked as the man responded with a agonizing nod. "Well Charlie, I'm not sure I can help you.

"The pain," he replied. "Help me."

"Stop saying that." Shelly pushed away from the desk at the man's renewed approach. "I don't know what you expect from me."

He stopped, his gaze locked on Shelly's face. Charlie opened his mouth and as his lips crumbled and fell free of his face in an avalanche of fine powder, he released an ear-piercing screech.

Shelly covered her ears, but the high pitched noise seemed to pass through her and reverberated in her head and chest. Tears pushed through her tightly closed eyes and cascaded down her face. Shelly buckled from the pain in her head. She unconsciously reached out to steady herself. Then the noise stopped.

Shelly did not move at first, as the sudden relief fell over her. She began to straighten her body and untwist her puckered face, when she felt a hand overtop her own. Shelly's eyes shot open and she yelped. As she stepped back from Charlie, she watched as a shimmering glow traversed his fire ruined body, healing the spectral man. Only then did she feel the energy passing between them.

She started to back away when Charlie squeezed her hand over his arm where she touched him.

"One more moment, please," he asked.

Shelly relaxed a bit, and left her hand on Charlie's healed arm. Eyes wide and glossy, she watched as the energy poured over him, fixing ghostly skin and tattered clothes. Her heart lightened and her head swam in a feeling she had never experienced. She was consumed by the outpour from deep within herself. The incessant need to heal this man, this stranger, this ghost. She felt joy and a sense of purpose.

As promised, the moment passed and Charlie lifted Shelly's hand from his arm and stepped back, smiling. "Thank you."

Shelly stared at him, taking in the transformation that took place from the moment she came in contact with his transparent form. She felt him as though he were a corporeal person. Though he was still clearly a ghost, he still held space in her room. He had substance enough in her senses that she felt him there as well as saw him.

"This is new," Shelly said and looked at her hands. "Why did you come here? Did you know I could fix you?" Shelly asked the question, but did not yet stop looking at her hands. They were still glowing.

"You sent out a call...Ms?"

"Shelly." She realized what Ma meant when she said her call was like a bullhorn at a pep-rally. Shelly moved to the window and looked out nervously. She gazed out at the yard and surrounding area, expecting to see a queue forming and patients taking a number to see the ghost healer.

"They aren't going to knock on the door you know," Charlie said, his voice normal now that his spirit formed vocal cords healed. "We pass right through them."

Shelly turned to face his smiling face. She saw the restrained laugh behind his pursed lips. "It isn't funny."

"Perhaps not to you, but between the joyful relief you have bestowed on me and the look of you staring out the window looking for sickly ghosts…it is a bit amusing."

A huff and grumble accompanied Shelly's deliberately wide path around Charlie to her desk. She sat down and laid her head on the surface, a bit harder than she intended. She held back the grunt of pain.

"What is going on?" Shelly mumbled.

Charlie stood in silence, not knowing if Shelly expected him to answer or if it was a rhetorical question she asked.

Shelly looked up and turned to face Charlie. "Well?"

"Don't look at me," Charlie said, hands held up. "I'm new to the dearly departed crowd. I just felt a compulsion to get here when your call rang out. Once I arrived I somehow knew you could help."

"And how exactly did I help you? I mean, I can see the transformation in your appearance, but you're still dead dude." Shelly moved closer, no longer troubled by his presence. "Are you going to cross over now or something?"

Again Charlie laughed. "You are too lovely to pass for John Edwards. Besides I don't feel any pull to be anywhere at the moment beside here. I think you need my help as much as I needed yours."

"How so?"

"I'm not sure. Perhaps if I told you the story of my demise, we might figure that out."

So Charlie took a seat and began to tell Shelly of his recent past and the events leading to his untimely death.

Charlie worked three jobs to make ends meet. On the weekends, he was a driving instructor at the DMV. That is where Shelly first met him, when she took Colby to get his first driver's license. A few nights a week he worked as a telemarketer selling insurance. And then there was his full-time job as a systems admin for MacroTECH.

Near two years past, Charlie's torment began. He became possessed by a life-force while at work. It was a day like any other at MacroTECH, or at least it started off that way.

Charlie was called up to a testing lab where a ticket was opened to fix a terminal connectivity issue. When he arrived, he found the lab empty. He called out for anyone to answer but only heard his own echo. He was busy that day, so many issues arising over failed computers and power surges, he decided to simply locate the effected terminal and fix the problem then head to the next one. That was his last memory of being…alone with his own body.

No sooner had he touched the keyboard and looked at the screen, a burst of light escaped a crack in the monitor and burned into his head. He recalled the blinding pain that burned behind his eyes. It only lasted a moment but felt as though time paused to prolong his agony. Through the pain, he felt the other thoughts, another mind. That mind pushed him to the side as though being shoved into the back seat of his own car while someone else drove.

"Have you ever sat in the back of your own car while someone else drove? Not only drove your car, but did so without consideration or care. It's like the bastard in my head parked me under a tree infested with pigeons filled to the beak and ready to blow!" Charlie was agitated and enraged at the memories racing through his spectral awareness.

He rambled on about how he felt being a passenger in his own head.

What it was like to be driven without control, yelling and screaming in his own head, only getting ignored.

Shelly was disgusted, not at his retelling but the torture he endured. "Were you aware of anything that happened?" she asked.

"Everything." Charlie spelled it out for her. He was aware of every moment spent in thrall of the oppressive presence in his mind. From the moment he first felt the chill race through his body and the other presence take control, he watched unable to do anything to stop his actions.

It began with small things, relatively speaking from knowledge of acts yet to come. The thing that bothered him the most were the teenagers. First time licensees of the male persuasion. The thing in his head was very interested in them. It was looking for something.

Charlie was forced to watch everyday as the monster in his head and in control of his body manhandled and assaulted the young men who he took on driving tests. He was torturing them to try and release a magic inside them. The creature wanted to awaken their connection to the Emassa.

Charlie never understood what the Emassa was or why the creature was so fixated on finding this thing inside these boys. It was't until he began working on some special program that he received any insight into wha the Emassa was.

He learned from the conversations he overheard while sitting in the back of his own mind, that Emassa was magic. Of course by now Charlie thought he was stark raving mad, but does a mad person actually think they are going mad? He retreated in his mind as often as he could to retreat from the madness, but during one of the few times he resurfaced, he caught his first glimpse of what had to be magic.

Magic was the only thing that he could connect with what he saw. He stared into a swirling mass of entangled energy that seethed with power and consciousness. It looked and felt like a nest of demons awaiting to be freed.

As Charlie spoke of the atrocities he witness and felt a part of, Shelly began to feel horrible for the man. While she relaxed at his presence and assured him none of those things were his doing, she placed a hand on his ghostly arm.

The more she spoke to him and he listened, the fainter his presence became. He began to accept her words and started to forgive himself, even though he was being controlled and manipulated. He thought he should have fought back, but Shelly explained that he couldn't stand against the Shizumu. A moment passed between them and Charlie was gone, but a feeling of peace remained and Shelly sobbed.

Chapter Ten

Colby stood outside Shelly's door preparing to knock when he heard the muffled sounds of conversation. At first he heard only Shelly's voice, but as he strained to listen, he began to make out a raspy whisper-like sound, not unlike white noise between radio stations or broadcast television. As he listened, he became aware of an energy field beyond the door. It was Emassa and it was making the hairs on his arms stand on end.

He raised his hand to knock and the conversation stopped. Colby looked at his arm, noticing the hairs drop with the sudden disbursement of the Emassa beyond the door.

"Shelly," Colby said, "are you okay in there?"

He listened for several heartbeats for a response. He could hear movement beyond the thin-veneered hollow door that separated the hallway from Shelly's room. He knocked again, hearing more movement and a sudden crash. Colby didn't wait for a response this time and barged into the room.

Colby saw Shelly sitting sullenly on her bed and looking down at the floor. He followed her line of sight and spotted the spirit board on the floor.

"What's wrong Shelly?" he asked as he approached her.

Colby watched as Shelly sobbed and shook her head.

"Nothing… go away!" she said. "Just leave me alone."

Colby stood there looking at the smeared eyeliner ringing his sister's glossy eyes. Shelly was not an emotional person usually, and something had her shaken. Without invitation, Colby began picking things up and attempted to straighten up the disaster that overtook Shelly's room, making it more a site for FEMA than usual.

"What are you doing," Shelly protested, her sniffling halted and was replaced by an irritated grunt.

Colby looked at Shelly from the corner of his eye but kept moving around the room, picking up clothes and garbage. He paused in his movements from time to time, looking around and sensing Emassa in the air. There was a static charge around the bed and Shelly's desk that were strongest.

Shelly noticed her brother pausing in the spots where Ma and Charlie first appeared. Sensing that Colby knew something was up, Shelly exhaled deeply and got up from her bed. She moved around the room, helping to straighten up the mess.

"You can feel something in the room?" Shelly asked, but there was no question in her tone.

Colby spared her a look but did not stop cleaning. "Ya, I can feel a charge in the air."

He didn't expand on his description, wanting to allow Shelly to tell him her story rather than guess at what transpired. When Colby didn't explain further, Shelly decided to tell him what happened.

As they continued to clean her room, Shelly retold her evening attempt at communing with Ma and what all happened. Though she had told her stories when younger of Ma keeping her up at nights ranting and babbling, the new experience of fully corporeal appearance and coherent expression was a new development. Then she began to talk about her second visitor, Charlie for the DMV.

The story of Charlie's visit was told with an unfamiliar tone in Shelly's voice, but to his credit, Colby listened intently and didn't interrupt or provide his own thoughts. Though a pang of guilt at hearing of Charlie's untimely demise filled Colby's gut, he had to hear everything first. He listened and took in all the information Shelly shared before deciding to interject.

"It's my fault," Colby said as he sat in the desk chair and lowered his head. "I released that thing from his body, and it came back to spite me."

"Seriously," Shelly spat. "Everything isn't always about you."

Colby looked up, surprised at Shelly's sudden shift in temperament.

"That Shizumu would have left Charlie when it was done with him, leaving a shattered man in its wake. His work at MacroTECH and the DMV left him vulnerable to another inhabitation at any time, so don't go beating yourself up over something you didn't start." Shelly was somehow angry and empathetic at the same time.

Colby shook his head. "You mean he worked at MacroTECH also? Doing what?"

"Tech support, that's how he got…infected."

Shelly continued her story of the conversation she had with Charlie, and how the software company was somehow involved in what had happened with the Blue Screen of Death attacks.

After listening to everything Shelly had to say, Colby was angrier than ever at the situation. "I wish I never had this power."

"Well wishes are like chasing rainbows little brother. Pretty from a distance, but the closer you get the more they fade and you only end up covered in the mud, and wet from the rain." Shelly offered a rare smile. "Besides, without you I wouldn't have been able to channel enough juice to send Charlie on his way."

"Wait…what?" Colby asked. "You sent him where?"

Shelly shrugged and went back to cleaning her room. "He crossed over or something. Somehow you're letting me siphon from your access to the Emassa and I could release him from this realm to the next or wherever spirits go."

Colby shook his head again. "Shelly, I wasn't channeling Emassa. I could feel it being used nearby, that's why I came to your door, but that energy didn't come from me. You did that on your own." He smiled at her.

Shelly stared at Colby and blinked then sat down on her bed. "What are you saying?"

"I'm not sure, but I think you're drawing on the Emassa all on your own."

"Maybe the little fur-covered blueberry will know more?" Shelly asked, referring to Fizzlewink. "I'm not sure I like this?"

"Why not," Colby asked. "You've been stomping around and pouting about me being so special, and me having the active ability with Emassa. If you can now access it without pulling it through me, then what's the problem?"

Shelly had no answer.

"Exactly," Colby said. "I know one thing for sure…I couldn't have sent that man's poor soul to the afterlife or wherever you sent him."

It was Shelly's turn to shake her head. "I wouldn't be so sure. You haven't begun to realize what you can do. You transported us home safely the first time we faced the Dreggs, and that was by accident."

"Yes, an accident. How many other accidents will I have before someone gets hurt?"

Shelly and Colby spoke for the remainder of the afternoon, cleaning her room in the process. While they talked, as friends, they began to find their bond growing and changing. While they shared the love of a sibling, it was the first time they spoke so freely and without reserve. Each one saying something to boost the other's esteem and reassure each other that things would be okay. They were in this together.

Once the room was well on its way to looking habitable, Shelly sat down at her desk to take a quick break. As she absently placed her hand on the desk, a charge of static shocked her and she looked down. She looked at the old book sitting there, recognizing the Journal as one of their father's that mom gave to Colby for Christmas. She ran her finger along the spine, watching the charges of energy jump between her finger and the book. For several moments, she repeated the motion until the silence in the room drew her attention. Colby was watching her and smiling.

"I forgot I brought that in here with me," he said.

"I imagine it has become a regular accessory these days, you've been taking it everywhere with you." Shelly lifted her hand and started to get up.

"Bring it over here," Colby said and sat on the bed. "There's something I want to show you."

Shelly took hold of the book and cringed as the energy it gave off shot up her arms before settling to a low annoying buzz. As she sat, she dropped the large tome down between Colby and herself.

"How can you stand the shocks that thing gives off?" Shelly asked. "Has it always done that?"

Colby shrugged, placing his hand on the clasp he already unlocked. "It doesn't do that to me, but maybe since I've started unlocking it, the book's spells are stirring."

Shelly's eyes lit-up at knowing Colby had opened the book. "What's in it? Is it a grimoire? Is there stuff that requires toadstool or eye of newt?"

Colby laughed. "No, nothing like that. I've only opened the first section." He pointed to the center and largest clasp that locked the journal. At his touch, the clasp opened and Colby turned to the first page.

Together, they read the personal note Jarrod left for Colby on that first page. When they reached the part about Shelly, she gave him a wink and squeezed his hand. Laughing at the cantankerous nature of their grandmother, they moved closer together. As they read on, through laughter and tears, a new understanding blossomed between them. It wasn't until they reached the part telling about the dual nature of their mother and the cut off part regarding Fizzlewink, that they each held a confused expression.

"Is dad saying mom is bipolar or something?" Shelly asked. "I know she's scattered from time to time, but I always thought it was the drinking."

"Somehow I think there is more to it than just her love affair with Jack Daniels," Colby said. "But I'm more interested in what's not here about Fizz."

"Do you think he can't be trusted?" Shelly asked. "Dad said Fizz was his oldest friend."

"Companion, not friend. And it's the 'but' I'm concerned about. It's all a bit fuzzy. The reference not Fizz's actual butt."

They both laughed.

"It seems as though the rest of dad's note was cut off or removed." Colby ran his finger over the final words. "What do you think?"

"I think we should keep that to ourselves unless something changes. If the little cat-faced 'fuzzy butt' starts acting weird, then we check it out."

Colby then told Shelly about the spell that accompanied his first reading of the words his father left behind. The vision of seeing his father in the study, writing in this very journal, the feelings he experienced, it was like his papa was still there sitting in his chair. After running her through the description, Colby turned the pages to show Shelly what he had read so far.

"Hey isn't that chicken pizza place where you're going in the spring?" Shelly asked.

Smiling, Colby corrected the name for her, 'Chichén Itzá', and showed her all the other events happening that same time. It didn't seem like a coincidence when they started putting the pieces together. As they began looking at the drawings, they heard a light knocking on the door frame. When they turned, Shelly invited Gary in to join them.

Colby gave Gary a rundown of what happened with the book when he opened it, then Shelly blurted out what happened with the spirit board and her visitors. After the initial surprise and excitement had worn off, the three of them got to work checking on what the drawings meant.

Gary got on Shelly's computer and began searching astrological web sites to discover that the dates of their trip coincided with a solar eclipse. This eclipse occurred moments after the equinox and the umbra covered the opposite area they would be visiting. Further research revealed a special festival going on at Chichén Itzá that took place on the first day of spring, but this was going to be an even bigger celebration due to the eclipse and super moon..

Gary began reading what he found. The pyramid of Kukulcán was the center of the cosmos for the ancient Maya and the equinox a special time of joining. This was when the setting of the sun caused a casting of a shadow from the steps to descend from the heavens down into the Earth. The construction was purposefully placed so that at this time of the year, the North of the pyramid was cast in shadow while the Southern side would be bathed in light.

"This is giving me the jeevies," Gary said. "Somehow you knew the place to go, even before gaining access to your father's journal. It's not just coincidence."

"I agree," Colby said. "But what does it all mean?"

Gary spun around in the desk chair to face Shelly. "Can you call up a Mayan spirit or something? Maybe they knew something."

Shelly grunted and frowned. "It doesn't work that way. Besides, do you speak ancient Mayan? I doubt an old native of that region would speak English."

"We need more information," Gary said. "There's gotta be something we're missing." He stared at the astrological data on the computer screen. "Do you have a globe?"

"Ah…no," Shelly said. "Can't you do a virtual one on the web?"

"Yes, but sometimes I like something more tactile."

Colby remembered something and jumped up. "There is a globe in dad's study, or at least there was in the vision." Without thinking first, Colby grabbed the journal and ran for the door.

Shelly and Gary called after him, but when their shouts went unanswered they decided to chase after him. They ran down the hall and toward the flight of stairs leading to the third floor where they saw Colby bound up two steps at a time.

Gary motioned for Shelly to go first with a grand bow.

"Cute," Shelly said then pulled his ear forward and guided Gary up the stairs ahead of her before letting go.

When they reached the top, they saw Colby standing before the closed door to the Study waiting.

"What are you waiting for?" Gary asked. "Open up and let's have a look."

Colby scrunched up his face and jiggled the handle of the door. "It's locked."

"Well mom carries that old key around her neck, maybe it's for the study," Shelly said. "I'll go get it."

Colby held up his hand to stop Shelly from leaving. He looked at the door and pulled a shroud of concentration over his mind. He lifted a hand toward the door and began to feel the energy pulling from the old wood door and begin licking around his fingers. A knowing smile crept across his face.

"I don't need a key," Colby said as he pushed his hand flat against the wood.

Power flowed from Colby's hand as he let the Emassa surge from the barrier holding his father's study door closed. Growing up, the kids never attempted to open the door, they simply walked past as though it wasn't there at all. While they knew of the room's existence since their father left that night so many years ago, no one dared attempt entering the room. Aria held a key to the study but never took it from the chain around her neck.

The magic flowed from the door and pulsated when it mixed with the raw energy Colby held within himself. After several moments of watching the lights coalesce they began to itch his skin and crawl up the length of his arm. Colby felt a tugging.

"What the…" Colby started and gasped as his hand began to sink into the door. A moment of panic gripped his chest. "It's pulling me in."

Colby reached back with his other arm and waved Shelly and Gary to take hold. They began pulling Colby away from the door until he shook his head.

"Just take hold. I think I understand." Colby nodded and gave them a reassuring smile. "It's a portal through the door."

The three of them stared at the door as the swirl of color raced out and enveloped them. In an instant, they were through the portal and the hallway was empty.

***

Aria stepped around the corner from the stairs and smirked at the sight of the three kids disappearing into the door. She raised a hand to the key around her neck and walked toward the door. Removing the key, she slid it into the lock and turned until she felt and heard the click. After a deep intake of air and slow exhale, Aria opened the door. The room was empty.

Aria stood at the threshold of her husband's study, concern slapping the smile off her face. The space looked the same as every other time she had snuck into the room unnoticed. Jarrod's few remaining things were scattered around the room.

The desk sat unused and covered in a thick layer of dust. A globe lay broken on its side near the window. Bookcases along the walls were bare except for the spider webs and grime. There was no sign of use, and beside the passage of time, it remained as she found it the day after Jarrod left. It was empty of all his important work and possessions. The children were also nowhere to be seen, but she could somehow feel them in the room.

Chapter Eleven

Colby was the first to fall through the portal and into the sunlit room, landing with a heavy thud on the floor. Before he had a chance to stand fully, he was pushed back to the floor as Shelly and Gary entered then landed on top of him.

At first the three of them slowly regarded their situation, then laughter broke loose while they pushed themselves free of the pile and sat up. As their laughing settled into giggles and finally quiet, they looked around the room and gasped.

Everything was as Colby described from his vision. The shelves were lined with old books. A work table was littered with scrolls and artifacts. Jarrod's desk sat to the side of the window, looking as though it had just been used. And the globe sat in front of the window on its large polished brass base, shining in the sunlight coming through the window.

As they got to their feet, they began looking around the room. Shelly went to the table to look at the artifacts and scrolls while Colby headed toward his father's desk. Gary spun the globe and looked out the window.

Colby lifted a stack of old papers and found another journal on his dad's desk. He set the papers down and reached for the book, but was stopped by the concerned tone in Gary's voice.

"Hey guys," Gary started, "you may wanna have a look out the window."

Pulling his attention away from the book on his father's desk, Colby joined Shelly and Gary at the window that overlooked the yard. Whatever he was expecting to see was nothing to what he witness. The vision was as wonderful as it was confusing to his mind. Playing out in the yard, was Colby and Shelly while Nana sat in a lawn chair talking to their mother.

As the three of them watched the scene play outside, realization began to set in that they were looking at the past. Beyond the fact that the weather outside was summer, while it was actually the beginning of winter, was the realization that the Colby and Shelly playing in the yard were much younger.

"What are we looking at?" Gary asked.

"Not what but when," said Colby.

Something changed from being in the room with his vision. Everything was setup like years past when his father was around. The room almost looked as though Jarrod Stevens only just left. Particles of dust hung in the air, not drifting on the air circulating in the room because there was no perceptible movement of air.

They could breath, but the air was stale and thick. It felt like breathing a thick fog. They could touch things and they moved in normal time, but it was what Colby saw outside that drew his attention. From where he stood he could see a bird flying past the window, or rather stuck in mid-flight outside the window.

Though the images in the yard moved in time or played like an old family video, the bird just outside the window was caught in whatever extended just beyond the glass. He resumed watching his younger self playing with a younger and happier Shelly. She must have enjoyed the scene as well from the light touch of her hand on his shoulder.

Colby raised his hand to the glass of the window as he watched through pained eyes. As his hand made contact with the surface, a jolt of energy threw him back and the room shifted as though ready to dissolve. When he sat back on the floor, he watched as the objects throughout the room began to shift and distort. Colby thought for a moment he saw the shadow of someone standing behind the desk. When he blinked, it was gone.

Shelly ran over to help Colby to his feet along with Gary, the three of them still watching the room warp before finally settling back in the way they found it.

"What just happened?" Shelly asked.

"I think this is some sort of time bubble," Gary said while looking out the window. "It looks like that moment of disturbance pushed things ahead outside."

Colby raced to the window. "From the looks of it, time moved ahead by at least a year." Colby pointed to the yard where a pool was being torn down. "I remember when mom finally had that above ground pool taken down."

Realizing the effect of contact with the boundary of the room, Colby decided they would need to limit their trips into the study. He figured there was a reason for this space being slowed down, but he needed time to figure out why.

"Let's do what we came in here for first, then we can figure out what to do next." Colby pointed Gary toward the globe while he moved back to his father's desk to retrieve the new journal he saw. It was not longer where he left it.

"Did either of you move a book from the desk?" Colby asked. "It was right here."

Shelly and Gary shook their heads. Neither had been near the desk. Shelly noticed things moved on the work table as well. Someone had been in the study during the year that the time bubble shifted.

Colby thought back to the apparition he saw while the distortions moved throughout the room and told the others what he remembered. Though he couldn't make anything out of the features, he could tell the person was tall and well built so it must have been a man.

"Could it have been a Dregg?" Gary asked. "They would be able to walk right through the barrier of this room."

Colby shook his head. "I don't think so. From our limited knowledge of their kind, I think a Dregg would have caused the whole thing to collapse. They nullify Emassa, remember."

Gary thought about it and looked doubtful, but didn't say anything. Instead, he went back to looking at the globe and took out two attachments from the lower drawer. He placed a moon and sun model on the sides of the globe, putting their long metal arms into holes of spinning rings that circled the sphere of the earth.

Remembering back to his discovery about the eclipse, Gary placed the positions of the moon and sun at the alignment and tilted the earth to the proper setting for the time of year during the spring equinox. He then pulled the curtains on the window and cast a hashtag spell upon the sun to light it from inside.

Forgetting about the mystery of the removed items in the room, Colby and Shelly joined Gary at the globe. As Gary turned the crank for the Moon, Sun, and Earth they moved relative to their actual celestial paths. After some adjustments, he had the pattern set for March 20, 2015.

As the motion slowed with his cranking, Gary pointed out the events as they will appear during the equinox and two weeks following. First they observed the solar eclipse over north-eastern hemispheres.

"The solar eclipse will be centered here," Gary pointed out. "Over the ocean here off the coast of the Faroe Islands, but the eclipse penumbra will traverse a large amount of Europe."

"Is that relevant?" Shelly asked. "I thought we were focusing on Chicken Pizza?"

Colby had given up on correcting her. "It may be important, what do we know about the areas that will be eclipsed?"

They all looked at the area of the globe when Gary paused the movement at the apex of the solar eclipse. In turn, they all listed anything they knew of historical significance. The only place they agreed upon, though not in the total eclipse, was the ruins of Stonehenge. Now they just needed to figure out what, if any, connection there was to Chichén Itzá.

"Well, let's look at what remains in the room for anything relating to all this or anything else that stands out," Colby said as he headed back to the desk. "I wish I had grabbed that journal when I had the chance."

"Maybe you weren't supposed to," Shelly said from the table. "You might have messed up the whole 'timey-whimey' continuum or something."

Both Colby and Gary looked at her with surprised faces.

She regarded them briefly before going back to sifting through the items in front of her. "Don't act so surprised, I happen to like Doctor Who."

They shuffled through papers, scrolls, and sketches for what felt like hours before Colby found something completely by accident.

While reaching down to pick up a pen that rolled off the table, Colby's thumb connected with a loose section of the carved wood along the edge of the desk. As he reached for the pen, he tightened his grip and the pressure from his thumb pushed into the section of wood. The give of the section of the desk under his thumb, accompanied by a click, brought Colby's attention to a small drawer that opened along the edge of the desk. Forgetting the pen entirely, he pulled the draw the rest of the way open and pulled out a velvet wrapped item hidden inside.

A familiar crackling of energy filled his thoughts as he cradled the object wrapped in the cloth. This item was meant for him to have found, he could feel it. He set it down on the desk and stared at it, not sure if he wanted to open the cloth.

"What are you waiting for?" Shelly interrupted Colby's thoughts. "It isn't gonna open itself…probably." She gave him an encouraging smile and nod.

With Gary and Shelly waiting on him from beside the desk, Colby began slipping the velvet wrapping off of the object from the hidden drawer. When he pulled back the final corner, he found something that had been flashing images in his head since the day he first saw symbols in his dream on the eve of his sixteenth birthday. He picked it up and now held the wheel of the year.

Colby explained what the symbol was as far as he knew, but beyond that he was unsure what the purpose was as it related to his personal quest. The artifact he held in his hands now made the images he had of it come to life. He now held the one thing that had eluded him every time he had a quick flash of it in his visions or on the screen of a computer.

It was Gary who made the connection. "It looks about the same size as the round indent of your father's journal."

Colby lifted the wheel and turned it slowly before smiling up at Gary.

"Shelly, bring me dad's journal from the table over there."

Shelly retrieved the book and placed it in front of Colby where he sat behind the desk. She stepped behind him, joining Gary at each side of Colby, supporting him and standing ready for whatever he needed. This didn't go unnoticed. Colby smiled at each of them. Shelly placed her hand on Colby's shoulder.

"Take the next step brother," Shelly said.

Gary nodded. "Yes…brother."

Colby's nostrils flared and his mouth turned down ever so slightly. As his eyes began to gloss over, he smiled and his chest puffed with the love he felt for that singular moment of acceptance and bonding. He felt the love from the two closest people in his life course through him and settle over his entire being. Gary had always been true from the day they met, but the catalyst was his sister Shelly. Colby always held the love between each other as siblings. Now, with their latest bonding after her conjuring of spirits and the complete change in her attitude with what was happening, they became closer than ever. He burst with love and acceptance.

Colby pulled the journal closer and moved his other hand holding the wheel over the slight indentation on the tome's cover. He held it there and drew in a deep lung-bursting breath. He felt the pull immediately as the power between the cover and the artifact called to one another with a longing to be together. The joy Colby felt within the new bond he shared with Gary and Shelly was reflected in the longing for joining he could sense from the energy flooding his system as he held the wheel above the journal.

Unable to withhold the pain of separation, Colby released the wheel.

The wheel of time slipped loose of his fingers and snapped to within an inch of the cover of the tome. It hovered for a few moments as the Emassa surged and encircle it, spreading blue and red light in every direction before coalescing into a deep purple glow. In the instant the color changed, the two met in a collision of light and force that pushed into the three onlookers and elicited a look of pure excitement on their faces. The light quickly changed from purple to pure white as the wheel continued to glow on the surface of the journal.

The journal lifted from the desk under the power of the light and Emassa flowing from the union with the wheel of time. As it raised several inches above the desk, the next clasp popped open with a powerful burst of Emassa that spread throughout the room and then drew back and into the three users within the room. Before they could react, the book flew open to the first page of the next unlocked section.

Light pour from the pages as though freed from eons of being bound to the parchment and sealed within the magically sealed tome. Secrets of the pages wanted freedom and they sought a receptacle for their knowledge. Now they had three. The particles of Emassa infused light leaped from the pages and seeped into the awaiting vessels.

Shelly was the first to react to the trance-like effect of the power flowing into them. Her head tilted back and her eyes glossed over as words fell from her tongue.

"Tick-tock of the centuries and the Sentries still stand. From the barracks, they gaze, observing the snakes decent through the gap of equal power's haze. The seal shall be broken within the turn of fourteen suns, but the enemy will be weak. The celestial signs will lead the way through the key of time. Turn the wheel to find the path. The return of the conquerors and the rise of the defender will proceed the clash of eternity. Look to the Ori, who shield, and the power that lies within the hunter."

Shelly drew in a long needed gasp of air before collapsing to the floor.

Colby and Gary came to their senses during her episode but were helpless to assist in preventing her fall to the floor. They watched as Shelly convulsed for a few moments before settling into a fitful unconsciousness.

Colby was able to move first, the effects of the onslaught of that pent up Emassa being absorbed into his body fading with every breath. He collapsed to the floor next to his sister and immediately checked her heartbeat and breathing. She seemed well enough, so he looked to Gary, who was starting to move sluggishly of his own accord.

"What was that?" Colby asked as he helped a waking Shelly sit up.

Shelly shook her head and then rubbed her temples. "It was really weird like someone was using my tongue to speak."

"Possession?" Gary asked. He and Colby looked at each other with the same expression of concern that a Shizumu may have been involved.

Shelly held up her hand to stop their thoughts as though she knew what they were thinking. "Nothing was possessing me, but the words just came on their own. I didn't even think them first or hear them in my head as I spoke. It was sort of like listening to a recording of my own voice, but not remembering ever making the recording to begin with."

"To tell the truth, I don't even remember most of the words anymore. They're fading from my memory."

Gary pushed Colby toward the desk and the stool he sat in prior to the release of power. He pointed toward the still open book, its pages pulsing with white light as words and images revealed themselves on the pages of the unlocked section.

"Looks like you won't have to remember them Shelly," Gary started, "they're appearing on this page here." He pointed to the book as he stepped up behind where Colby was taking a seat.

Shelly soon stepped in behind as well to join in reading what was on the newly unlocked pages. She listened as Colby read through the cryptic words on the page, reciting the same message Shelly had spoken aloud when the stored Emassa of the pages was released. As Colby continued to read, Shelly felt more at ease finding out that her temporary lending of tongue was a result of the energy released as a security measure against forceful opening of the book.

The pages did not elaborate on what would have been the result of an unwanted breaking of the locks by someone not meant for the information the book contained. It was explained briefly that only the rightful owner of the journal or his proxy were allowed to unlock and read the pages. Each remaining section required a specific set of conditions to be opened based on a location, time, and position of the wheel on the tome's cover.

Colby soon discovered the next section would not open until they were in Chichén Itzá. Before he could read more, there was a rattling at the door to the study.

Chapter Twelve

Aria exited the empty study and attempted to re-lock the door as she left. The key would no longer turn as though something was pushing against her. After several attempts, Aria pulled the key away and placed it back around her neck. Finding the room nearly empty, not just of the kids, but all the items that Jarrod had left behind, this rattled her nerves more than anything. At one point or more, someone had entered the study and began removing Jarrod's things. Just then, a knock at the front door stole her attention so she made her way down the stairs.

Colby lead the way out of the study though he was no longer required if Shelly or Gary needed to enter. Colby found the runes in the front of his book was actually the spell to create a passage through the time field. They now had the ability to use the room as needed. Though they all agreed to wait until necessary to enter again to test the theory that every disturbance of the barrier would speed time up in the room, causing more things to vanish or perhaps worse.

Unable to find the cause of the noise from the door, Colby, and the others made their way downstairs, where they were greeted by Darla and Rhea sitting in the living room talking to Aria. The girls looked up and waved at them as Colby, followed by Gary and Shelly, made their way in and sat down. Darla and Rhea both gasped as Colby drew nearer.

"You have visitors," Aria said, interrupting the tension. "I'll just pop into the kitchen and get you kids some refreshments."

"I need to get ready for work at that horrid diner," Shelly said.

"Hello ladies," Gary said. "What brings you over today?"

Rhea looked at Colby and then at the floor. Darla, on the other hand, looked at Colby with a knowing stare and smiled. "You are one of us aren't you," she said. "I knew it."

Shelly paused at the stairs and changed her mind about getting ready for work.

Colby knew what she was talking about but wasn't sure how to respond. Before he could answer, Darla moved to sit next to him, causing more anxiety.

"It's okay, I get why you never said anything. It's not like you can go around telling people you have magic. If you had, however, you'd be surprised how many people around here might just listen." Darla gave Colby's knee a squeeze and jumped at the surprising surge that left him and entered her body through her hand.

An involuntary grunt escaped Colby as he pulled his leg free of Darla's hand and stood up next to the fireplace. "I'm not sure what you're talking about Darla."

Darla giggled and looked around the room. "Everyone in this room has a power, I can sense it. It's also why my own power has never quite worked on you." She gave him a wink before continuing. "My gift is the ability to influence people's minds. Rhea, well she can heal people and see into their bodies like x-ray vision." She walked back to her seat and plopped down, tucking a leg under the other. "What are your gifts?"

Silence filled the room until at last broken when Aria returned with a tray of cookies and juice. "I believe Darla here asked a question."

Colby looked at his mother with eyes wide and shock written across his brow.

"No need to be shy now my boy, the girl has Emassa about her as the rest of us. She already knows what it is I'm sure, knowing her parents." Aria nodded for the group to continue before leaving the room again. She went to the kitchen but still within hearing distance. Nana and Fizzlewink sat at the Island listening as well.

"So…" Darla started, "what is it you guys can do?"

"Darla, I really don't think-" Colby started.

"Listen Colby, as part of my gift I can read people's intent. And your intentions have always been honorable and pure, except when you get angry like in the halls at school." Darla saw she had Colby's full attention. "I saw everything. I just figured that you would come around sooner or later, but with everything that's going on…well later has become sooner. So spill it."

Colby told the girls about how his power came back on his sixteenth birthday and how his father had hobbled him at an early age to protect him from forces that would have used him for their own needs. As he spent the next half hour summarizing the events that had taken place over the last several months, the girls listened intently and hardly interrupted. After covering the instances of BSOD and their link to the Shizumu, Colby finished with the night of the Halloween fundraiser and the visit from the Dreggs.

"Holy crap Colby that is CRA-CRA," Darla said. "Those giant ghoul things were real? Why haven't my parents ever told me such things existed?"

"They may not know. The Dreggs haven't mixed with the magical community for generations. It's because of my opening the way to the Emassa that they are drawn to me. Along with other things we have yet to encounter I imagine."

"So those costumes you and Gary wore, the goblins, they were so real. Did you guys turn yourselves into them?" Rhea asked.

Colby laughed. "No, that was a spell using the runes we use in the games at school."

"Those ruins are real?" Darla asked. "Does the school know?"

Colby only now wondered at the connection. "I hadn't thought of that. Why would there be such a popular game at school using the ruins mastered by the Nefslama eons ago?"

"Another question for another day," Darla said. "So you can do spells with the runes. What can you do on your own? What is your given gift? It must be fantastic with the way you glow."

Colby looked at Gary. "Well Gary can manipulate the energy of objects so far. And Shelly-"

"I see dead people," Shelly said. "I've been waiting to use that."

"What can you do Colby?" Darla asked.

Colby paused to think. He never really thought about a label for what he could do. As a matter of fact, with every passing week, it seemed he could do more and more. Before he could answer, someone did so for him as he made his way from the kitchen.

"He could do anything he could image if he were disciplined enough," Fizzlewink said. He walked into the room and plopped down on the arm of a chair.

Darla shrieked and Rhea stared open mouthed but silent.

Fizzlewink regarded the two girls and looked at Colby. "In for a penny, in for a pound."

"Did you turn a Smurf toy real?" Darla asked.

After everyone save Darla, Rhea, and of course Fizzlewink had stopped laughing, Colby continued. Colby held his side and tried to explain what the little blue man was. After he finished explaining about his part in everything happening and that he was a Nefslama, the girls started to relax.

"Now that the cat's out of the bag," Shelly said while glaring at Fizzlewink. "Maybe it's time we start figuring out what to do about MacroTECH and those behind all of these terrible things."

Aria cleared her throat, getting everyone's attention. "One step at a time my dears. We first need to know who the players are."

"Isn't it obvious," Colby said. "These things start at the top. It has to be Mr. Bodine. Even through the TV I could feel his dark energy."

"Probably, you are correct," Nana started, "but this is much bigger than just what has been happening with the computers and a few possessions. Something else is brewing and I can feel it stinging like a tack in the ass."

"So then where do we start?" Darla asked.

Nana popped up from the couch with more energy than expected for one of her advanced years. "We start with education and infiltration."

Confused looks passed between everyone including Fizzlewink. He stood up on the chair so he was eye level with Nana. "What are you blabbering about old witch?"

Nana squared off with Fizzlewink and waved a hand at him, sending him hurtling back into the chair.

No one was more surprised than Nana. "Oh dear!"

"Mother!," Aria said. "When did your power come back?"

Nana stuttered. "I'm not sure…I had an itching earlier this afternoon but didn't think anything of it."

"It's because of me," Colby said.

Everyone had looked at him for several moments before he continued.

"When I placed the wheel on the journal and that energy burst free of the book, I felt something burst free from me as well. I think I have changed."

It became obvious to everyone in the room in that instant that Colby was correct. They could see the Emassa flowing off of him through the glow that was visible since he left the study. Only now did it begin to make sense.

"I think that just being around me is awakening things in Nana and everyone else." Colby looked at Darla and Rhea then back at Fizz. "You should look like a cat to the girls, yet they saw you the instant you came into the room."

Fizzlewink smacked himself in the head. "How did I miss that?"

"What does this mean?" Shelly asked as she walked up to Colby and took his hand.

"It means he has his power…all of it. But now he needs to learn how to use and hide it." Aria said with a tone in her voice that seemed alien to everyone in the room. She looked away and then sat down.

Nana looked at her daughter and grunted. "Education and infiltration. We get Colby the learning he needs, and these girls have obviously not been taught anything from their parents on the real origins of their magic."

"What about the infiltration part?" Gary asked.

Nana grinned. "Aria already has a job at MacroTECH…we need more eyes on the inside."

Darla cleared her throat. "Shelly, it sounded like you hated working at the diner…"

Shelly looked at Darla, eyebrows raised. "And?"

"Well don't they have an in-house restaurant? Maybe they need staff." Darla offered with a hinting tone.

When no one seemed to get where she was heading, Darla huffed and filled in the blanks. "People feel more relaxed when they eat. When they are hanging out with people they trust, they talk…freely. Where better to listen and overhear things not meant for others to hear?"

"I like her," Nana said. "I really like her."

While everyone began to settle after the initial shock of all the revelations, they began to formulate a plan for dealing with the perceived enemy. They talked about what happened with the BSOD in the lab that day when Colby intervened and how the Girls thought their awareness heightened that day. They had been more drawn to Colby ever since and now they understood why.

"What about Jasper?" Colby said suddenly. "He was also in the room that day."

Gary stood in a defensive posture. "What about him, he's been the same if not a bigger prick since then."

Darla looked at Colby and immediately understood what the others didn't. "You leave Jasper to me. I'll figure out what is going on. I know you two were once very close and suddenly he became a complete jackass. There has to be a reason."

Colby smiled at Darla and they shared a moment of understanding that went unseen by the others.

While the others continued to make plans to understand their enemy, Nana slipped off to the kitchen. She was concerned about the changes taking place, especially those that caused her active magic to return.

"Worried?" Fizzlewink said as he followed her into the kitchen.

Nana grunted at him and went about cleaning the counters. "Worried about what?"

Fizzlewink just sat and waited.

"Listen you old sorry excuse for a cat, I don't know what game you're playing, but I'll not see you use my grandson as a tool for your war with the Shizumu."

"I am not here to see him used…at least not by me," Fizzlewink said.

Nana stared at the little blue man for several moments. "What are you getting at." She raised a frying pan as a threat.

"You know as well as I do that he is not entirely your grandson." Fizzlewink stared her down.

Nana slowly lowered her arm and set the pan down on the stove. "He is my grandson, my daughter gave birth to him."

Fizzlewink tittered at her answer. "She may have been the vessel, but we both know who was really in residence during the conception."

Nana stared daggers back at Fizzlewink. "How could you know such a thing?"

"Do you think Jarrod would not know, and that he wouldn't eventually confide that in his dearest and oldest friend."

"Friend?" Nana huffed. "You use that word as freely as a politician would use the word promise. What do you know of true friendship?"

Fizzlewink started to retort but held back. "More than you could possibly know human. Your life and experience have gained you little in respect to what I have witnessed and endured. To see what Jarrod has done to try and free our people is beyond your comprehension. Do not question my dedication to the eradication of the Shizumu threat."

Nana shook her finger back at the stone-faced Fizzlewink. "You think to throw your prejudices around as reasons for your fight. Those lines are no longer black and white. If that boy learns the truth you can kiss your usefulness goodbye!"

Fizzlewink remained silent as he hopped down from the stool and headed back to the living room. "We shall find out soon enough. The truth always has a way of unburying itself."

Aria glared at Fizzlewink as he returned to the room, her eyes shifting from him to her mother. She didn't seem placated by the reassuring smile her mother gave her from the other room, but smiled back none-the-less. She turned back to the room where she saw everyone smiling and smirking as they schemed to take the offensive against their common foe. The only one taking notice of her was Shelly, who stared at Aria with a questioning glare. 'That one will be a problem,' she thought to herself.

"Okay," Darla interrupted. "So Shelly will try and get that job in the employee restaurant. Mrs. Stevens will continue to 'make friends' with co-workers. Gary will tap into the internal systems with the help of a trojan that Mrs. Stevens will introduce on this thumb drive." She handed the drive to Aria. "Rhea and I will try to find out who else at school is a team player…so to speak. And the rest will take all the information and process it."

Colby finally sat up and looked at the people around him. He couldn't help but feel as though he had his own private army. But he also couldn't help but feel a slight itch when he looked over at his mother and watched her forced smile. Something was wrong, but he couldn't place the feeling. When he looked at his mother now, for the first time since absorbing the power from the release in the journal, he saw something new. His mother was surrounded by something different. Not red or blue, not dark or light; a grayish purple haze surrounded her.

Chapter Thirteen

Shelly's first day in the employee cafeteria at MarcoTECH started out simple enough. The staff was polite and helpful with getting Shelly accustom to the way the kitchen operated. The workers moved around each other in a frantic yet coordinated effort that at first glance seemed confusing, but as Shelly watched further she noticed a collaborative movement.

The choreographed and effortless movements impressed Shelly so much that she became mesmerized and joined in the dance. She stepped in and filled a spot moving things from one station to the next. Shelly found, as if by magic, places where she could improve the timed movements and felt things speed up and efficiency increase. This immediate change was noticed by her supervisor and by the end of the day, Shelly was running the cafeteria.

As she worked and managed the staff over the days that passed, Shelly began to use the instruction Colby gave her for seeing beyond the normal and into the Emassa. It was difficult as she strained her eyes and squinted trying to see the unseen. On several occasions, she thought she may have caught a vision of the aura that surrounded all things. It was during one of these moments of fleeting clarity that she saw a dull haze of grayish purple but when she blinked it was gone. Standing before her was Aria.

"How are things progressing here?" Aria asked.

Shelly blinked rapidly for a moment before answering. After shaking away the fog, she regarded her mother. "Well the cafeteria is running fine, but I haven't figured anyone out who might be on either side."

Aria smiled and sat at the long counter next to Shelly. "I'm sure you will in time." Aria smiled sweetly and patted Shelly's hand.

Shelly saw something in her mother that seemed patronizing, but she dismissed it…for the moment. "What have you managed with the e-mail guy?"

Aria smiled and withdrew her hand. "I have indeed gained a list, be it small, but a list of names which are connected to the e-mail subject of 'Transformational Physics'. It is a starting place for the little gift Gary created." She placed a finger on the tiny USB drive that was disguised as a pendant on her bracelet.

"And how are you going to get them onto these people's computers?" Shelly asked.

Aria smiled. "That's where you come in. You've been afforded more access to the people who work here than I." Aria motioned around at the people dining. "Look for the people who have the tech support title on their badges. Once you find the right person, a trustworthy person, set them on the path." Aria slipped the charm bracelet off her wrist and pushed it toward Shelly before turning around in her swivel chair and heading off toward the exit.

Shelly watched as her mother left and suddenly the hazy purple became apparent. It was when her mother left that Shelly saw the old man in the corner by the door. He stared back at her and smiled as his eyes flicked down toward the bracelet. Shelly saw no color around the man. He had no aura at all. Even the dead had an aura. Shelly spared a moment to look down at the bracelet. When she looked back up, the man was gone.

Shelly walked over to where the man was seated to find a young man sitting there typing away at his keyboard. He sat alone, opposite of the position the old man appeared moments before.

"Can I help you?" the young man said from behind his thick glasses.

Shelly looked back at him, noticing his awkward smile and nerdy attire. He sat in front of three laptop computers and held a bright blue glowing aura. She noticed the anti-virus discs he fumbled to insert into one of the computers, then saw the title on his name badge, Computer Technician. She smiled back at him and removed the bracelet from her pocket.

"Perhaps I can help you." Shelly smiled, batted her lashes and sat down. "My name is Shelly."

***

As the weeks passed, the information began to trickle in before finally producing something more useful. Gary sat in front of the laptop accessing the many computer systems that gained him entry into the larger network at MacroTECH. He watched as the image on the screen began to grow and spread, creating the latticework of a topology in the internal network connecting all the computers.

"This will take longer than expected," Gary said. "But at least we're in and will eventually find what we're looking for."

"And what are we looking for?" Darla asked.

"The epicenter of the BSOD programming and source." Colby answered. "Shelly you found someone to help quicker than I expected."

Shelly shrugged. "It was pure chance and dumb luck I think. If that old man hadn't drawn my attention then disappear, I wouldn't have ever noticed the dorky guy."

Colby's eyes narrowed at the mention of the old man. He immediately insisted on a description of the man. He sat down where Fizzlewink perked up and twitched his ears

Shelly described him as best she could remember. She included the way his gaze fell upon her as though he knew her or what she was thinking. When she slipped into the second vision to search his aura, she described how she saw nothing, not even the shimmer of the departed hung over his form.

"So this old man," Colby started, "he showed you what you needed and then was gone. You haven't seen him since?"

Shelly shook her head.

"Sounds familiar," Gary said looking at Colby.

"What are you talking about?" Fizzlewink asked.

Colby told everyone about the old man from the park which called himself Jenkins. Fizzlewink shifted at the mention of that name and Colby saw it but said nothing.

"He helped me with playing Runes. At first I thought it was Gary helping me, but even he said he only planted tingling sensations into tiles. That never explained the glowing of the runic symbols and thoughts in my head. I had seen him only a few times before he disappeared.

"Now that we have Shelly's account, I think we can say he's likely the same old man. I only wish we knew who…or what he is. I have gone back by the park many times, and Jenkins is never there. No one in the park seems to know him or have ever met the man."

Colby paced the floor all the while he spoke. From time-to-time, he looked at Fizzlewink, who failed to keep eye-contact.

"It's too bad that old man isn't around to coach you anymore," Darla said.

Colby turned to Darla, his face squinted up as he looked at her quizzically. "What do you mean?"

"Well," she whined, "I spoke to Jasper and…well he sort of wants a rematch."

 Colby was dumb-struck. He stood staring at Darla with his mouth agape, but nothing came out. Of course, he knew that eventually he would have to face Jasper again in Runes since the day he left the tournament before playing against him. The rules required an official to accept a concede, but only after a match actually begins. Jasper could not be officially recognized as the winner until Colby started a game.

"We'll accept," Gary said facing Darla but looking sideways at Colby. "It was a team match, after all."

Colby stuttered and stopped, unable to express what was playing in his head. He sat hard on the couch next to Darla. When she put her hand over his, he turned to her with glossy eyes.

"It'll be alright," she whispered. "He is starting to come around to dealing with his little…problem."

"What do you mean," Colby asked quietly.

"That is for Jasper to explain." Darla said and got up with a wink and giggle.

Colby was left on the couch, confused and terrified. He had no idea from where the fear was coming. He flashed back to all the images of the times he was tormented by Jasper. The locker stuffings. The stolen homework. The wedgies. It all came crashing in on him like weights piled upon his shoulders.

While these visions danced across his awareness, something else began to push harder from the opposite direction. His heart thumped painfully against the inside of his chest as he delved deeper into his memories of Jasper Bodine.

Long ago, when he was a pre-teen, Colby had a single and best friend, Jasper Bodine. Colby and he were inseparable. If his parents couldn't find him, they knew to check with Jasper's parents. The same went for the Stevens. Aria always knew where to find Colby, though it was usually Nana who hunted him down. Aria was usually working or tying one on with one of the three J's: Johnny, Jack, or Jose.

The two found trouble anywhere they went no matter how they tried to be good. Between sneaking around and teasing Shelly and her friends, or hiding in the house and listening to the adults talk, those boys were two sides of the same coin. But that all changed around the time Colby was ten years old.

Mrs. Bodine became very ill and things went from bad to worse in a few days. Colby remembered very little about the funeral, only that it was the last day he saw Jasper as his best friend. His father took him away and never said where they were going. Colby's mother refused to help him find Jasper and Nana got tired of fighting Aria over the whole situation.

Some time later, Colby used the Internet to track his old friend down. He tried reaching him on various social media sites, but his friend requests and messages when unanswered. Except one. It was a simple and to the point message, 'LEAVE ME ALONE'.

Colby never understood what happened. When the day arrived that he was reunited with his old friend, he was happier to see the familiar face walk into his class than he could ever remember being. But Jasper ignored him and sat on the opposite side of the room. It was later that day when Jasper confronted Colby for the first time.

Jasper called him names Colby didn't understand. He pushed and threatened him. That wasn't the boy Colby remembered like a brother. Something had changed him and not for the better. The years that followed, Jasper continued his tyrannical reign over Colby and soon began taking his lunch money and homework. That ended now that Colby had his magic. That changed further on Halloween when Colby finally let go of the hurt and fear.

Now Jasper was warming up to him and it felt odd. Good on one hand because he might rebuild a friendship. On the other hand, his father was the head of MacroTECH and there could be ulterior motives involved. First he had to face a rematch in Runes with the boy. Afterward, if he survived the embarrassment of an inevitable loss, Colby would decide what to do next.

Chapter Fourteen

The day of his rematch with Jasper would eventually arrive. The thought of that day, when Jasper will ask for the game 'officially', brought with it a dread that made the bottom of Colby's stomach fall out. He spent the first few weeks after returning to school post-holiday break building up the encounter in his head. He ran through scenarios of what would be said among them. In some cases, it went well enough. In other flights of fancy, Colby chased Jasper through the halls, sending bolts of energy from his hands into the other boy's backside.

Colby stopped at his locker to grab the books for his next class, when a tingle crept under his skin at the base of his neck. With a sudden shiver that shook his upper body, Colby felt as though someone was watching him and turned. Down at the end of the corridor, Colby's eyes locked with Jasper's and the tingle spread to the ends of his fingers and toes.

The two boys continued to stare at one another for several moments and all other activity in the halls melted away. The clatter and noise of lockers and talking faded as it was replaced by a light high-toned ring. It wasn't an unpleasant tone, but neither was it an imagined one.

Colby began to feel something altogether different than the tingling of his digits. His teeth began to chatter and his palms became moist.

Colby shifted his books around as he wiped each hand on his pant legs, never dropping his gaze from Jasper, who began to move toward him tentatively. Colby's shaking increased and he couldn't seem to slow the strange sensation taking over him. As Jasper continued to close the distance between them, Colby started turning away and backing toward the lockers. He nearly tripped as he stumbled into his open locker and quickly turned to slam it shut only to then jump at the smiling face revealed lurking behind the door.

"Darla," Colby squealed. "Jeez, you scared the crap out of me."

The shuttering waned as he caught his breath. Only at that moment had he realized that he was holding his breath prior to her appearance.

Darla grinned as she looked past Colby. "What's got you all jittery Colby?"

"Nothing," he said noticing her averted eyes. "I-I um…I need to get to class."

Darla looked back into his eyes. And time slowed down as her gloss covered lips twitched and parted. As the next few words flowed across the curved and pouty flesh of her mouth, a musical whisper echoed behind each syllable, reinforcing the statement as though it were a command.

"Turn around Colby and talk to Jasper. You know you want to." Darla's lips twitched as the corners of her mouth curved slightly into a sultry grin.

Colby's eyes lingered on her lips for barely a moment before he smirked and narrowed his brows then looked her eyes.

"Don't try that on me again," Colby said flatly. "You have no sway over me as you would someone without my power."

Darla held back her giggle. "It has nothing to do with your power Colby." She grabbed him by the shoulders and turned him around. She leaned into his down-turned head and whispered into Colby's ear. "Just listen to him then, and stop being a chicken shit."

Colby started to turn back in protest, but a stronger sensation caused his head to jerk up and stare into the eyes of his nemesis.

Jasper stood inches from Colby with his hand gripping Colby's wrist. The presser was light and non-threatening, but that didn't stop Colby's shiver from returning.

"You got a minute," Jasper said in a cracking voice. His tone was flat but did not instill malice or threat of any kind. He cleared his throat and turned his eyes away from Colby's. He looked at his hand wrapped around Colby's wrist and felt the shiver. Releasing his grip, Jasper reluctantly stepped back to give Colby some space but did not look him in the eyes. "I just want to talk."

Darla patted Colby on the shoulder before stepping away. "I'll see you later." She winked at Colby's pleading gaze before spinning around and bouncing off down the hall.

Colby turned back as Jasper cleared his throat again. He pushed down the strange fear he was overcome by. Colby could not understand what was happening. After Halloween, he had not felt any fear or dread about Jasper. Even his anger had subsided, but now as he looked at his childhood friend, he saw something long forgotten and hidden away.

"Look," Jasper started.

Colby backed up from Jasper and steeled his nerves.

Jasper saw the sudden stiffness take over Colby and slouched slightly. He looked at Colby with an unfamiliar feeling, but suddenly stood straight and took a step back.

"I wanted to ask if you would sit for a rematch at Runes, that's all." Jasper was abrupt and the former pleading in his eyes gone. "After school tomorrow."

Colby, confused by the sudden change in Jasper's countenance, nodded. "Name the place, but I'd rather not have an audience."

Jasper agreed with a slight nod and raised an eyebrow. "We'll just have an official and our teammates. Meet me in the student council office after the last bell."

Jasper nodded once to Colby and turned to leave. He paused a moment and muttered a thank you before quickening his pace back the way he came.

Realizing he would be late for his last class, Colby shifted his books and backpack before racing down the hall. He didn't notice Gary standing behind a display case watching him pass.

***

When Colby caught up with Gary after school to walk home, he noticed his friend's chilly stance as he stood at the school exit.

"What's up with you?" Colby asked.

Gary snorted. "Anything to tell me, dude?"

Colby gave him a confused look as he grabbed his arm and pulled Gary out the door. "Ya, we have a rematch at Runes tomorrow."

Gary allowed himself to be pulled along. "Dude, what's the rush?"

"I wanna get to the park and see if Jenkins is around."

Gary yanked his arm free and slowed down. "Why would he show up now? He hasn't been seen in months."

Colby grabbed Gary's arm again and pulled him along. "Because we have our rematch tomorrow and something tells me the mysterious old man will show up."

Matching Colby's pace toward the park, Gary decided to push aside his nagging feelings and concern to follow his best friend on the hunt for Jenkins. He was the old man who first started Colby getting interested in his new found skills at Runes.

When they arrived at the park and made their way through the maze of paths and bushes to the open area where retired men and a few school kids gathered to play Runes. The place was full of players and sounds of tiles slapping against the stone tables as they made their moves.

Colby and Gary decided to split up so they could search the dozens of tables to find Jenkins. They each strode from table to table looking for their quarry. Though they aroused some irritation from their interruptions and questions, there was no sign of Jenkins. No one they spoke to was familiar with the old man with young eyes and teeth that rivaled any Hollywood smile.

"We could just sit in on a few matches here," Gary suggested.

Colby shrugged. "No, I'd rather just go back to my house and practice constructs."

Gary followed Colby toward home, muttering to himself. "I don't know why you're so worked up all of a sudden."

***

Colby ran through constructs all the next day at school rather than focus on his classes. More than once throughout the day teachers called his attention back to class. At lunch he couldn't eat for fear he might return it immediately after swallowing because his stomach was performing the acrobatics worthy of an Olympic gold medal. When he finally made it through to the afternoon, his nerves were a bundled knot in his chest and he felt like he couldn't remember anything he studied all that morning and afternoon.

Gary met Colby outside his last class and pulled him blindly along toward the student council office. As they rounded the corner, Colby halted their progress at the sight of dozens of students and teachers milling around the entrance to the office. Word had obviously spread about the rematch and a gathering of hopeful spectators gathered, awaiting the chance to attend.

"Who opened their fat mouth?" Colby said. "This was supposed to be a closed match."

Gary shrugged and yanked Colby's arm toward the office. They walked past the people looking on and wanting a seat inside the office.

"Deep breaths and keep your cool dude."

Colby and Gary sat down at the table which sat in the middle of the room and where Jasper and his partner were already waiting. Colby could read nothing from their opponents' expressions or posture. He found this remarkably unsettling as Jasper was one to always present himself an imposing and overbearing adversary. This sudden change in him made Colby more nervous than if Jasper were acting the bullying jerk he usually was. He even had his pants pulled up properly for a change though that might be due to the fact his father was likely in the audience.

Both teams were ready and the game was started. Jasper started with laying out some tiles in preparation for building full constructs called partial casts. It was a basic strategy to begin a match by showing strength, and Jasper excelled at quick strategy. As he set the tiles together on the table, he looked up several times at Colby, gauging his reaction.

Colby watched but did his best not to react or give the impression he was concerned. The tiles Jasper was revealing could be a distraction or his way of pushing Colby and Gary into a forced show of their weaknesses. Based on the tiles they had to start off with, Colby was feeling insecure. He looked at Gary and they began shifting runes around to prepare for their first move.

Rather than reveal any of their available preparatory casts, Colby agreed with Gary that they should make a full construct. With what they had, it was likely to be an easily blocked move, but it would give them much needed replacements and a chance for better runes. Colby laid the six tiles out and formed a spell for pushing a wall of fire at their opponents.

As expected, Jasper's teammate pulled two tiles from their prep zone and combined them with another set from their reserve to form a saltwater trench. This move both nullified the spell Colby set and gave a lead in points. As both sides replenished their tiles from the draw piles, the game began to speed up.

Construct after another was set down as points racked up on both sides. The game was evenly matched until Jasper and his mate placed a set of advanced runes down that created two spells at once and gave them a forty-point lead.

Colby was beginning to become flustered and began looking out at the crowd. He felt as though everyone was staring directly at him. He could hear whispers in the growing stream of people entering the room. How had so many heard about the rematch? Did they all come to watch him loose, or did they expect him to bolt for the door and give up. If he did that again this time, he would have no option for a rematch. The game would be lost and he would be a laughing-stock. Colby couldn't let that happen. He wouldn't do that to Gary.

Determination set in his gut as Colby clenched his jaw and looked over the table. He had few options for taking any points. He could throw together some precasts, but that would only reveal the weakness in available tiles from the standard set they had. Colby had no choice but to look at his advanced tiles, the ones he created. He was still uncertain what most of them even represented.

Looking at the runes, their curved and squiggly lines causing his eyes to loose focus, Colby took a deep breath. He reached first for a few runes and as his hand drew nearer they gave off a slight burning tingle. He withdrew his hand and moved on to others. As he moved around the tiles placing them next to one another, hoping for some sense of what to do. He suddenly found himself with four tiles standing on their ends facing him.

At first Colby didn't know what they were. He looked at Gary, who shook his head. Though he didn't know what they were exactly, Colby knew somehow they were the ones he needed. Four rare and advanced runes that he needed to find a spot on the playing area to place them. As he looked at the runes played out around the center of the table, a spot seemed to glow with a faint purple haze. Four spots to be precise.

Colby moved the tiles from before him and placed them, in what he felt was the correct order, on the table between several other constructs. After he had laid the last tile down, he sat back and looked at the game official, Rigel.

Rigel looked over the tiles and his eyes widened slightly. He looked closer and nodded his head.

"That's game and match."

"What? In just one move," Jasper's teammate stood and said. "That's not even a construct."

Jasper looked at the construct and even though he held a confused stare, a slight curl formed at the corners of his mouth.

"Sit down dude," Jasper said. "Colby just won."

Rigel stood behind Colby and Gary as he announced their win.

"By placing an unraveling spell with advanced runes including one for time control, Team Stevens and Connor have reversed three spells, taken control of another and stolen those points from their opponents. By also reversing time itself in a move, they have nullified all precasts placed by their opponents between those moves and gained a three-hundred-point lead. That is more than adequate for a full match win."

Jasper stood and reached out to shake Colby's hand. It was an unexpected move, and Colby felt more nervous now than before the game started.

Colby began to reach for Jasper's hand, but Gary took it first. He shook the hand and twisted Colby away from Jasper. As he pulled Colby along, Colby turned his head to look at Jasper, who nodded and still had that slight smile on his face.

"Very impressive constructs Mr. Stevens," Rigel said as he patted Colby on the shoulder.

Feeling uncomfortable, Colby shifted out from under the 'friendly' hand of Rigel and turned to face him.

"Thank you," he said. "I think I'm starting to get the hang of strategy and counter moves."

Colby stared directly into Rigel's eyes at his last words. Something about this man always put Colby on edge, but lately those feelings were getting stronger, yet he didn't understand why.

Rigel held eye contact for a few moments before blinking and glancing away. "I have to admit, there were a few moves there I hadn't seen the like of since your father's time as champion. You didn't happen to find them in his personal notes did you?"

Colby measured his next words, wanting to both elicit a reaction, and put an end to the constant requests for information about his father's personal journals and notes.

"As a matter of fact, I may have borrowed a few things from some of my dad's notes. I'm very glad he left me his personal journals for my private use. I expect he'd want me to keep them private still."

Colby watched as Rigel's expression went from an imperceptible grin to one of bitter disappointment. That made him feel good, but still curious about what this man wanted.

Rigel forced a weak smile and nodded back to Colby. "I'll see you tomorrow at the fundraiser. We already have quite a lot of folks signed up for your computer and device scanning slash virus protection services."

Colby nodded back and turned toward to his friends and classmates who continued to congratulate him on his and Gary's triumph at the Runes match. He looked back for a moment to catch Jasper leaving with his father, berating him, and felt sorry for his long ago best friend.

Chapter Fifteen

The queue filled rather quickly when the doors to the computer lab opened the next morning. Although there had been no reported cases of BSOD associated incidents lately, people were not taking chances and wanted their laptops, computers, and personal mobile devices scrubbed clean of any possible virus or malware. The fundraiser was well under way with the promise of a successful day's work.

Colby and team had only just completed setting up the required equipment when the first of the computers was placed on the table. Rhea stood at the receiving line accepting devices and passing out claim slips for the owners to use when returning to pick-up their cleaned and protected electronics. The devices piled up quickly.

The kids moved through the bins of devices, each grabbing a tablet, phone, or laptop. Using a supply of SD cards and thumb drives, they began rebooting the computing devices to run a special program from the alternate source that would scan and eliminate known viruses and identify suspicious software.

There were countless personal devices to get through and still many people showing up to drop more off for repair. The recent sensationalized reports on the news and in the tabloids had people scared they would encounter a BSOD and get vaporized or end up in a vegetative state at some hospital. It was the best marketing a little fundraiser like this could get. People scared into paying for their services.

Colby was just about to grab a phone when a hand reached over the counter and rested on his. Colby looked up to stare into Jasper Bodine's eyes. He stood there momentarily dumbstruck. When it finally registered, Colby pulled his hand back and shook his head to clear the fog.

"Did you have something to drop off Jasper?" Gary said from behind Colby.

Jasper's eyes never left Colby as he responded to Gary. "No. I thought I might volunteer to help."

Gary snorted. "What? Your daddy send you to spy on us because his software is killing people?"

Colby turned his head to Gary. "That's enough."

Colby invited Jasper into the lab and pulled out a phone from the 'to-do' pile and then grabbed an SD card. He showed Jasper how to re-seat the SIM card on another device as well as how to use the thumb drives on laptops. Satisfied that Jasper had the process down, Colby moved to the other side of the lab and worked on his own stack of devices, looking up from time to time only to find Jasper looking back.

Jasper was no computer genius compared to Gary and Colby, but he knew well enough to follow a brief set of instructions and did his share.

After what felt like hours, Gary found something on a rather sleek and stylish appearing laptop. The unbranded machine was deceptively light and durable and unlike any other with the exception of the operating system. It was still running the MacroTECH system and Gary wasted little time examining the machine before plugging in his thumb drive and rebooting it to install the virus cleaning and protection software he and Colby designed. Once the system was running, the odd display got his attention.

"Got one!"

Colby stopped what he was doing and hurried over to Gary's side in time to see his friend begin to convulse. He wasn't the only one. Darla, Rhea, and even Jasper had all turned at Gary's shout and were now fixated by the swirl of symbols and flashing light. Only Colby seemed to be immune.

Colby looked at the screen and began to focus his attention on the pattern, looking for the weakness. He began pulling on the Emassa. He looked down at his phWatch and prepared to enter a hashtag spell. It dawned on him, as he searched his mind for a solution, the last time he stopped this attack it was by will alone. An instinctual reaction that was pure magic, not his app augmented construct.

He first moved to grab the laptop and pull the battery, but was shocked by the energy being emitted from the device. He struggled to hold onto it, but couldn't put it back down seeing his friends begin to worsen. As he fought the repulsive bursts from the screen, Colby examined the underside of the laptop to find no battery to pull. It must be inside and would require taking off the bottom. No time.

Colby unceremoniously slammed the machine down on the table, noting its rugged design when nothing happened. He stepped back a moment and tried to clear his mind in effort to reproduce what he felt in the past, when he stopped the attack last summer. His thoughts were being clouded. He felt a trailing energy wrapping his arms and noticed streams of red light coming from the computer screen and entangling his wrists.

A rising heat in Colby's hands accompanied a faint scent of ozone.

Concentration faltering, Colby looked at his wrists to see the hairs begin to curl and shrivel. He was beginning to burn as something was trying to penetrate his skin. A Shizumu.

A shudder ran through Colby and a tingle pushed up from his toes all throughout his body and centered on his gut. It felt cool and inviting, calling to Colby's soul. He wanted very much to retreat into that place. He could be safe there, but that wasn't right. Somehow, Colby knew that he shouldn't go there, he should fight it. In a moment of clarity, Colby saw that it was a trap, a misdirection used by the Shizumu to take over and suppress him. Colby broke free and screamed out in rage against the intrusion in his mind.

Colby's face reflected his anger as his skin radiated a purple glow. Tendrils of Emassa coalesced and slithered along his skin toward the gripping red energy. Colby was so focused on his own fight, he failed to notice his friends all ignored by the attack and now watching Colby in awe of his power.

The room grew brighter as Colby struggled against the Shizumu. Though his body temperature returned to normal, he still felt the prickling of his skin as the Shizumu searched for a weak-spot.

It finally found one.

Colby jerked back as he felt the sting on his wrist around his phWatch. At that moment, the struggle for dominance shifted in favor of the Shizumu, but Colby's anger doubled. With a final effort fueled by burning rage, Colby broke free of the red energy and burst forth into a purple light that filled the room. Panting for breath, Colby leaned against the table staring at the laptop as it spun in circles and stopped. A single flashing line in the top right corner of the screen was replaced by the boot menu of his program.

A firm hand on his shoulder brought Colby out of his daze. He turned, expecting Gary supporting him as he straightened up, but found himself staring into Jasper's eyes. Again.

"That was awesome," Jasper said with a grin.

Colby, momentarily stunned by Jasper's accolades and handsome grin, smiled back awkwardly and shrugged away. At the same time, he rubbed his wrist around his phWatch where he received the sting from the Shizumu tendrils.

"You saw that?"

Gary cleared his throat. "We all saw that." He glanced away toward the girls.

Colby followed Gary's glance and saw the smiles on Darla's and Rhea's faces.

"You saved us from that…whatever it was," Rhea said.

"Again," Gary added.

All eyes focused on Gary's revelation.

"What are you talking about? This has happened before?" Jasper asked.

Colby released the breath he held since turning around and finding Jasper holding his shoulder. He stepped back and gestured toward the laptop, now harmless, and explained what happened minutes ago. He then elaborated and described the last time it happened to each of them when they shared detention.

He revealed the events of that day for Jasper's sake, the day the BSOD occurred in the very lab they now stood. Colby explained how he somehow sent a burst of energy at the shared power strips that surged the computers and rebooted them. This effort interrupted the effects of the attack, thus stopping the seizures and convulsions they each suffered.

Rhea began to piece more things together. She looked at Darla who nodded in agreement. They both turned to Colby.

"That's when it started remember," Rhea started, "when we started having stronger power and use of our magic. Not only did you give us a connection to your flow of Emassa, but you sparked what we already had."

They all looked at each other, knowing this as truth. They then turned their attention to Jasper, who took a step back to lean against the table.

"What are you all saying?"

"We're saying that we all gained our gifts that day or greater access to them anyway. What did you get?" Darla moved toward Jasper, staring intently into his eyes.

He began to mumble something as he stared back at her intense gaze. As he began to slump, he started blinking and stood straight again then scowled at Darla.

"I got stronger," he said. "And that thing you do doesn't work on me any better now than it did a few years ago."

Darla, painting her most sincere and innocent face, backed away. "I don't know what you mean."

"Oh save it girly, you're an empath. I've known for a while now. My father never kept the truth of magic from me, or at least some of it."

Jasper began to doubt his own words as they fell from his tongue. He looked back at the laptop on the table, the one that nearly caused everyone to get possessed, and noticed something on the side. A small blue label with a barcode and company name, MacroTECH.

"Perhaps he hasn't shared everything," Jasper admitted softly. "This computer is my father's new prototype."

Before anyone could ask the questions that showed on their faces, the screen on the computer flashed with an alert from Colby's and Gary's special program. It was still busy scanning the machine since Colby repelled the Shizumu attack.

"Quiet," Colby said. "Gary look at this and tell me what this is."

Gary stepped beside Colby and watched the screen as the others huddled around as well. They all watched as lines of numbers and names scrolled on the screen, sometimes interrupted but asterisks. One line at a time, output on the screen began to display what the program was ultimately designed to accomplish. A trace.

"It's a trace route," Gary said. "It's working." He turned and smiled.

The looks on everyone except Colby's faces told Gary they had no clue what he was talking about. He explained how the boot program was designed to find the virus, in this case, the Shizumu, and trace it back to its origin. The program had identified its target and was tracing it back to where it came from after the program had started its scan.

"You must not have defeated the Shizumu, but sent it running."

Colby grinned. "The path is broken in places but I can assume it is trying to mask its trail."

"Perhaps," Gary added. "It may be unregistered proxies or other routers, but our program keeps picking up the path."

"Can you trap it?" Jasper asked.

Gary looked back at Jasper incredulously. "Why would we want to trap it? We want to know where it lives."

"What if it knows that it's being followed and is leaving a fake trail? That's what I would do."

Again Gary narrowed his eyes at Jasper. "What would you know about it? Is it something your father shared with you?"

Jasper felt the sting of Gary's accusation but didn't back down… much. "He stopped talking to me about magic shortly after my mother died. He hardly talks to me at all. I know strategy, and sometimes in order to get what you want, you have to mislead."

Gary raised an eyebrow, but it made sense. "Maybe."

Gary began chasing the path and tried intercepting the Shizumu as it moved through the internet. He watched the networks it entered and tried hacking them to gain access and prevent the Shizumu jumping to another. He kept missing his chance. Each time he entered a network, the Shizumu would jump out sooner and sooner until it finally jumped beyond Gary's reach. He started to formulate a new plan when the sound of a throat clearing broke his concentration.

"How many of you does it take for one computer?" Rigel asked. "We aren't going to make much money for our trip at this rate."

Following Rigel's pointed finger to the stacks of devices awaiting service, Colby, and the others broke from Gary and began tackling the backed up work.

Rigel walked among them and stopped near Gary, who noticed his approach and closed the computer lid and moved to grab a new device.

"We'll be done with these in no time sir, just admiring the new model MarcoTECH machine." Gary watched Rigel's reaction, hoping he wouldn't open the lid and look closer at the machine. He didn't, so Gary got to work on the next laptop and let the program run uninterrupted on Mr. Bodine's computer.

The kids toiled all morning and well into the afternoon. They completed their work on well over one hundred laptops, tablets, phones, and even a few desktops. All machines had a clean bill of health and an updated system BIOS that would prevent the BSOD virus from affecting their equipment.

Gary had only just removed the thumb drive from the MacroTECH laptop when people began arriving in order to pick-up their property. Everyone was very grateful for the services the kids did and many overpaid and tipped well. Smiles spread across everyone's faces when they saw the money start coming in but were more pleased they could do something to help stop the Shizumu from spreading.

"That's all of them," Darla said.

Colby turned to the empty tables and saw that even the MacroTECH computer was gone.

"Who handed off the MacroTECH laptop?"

Everyone looked at one another with blank expressions. They each admitted that not one of them remembers a claim for it, especially as busy as they were. They wouldn't have forgotten how important that machine was, bit somehow it disappeared.

Gary gave Jasper a sideways glance but didn't question him. "Well it couldn't have just vanished or walked away."

Colby shrugged his shoulders. "I have a talking cat. Stranger things have happened."

Chapter Sixteen

"So tell me about this talking cat," Jasper asked Colby.

The two of them walked ahead as the group of five headed to the Stevens' house after the fundraiser. Colby offered some refreshments and conversation about what happened that day back at his house. Everyone agreed and Jasper was especially happy to be invited.

"He isn't really a cat…Well sometimes he is. Sometimes he's a little blue man. But most of the time he's a pain in the ass."

Colby told Jasper about the Nefslama and the Shizumu as they walked. He was surprised at how much his own father didn't tell Jasper about the source of magic and the fight for power between the two races.

"Why do you think your father hasn't told you about the other magical races and such. If he knows about the Emassa and runes, he should know about them?"

Jasper turned away from Colby at the mention of his father. "I really don't know. He usually only tells me what is important to himself and even then he's always mad about something."

"I'm sorry."

"For what, you didn't do anything. I should be the sorry one. I listened to my dad all these years not knowing what to think." Jasper looked at Colby for only a moment before looking away again. "I still don't know what to think."

Before Colby could say more, they reached Colby's house to find Nana digging in the side garden and singing…not pretty, but loud. She kept digging and planting and singing as the kids gathered and watched, trying to hold back their laughter.

Rhea couldn't hold back well enough and snorted. This caused the others to burst out laughing.

Nana stopped singing as she turned to find an audience. Nana's face was splotched with dirt and her hair was winning a war against the scarf wrapped around her head in an attempt to hold the tight wiry curls from springing free. It was a hopeless cause. She wiped her hands on her apron as she stood and giggled to herself.

"Well," Nana said between Rhea's snorts. "How did it go today?"

"Very well," Colby said. "What are you doing in the garden?"

Nana looked back and shrugged. "A little something I haven't done in years. A special herb garden." She winked back at them. "I wouldn't suggest eating any of them though if you catch my meaning."

The laughter stopped and puzzled looks replaced smiles.

Nana decided to avoid questions and pushed them along to the back door. "Come on inside and have some snacks. You can tell me how the day went and how Mr. Bodine happens to be tagging along with you."

Nana gave Jasper an appraising eye but said nothing more as she followed them all into the kitchen and closed the door tight. Spring was coming but not fast enough for her old bones. It was the time between winter and spring where the weather was highly unpredictable in Chicago. The morning could be warm and sunny and by afternoon freezing and pelting the area with ice and sleet.

She made her way to the oven to put on a kettle for making hot chocolate, one of the few things Nana never screwed up, and pulled some cookies from the cupboard.

"Sit children, and tell ol' Nana how things went today." She smiled and sat down. Her eyes seldom left Jasper. "How did the 'fundraiser' go?" she asked with an emphasis on fundraiser.

Nana didn't want to speak about the true intentions of the event without knowing why Jasper Bodine was suddenly among her grandson's closest friends.

Colby saw the look Nana was giving Jasper.

"It's ok Nana, Jasper knows about as much as we do, and he was there when something happened."

"What happened?" came a voice from nowhere.

Jasper jumped as he looked down and saw the bunched up blue face of a small man with long white hair and eyebrows that he twirled with his long pointed fingernails.

"What the hell?" Jasper said. "Is this the cat…"

Fizzlewink rolled his eyes and leaped up onto a stool at the island. His eyes darted from Colby to Jasper and back before resting on Gary's sour expression and grunted.

"I am 'not' a cat."

"He just plays one on TV," Colby said and laughed.

"I have never been on the television boy. I could never understand that mind sucking contraption-"

"Anyway," Colby interrupted, "we were doing fine with checking-in devices and such for scanning and virus protection. When we began working on the equipment, we found one that was…special."

Colby replayed the events of the morning when the Shizumu attacked while the BSOD prevention software started scanning the machine. As he gave a play-by-play, Colby became more animated and the Emassa began to flow off of him like a purple mist, spreading out and being absorbed by everyone in the room. His story, as he retold it, was nothing worthy of a great oration, but as the Emassa flowed and the words poured out, no one could take their attention from his recount. He was inadvertently casting a spell that left everyone in his power.

When he finished speaking Colby caught his breath and waited for a response, but not a sound was made by anyone. He looked around to find everyone staring at him, eyes glazed over and a stupid grin on their faces.

"Hey! Earth to everybody."

Fizzlewink was the first to snap out of the trance and after shaking his head, looked around the room to observe the others slowly clearing the fog from their minds.

"That was peculiar," Fizz said.

"What?"

"You seemed to have enthralled us. All of us." Concern fall over Fizz's face. "That has not ever been accomplished upon my kind."

Colby was confused. "You mean like what Darla can do?"

"Hardly," Fizz laughed. "What she does is influence one's mind. A mere parlor trick compared to what you have just done. Had you fully completed the enthrallment..."

Fizzlewink stopped himself and grabbed a cookie from the tray. "Did you say the Shizumu came through the laptop and attacked without the actual blue screen thing happening?"

Conversation back on track, Colby continued with his theory that the Shizumu must be using the devices and connection to the internet to spread from some other location.

Fizzlewink shared his opinion of doubt, explaining that the Shizumu were few and could not reproduce. If somehow they were released from their prison, they would not need computers to infect the population.

Rhea began a speech on the evolution of species and how after however long the Shizumu were imprisoned, they could have learned how to procreate. This of course led to a full debate on the evolution of man and Darwinism.

Fizzlewink took his chance to sneak away and headed for the doorway to the living room when he stopped and stared off absently for a few moments. He began shifting back into cat form and ran off toward and up the back stairs to the upper floors.

Nana watched Fizzlewink's odd behavior and squinted past her thick glasses and cataract covered eyes. She moved to follow him when the front doorbell sounded. She took one final look at the path Fizz headed and then waddled to the front door to see who was calling.

Moments later while the kids were still talking, laughing, and eating junk food, Nana came back in the kitchen with a sour look.

"Jasper, your-"

"Jasper, why were you not at the appointed pick-up location this afternoon. Driver was waiting for you?" Mr. Bodine boomed as he pushed his way past Nana and into the kitchen.

Nana looked at the man and then back toward the front door where she had left him waiting. Her face pinched up as her face reddened. Not only did the man invite himself into her kitchen, but he also pushed past her as though she were a servant in her own home. She raised her right arm and pointed an arthritic finger toward him. Sparks of purple began to fizzle around her fingertip as she took a few steps toward him.

Colby's face drained of color as he watched the possibilities flash before him. Nana was developing a reuse of magic after however long she was unable. Someone she openly despised barged past her and entered her kitchen. And she was pissed. Before he could stop her, Colby was relieved to see Darla jump up and pull Nana's hand down and point at her finger.

Nana's face of rage contorted into one of shock, shame, and horror as she watched the sparkles of purple dancing on her finger and slowly die out. She shoved her hand into her apron pocket and shuffled off to the back table, sinking into a chair and looking away.

Colby wanted to figure out what was wrong with his grandmother, but he couldn't help feel bad for Jasper as he looked and saw the sulking face on him. He was only now beginning to feel something in the return of his one-time best friend. Now Mr. Bodine was here filling the room with a toxic mix of loathing and displeasure that oozed of his every word and movement.

"Well...answer me boy."

"I forgot. We all had so much fun today at the fundraiser and when they invited me back I guess I just-"

Mr. Bodine sighed. "What fundraiser?"

Jasper told his dad about the fundraiser and how they were helping people update their virus protection. As he recounted the day, leaving out the encounter with the Shizumu, he began to regain the smile he had held before his dad showed up.

Colby couldn't help but smile as well while he watched his friend show a happy side at the time they spent together today. But when he felt a tingle across his skin, Colby looked up to stare directly into Mr. Bodine's eyes. He saw such hollowness behind those eyes. Colby's smile fell.

"I was not aware you were once again friends with the Stevens boy… and these others." Mr. Bodine painted a false smile and nodded slightly at Colby. He never spared a glance at the others.

"What kind of virus protection were you using on these machines? I only ask as my own people, people highly trained, educated, and paid well, have yet been able to identify anything related to this BSOD virus, as it is being called."

Colby faltered for only a moment. "We didn't say anything about the BSOD virus particularly."

Now Mr. Bodine was caught off-guard, only for a millisecond, yet long enough for Colby to sense.

"I must have seen your flyers or some other advertisement. That is what you were billing this service as was it not, protection against the Blue Screen of Death?"

"We used it for-" Gary started.

"I was asking Mr. Stevens, Mr. Conner."

Mr. Bodine didn't even look at Gary, but everyone in the room felt the slight.

"A marketing ploy I guess Mr. Bodine. Much like advertising a new operating system so advanced and innovative, even though it might be a poor man's copy of competitor's superior product not prone to viruses."

Mr. Bodine smiled. Not a happy smile, but one a viper might give a mongoose as they squared off.

"Touché."

Mr. Bodine looked at the back stairs and frowned.

"Jasper, say goodnight to your 'friends'. I will be in the car."

Mr. Bodine headed for the door, but then turned and regarded Colby…coldly. "I image we might be seeing more of you again Mr. Stevens. Good evening."

Jasper looked at the others and had no words. He grabbed his bag and nodded before mumbling his goodbyes and followed after his dad.

"Did it just get warmer in here?" Gary asked and looked at the others.

"I felt it too." Darla said.

"What an asshole," Gary said.

Colby looked at Gary. "There is something weird about Mr. Bodine, but he is a busy man."

"I meant Jasper, but his father is a bigger asshole."

That started an argument on the merits of letting Jasper getting involved in the first place. When he arrived at the fundraiser, Gary was against him helping from the start. Why, after the last few years of torment, would Colby consider extending an olive branch. He was trouble and was probably spying for his father. How else had the MacroTECH computer gotten there. Where did it disappear to when nobody remembered getting a claim ticket for it or even receiving it in the first place. And wasn't it Jasper who identified it as being his father's new prototype.

Colby refused to believe that Jasper was involved. Mr. Bodine, definitely, but Jasper? No.

Gary stood up and grabbed his bag. He pulled out the thumb drive that recorded the data from tracing the Shizumu and tossed it on the counter toward Colby.

"I have to go."

Gary looked at the girls and huffed before heading out the back door.

Darla got up and rested a hand on Colby's as he watched Gary storm out the door. "He's just upset. He'll come around."

"Upset at what?"

Darla smiled and looked at Rhea knowingly. They gathered their belongings and each gave Colby a hug and left.

Colby sat at the kitchen Island wondering what had just happened when he heard the sobbing coming from the table at the far end of the kitchen.

Nana sat hunched over the table, crying into her arms.

Colby hurried over and rubbed her arm. "Nannie, what's wrong? Are you upset your magic was weak?"

Nana sobbed harder before finally sniffling and sat back straight as she could have the sagging shoulders and curved spine of an elderly woman.

"It wasn't weak at all my boy."

"So why the water works. You should be happy."

Nana laughed with an uneasy air. "Me having magic back is not something to be happy about. If your grandfather were still around, he could attest to that. It causes me to not be quite myself."

Nana got up and pushed past Colby, heading toward the stove. She turned on the burners and moved a pot on with something that smelt like dirty gym shorts. She began stirring the mystery stew and brushed back her tears and fluffed her hair.

"Dinner will be ready soon. You should go wash up."

Colby left her there, preparing a dinner fit for a green garbage can dwelling monster, and headed up to his room to install the thumb drive and begin analyzing the data from their encounter with the Shizumu. He was tired, and with school and Archeology Club the next day, he was ready for a good night sleep.

Chapter Seventeen

The next meeting of the Archeology Club started with a counting of funds required for the trip and what they made at the fundraiser. Colby sat at the table glancing at Gary, who decided to sit at the other end of the room, and spun his finger around the face of his father's watch mindlessly. He had been wearing the watch on his right wrist opposite his phWatch on the other for weeks now. Colby hadn't remembered why he started wearing it again, but that wasn't what he was thinking about at present.

Colby stared at Gary, brooding over in the corner. He just couldn't understand what was going on with his friend. They had never fought or argued about anything. Colby knew that Gary didn't trust Jasper, and he understood why. He wasn't certain he trusted him entirely either, but there was something else going on that Colby just didn't get.

Gary finally looked over at Colby and gave him a weak smirk. He began to get up and move toward Colby when the door to the classroom opened and in walked Jasper, grinning toward Colby. Gary sat back down and glared at him as Jasper walked past and moved in next to Colby and sat down.

"Ah Jasper, glad you decided to join us, after all," Rigel said as he stood then walk out from behind his desk. "I only now finished tallying or final kitty for our little trip and I think it only fitting you arrive to share the best news of all."

Jasper held the same confused look like the others when they looked at him. He shrugged and looked back at Rigel as the others now did, awaiting this big news.

"As you all know, the first fundraiser didn't come close to what we needed for the trip to the Yucatan. And the Second, although much more successful, still left us shy of the funds we would need to provide for all the lodging, food, travel, and miscellaneous. With our newest member Jasper, those funds have become even further desperate."

Everyone sighed, and Gary grunted as he glared at Jasper.

"Not to worry," Rigel said, "we have a special and most generous donation to our trip that means we have more than enough to complete our planning."

Rigel stepped forward with a letter and handed it to Colby. Colby took the letter and read it to himself before turning toward Jasper and handed it to him.

"What is this all about?" Colby asked. He held a hint of skepticism on his tongue.

Jasper took the letter and read it. He handed it back to Rigel and shook his head and looked at Colby.

"I know nothing about this. You have to believe me."

Colby looked at him with doubt for the first time since their reunion as friends. "Why would he do this?"

"I really don't know what motivates him these days, but something has him interested, and it can't be good."

Colby seemed appeased for the moment.

"Colby, do you want to share the good news?" Rigel asked, ignoring the boys' exchange.
Jasper placed his hand on Colby's, who jerked slightly but didn't pull it free. "Let me please."

Colby nodded.

"It would seem, that for some dubious reason, my father has granted the club unlimited access to the MacroTECH corporate jet for the spring trip to Chichén Itzá." Jasper frowned while he said the words.

The room had remained silent for several moments before a grunt from the far end drew everyone's attention.

"I suppose that is your ticket to joining the club?" Gary asked.

Colby frowned at Gary. "Don't be a jackass. Jasper had nothing to do with this and I think you know it."

An argument erupted between everyone except Rigel, who stood back and watched and listened. Smiling. After several minutes of bickering, Rigel's smile faded into a smirk and then folded into a frown. He held a hand to his temple while the other extend outward.

"Enough!" Rigel shouted over the other voices. "For whatever reason, we have been granted a boon. Let's just accept it and move on to planning this trip. I'd like to get there as not to miss the equinox and solar eclipse."

While everyone muttered and settled down. Colby focused on Rigel's comment about the eclipse. Though the kids had discussed the ramifications of the celestial events occurring on the equinox, they never brought it to Rigel's attention.

"So you realized there is a celestial event happening while we're there professor?" Colby asked.

Rigel looked away and moved back behind his desk. "I am aware, yes. It is a significant time of year regardless, but I did research, as any trained archeologist would do, with the full scope of when and where we would explore."

'Smooth' Colby thought, but he saw through the façade. Rigel knew more than he was letting on, and Colby was determined to find out one way or another. This man was really starting to get under his skin. But now he also had the building animosity between Gary and Jasper. This growing divide was more than the relation to past treatment from Jasper and his former pack of bullies. Gary was being spiteful purposely rather than getting beyond the past history. Colby was beginning to wonder if Gary was going to pull farther away than he already was. It was lowering his spirits over finally having the chance to rebuild a friendship with Jasper. Would he have to lose Gary?

Thankfully, his despondency was interrupted by Darla asking about who all would be traveling beside the students and Professor. She suggested they have at least one other chaperone. A Female because the boys outnumbered the girls. When Rigel asked who might be able to take the time to accompany them, Darla was too quick to suggest Colby's sister Shelly.

"Why would you suggest Shelly? Have you already asked her?"

"She may have suggested it to me herself," Darla admitted. "Several times actually."

Darla glanced over at Rigel and smirked. Colby understood immediately and stifled a laugh before remembering Shelly had a boyfriend Bruce, who might not like the attention she was directing toward the Professor. Then again, he hadn't seen Bruce around lately, not since Shelly left her job at the diner to work at MacroTECH.

"Hey guys, since we are done here," Colby turned to Rigel, "we're done here right?"

Rigel nodded and waved Colby and the kids off. "We'll firm up plans next week. I'll take care of all the ground travel and accommodations."

Colby grabbed his bag and motioned for the others to follow. "Let's stop by the diner for some food and then head to the warehouse."

"Ya," Gary said looking at Jasper. "I feel like some target practice."

Colby looked at Gary and frowned. He didn't like this side of his friend.

When they got to the diner, they each placed orders for takeout and sat at the counter while they waited for their food. Seeing Bruce in the kitchen staring at them over the food counter, Colby smiled and waved. Bruce smiled back and headed out from the side door.

"Hey kids, what's the news?" Bruce said. He looked over to see Jasper sitting next to Colby and tilted his head, but said nothing.

"Not much," Colby said.

"Not much?" Darla said. "We just made a killing at our fundraiser is all. People from all around the area and some further out, all came to drop off their computers and phones and tablets and such. We had more things to fix than I thought we could manage. Thank goodness Jasper showed up to help." Darla smiled at Jasper, who just smirked back and looked down.

Bruce looked again at Jasper. "Ya, I'm sure that helped a lot." He looked back at Darla. "Shelly didn't help out?"

"No, she's too busy you know. She has that new job at MacroTECH. It keeps her really busy." Darla batted her eyes as she looked at

Bruce.

Colby wondered what game Darla was playing.

"Not too busy though that she can't come with us to Mexico on our spring trip." She leaned forward and swung her foot under her bottom so she could sit higher and at eye level with Bruce. "Yep, it's gonna be totes amazeballs. All of us are gonna have so much fun, digging around ancient ruins and then shopping for silver and turquoise…"

Bruce was turning red in the neck. Colby watched him begin twisting the towel he held in his hands.

"It's not going to be all that fun Darla. We will be there to do work for school you know. Shelly is just going to be an adult supervisor because we needed another chaperone."

Darla shrugged. "Ya I suppose while us kids are doing our homework, Shelly will have to hang out with…what did your grandma call him? Oh ya, Professor yummy pants."

The ringing of the service bell saved Bruce from blowing his stack. He nearly jumped when it rang. He turned and grabbed the styrofoam containers and began shoving them into plastic bags. He pushed them forward on the counter toward the kids and told them they could pay on the way out.

Colby grabbed his bag and pulled out his wallet. He opened it and sighed at the meager contents. "I miss her not working here. I'll miss the free food."

Jasper grabbed Colby's check, then the others. "Let me get lunch…as a thank you for letting me join you today. And the other stuff that's happened too."

Before Colby could argue, Jasper was standing at the register handing the cashier money. He turned and looked back at Colby and smiled.

Colby felt an uncontrollable shudder go through him from the feet up. Not one of those ghosts walking on your grave shudders, but something more…intimate. He shook his head and walked out after Jasper and the others.

Darla looked at him and then smiled. She skipped out the door, turning to wave goodbye to Bruce before catching up with the others outside.

"What are we going to do about Bruce, he's gonna go apeshit crazy about her being near Rigel?" Darla asked. She batted her eyes again knowing she was purposely brewing up trouble.

Girls. Colby sighed and frowned. He knew Darla was playing with Bruce. "Not my monkey not my circus, as Nana would say. He's Shelley's problem."

They took the number eight bus down Halsted Street all the way to Goose Island where they got off and walked the rest of the way to their special practice location. The warehouse. Rhea and Darla had many times tried to offer up a new name for the warehouse, but Colby preferred the name as it was. He thought it sounded very 'secret agent'.

Meet me at the warehouse. We have to check in at the warehouse. These thoughts and the fact that the place was protected by magic made Colby feel special. Feeling different all his life now began to make sense and having a special place with special gifts and equally special friends, Colby felt a sense of belonging building inside himself. It was his warehouse, plain and simple.

Once inside, the kids found a place to sit and eat their late lunch. After they had eaten, Jasper poked around the place, admiring the remains of targets that Colby, Shelly, and Gary had left behind on previous visits. Darla and Rhea found some old brooms and began sweeping up the floors and clearing as much debris and dust as they could. Their looks of disgust at the filth left in some corners amused the boys.

Gary demonstrated a few of the things they had learned and what they did with the hashtag magic app while Colby loaded the app on Jasper's phone. He figured that Jasper was one of them now and he needed to be included in on everything. Though Gary protested, vehemently, Colby insisted and trusted Jasper.

It wasn't that Colby was taking Jasper at his word that he was true, it was a feeling. Colby felt a spark renew between himself and Jasper. An old friendship that fell apart but was on the mend. The measure of true friendship is when two people can disagree, fight, and even have a falling out. Then over time, that which brought them together in the beginning will resurface and rebuild on the foundation that could never be destroyed.

Colby smiled and handed the phone over to Jasper. His face lit up as he typed in his first hashtag spell and watched the blue mist swirl from his hand and create a stream of lights that shot up to the ceiling and burst out in all directions. The lights sparkled and fell back to the ground akin to a fourth of July display at Navy Pier.

Darla and Rhea laughed and shouted mock 'oohs and aahs' at the display. They danced with their brooms under the falling lights, giggling the entire time. They cast hashtag spells on them and rode the brooms like the witches of storybooks. Colby couldn't hold back his own laughter as he smiled at their jovial dance and flight through the warehouse. He felt Jasper's strong arm wrap around his shoulder as he laughed along.

Gary stood by the charred remains of targets. Bottles and cans all freshly pelted with shots of magic. He glared at Jasper worming his way into their group. Colby was Gary's friend now. Jasper may have been his friend first, but that was a long time ago and he blew it.

Colby felt the icy stare coming from the corner and looked to see Gary sulking. He waved him over and felt puzzled by his friends unusual behavior. Colby walked over to Gary, who started walking away.

Gary grabbed his backpack and waved off. "I'll see you guys later. I have to head home."

Colby stood there speechless. Gary always came back to his house after they did anything. His parents were never at home so he always had a home at the Stevens' house.

"What's his problem?" Jasper asked.

Darla stood on the other side of Colby and looked at Jasper, then at Colby. She looked then at Gary as he left and glared back in their direction.

"He looks a little green to me," she said.

Colby looked at her. "How can you tell? I can't even tell when he's sunburnt."

Darla shook her head at Colby and smirked. "Boys, sometimes I wonder how you manage to walk upright without a girl telling you how."

Rhea giggled with Darla as they put their brooms away and grabbed their own bags. Colby and Jasper followed behind and they all left the warehouse.

"We can have some real lessons next week if you guys are free," Colby said. "We usually come here just after dawn and spend the entire day."

Jasper and the girls agreed happily and Darla said she would pack a picnic with plenty of food and snacks. She enjoyed any excuse for a picnic. All organic, of course. Rhea agreed as well but insisted on bringing some cleaning supplies and better brooms.

"Those brooms in there just don't have the right balance," Rhea told them as they walked to the bus stop.

"What balance do you need for sweeping?" Colby asked.

"Not sweeping silly, flying."

Colby laughed. Magic, monsters, and flying witches, what next?

Chapter Eighteen

Everyone met downtown outside the warehouse on Saturday morning shortly after dawn. It was still the tail end of winter though there was little to no snow on the ground. The winters in Chicago are very unpredictable and this year it was no exception. The sun was peaking up over the horizon casting a long rippled reflection on the Chicago River. The river bent and weaved through the city breaking up metropolis into large island-like sections and the smaller one that few people realize exist.

Goose Island is a minuscule section of land surrounded by the North Branch Chicago River and the North Branch Canal. Colby had not realized at the time, but his choice of warehouse nestled on this one hundred sixty acre plot of land was special beyond the obvious seclusion it allowed. Being surrounded by water provided a basic barrier to their magic, one that masked their use to all but the Dreggs.

Colby still wasn't certain what the Dreggs wanted, but was aware that they were watching and waiting for some reason. They were a curious race, created by the Nefslama for some purpose not fully explained by Fizz. Fizzlewink has avoided explaining quite a bit and much of what he has said has sounded suspect.

The story of how the Nefslama and Shizumu came to be on Earth was one such story that Colby and Gary both did not believe entirely. There was something missing and both boys could sense it but they simply did not have all the information. Time would tell, they just hoped that things came to light before anything disastrous happened.

When Darla and Rhea arrived to meet Colby, Gary, and Shelly, Gary turned to go toward the back entrance of the warehouse when Colby stopped him.

"We are still waiting for Jasper. He should be here any second."

Gary faced Colby, glaring. "What is he coming for?"

"Because I asked him to. He has magic and is part of the Archeology Club now, so stop being a jerk. It isn't his first time here, what is the problem?"

Gary huffed and kept walking. "I'll be inside."

Colby turned at the sound of steps crunching down on the pebbled surface beside the building. When he turned to find Jasper walking up, Colby smiled. His smile faltered momentarily however when he realized that Jasper must have heard Gary's remark.

Jasper slapped Colby on the shoulder and nodded in the direction Gary went. "We're gonna have a full set of lessons today from the smurf?"

"Yep. We should head in, it's frikkin' freezing out here. I think I'm turning blue as well."

The girls, arms folded and shifting their torsos side to side, agreed through chattering teeth.

The warehouse was much as they had left it last time. Colby and the others were ready to start practicing magic. The only difference was that Fizzlewink added some new obstacles and targets. For some reason, he added large cutouts of the Dreggs. Colby moved to them and pulled them down.

"Fizz! What the hell are you thinking? They're not our enemy."

"Are they not?" Fizz asked and frowned at Colby's doubtful stare. "You know nothing boy."

Colby continued removing the images of Dreggs from the target range and replaced them with generic figures of dark cloaked assailants.

"The Dreggs have done nothing to hinder us," Colby started. "Sure we had an awkward introduction, but they saved me and Gary from that seeker on Halloween."

"The Dreggs do what serves them."

Fizz grunted at Colby's handy-work before hopping down from a barrel and stepping into the middle of the target area.

"We don't have the luxury of time, the proper amount of time it takes to master runes and the magic of Emassa," he added with a hint of haste. "What we have is Colby's hashtag magic and your devices to speed things along." He sniffed and scowled. "This will have to do for most, but I expect you to all master your core gift."

Fizzlewink began the exercises by having Colby and Shelly show the others the hashtags they would be using. He advised them to play to their strengths. Each one of the kids has an affinity to a particular gift, something that came naturally to them and required no augmentation from the #Magic app. Fizzlewink was no fan of the use of their electronics. He wanted them to learn to do without them, but he knew that would take more time than was available before having to face what was coming for them.

They were perplexed at first, not knowing what Fizz meant exactly.

It was Shelly who spoke first and said that her core talent was summoning and speaking to the dead. She could do this without the use of #Magic. It was difficult, but with practice she could pull the Emassa and channel its power into her summonings much easier.

Gary was adept with manipulating objects in a way that allowed him to move or alter them. He would practice his abilities with kinetics without the app.

Healing is what Rhea decided must be her natural affinity. She never got sick. The few occasions she thought she cut herself, her skin closed right up and never bled. And she remembered a time when her family dog got hit by a car. She ran to him and lifted him up crying and felt a warmth spread through her. Her parents never said more, but their reaction to her story at the time was dismissive. The dog had no injuries when they took it to the vet.

Everyone knew what Darla could do, with her persuasive thoughts and movements. She was an empath who could sense emotional states, as well as affect others, and plant ideas. She had tried this multiple times on Colby without success.

Colby was immune to Darla's influence and she could not read his energies or feelings, but the reason was not clear. He figured that was part of his natural gift, but Fizz disagreed and told him they would need more time to figure out his true extent of natural talent. His ability to teleport was only part of what Fizz said would be his primary gift, but that was difficult to tell.

That only left Jasper to share what his gift was. He thought about it and suggested it had to do with the exercises his father constantly made him perform. Drills that would make him run faster, jump higher, lift more weight. He mentioned he felt that his dad wanted him to be some Olympic athlete or something until the first day he pushed Emassa into him.

"He did what?" Fizz asked.

Jasper explained how his father pulled Emassa and fed it into Jasper's core, telling him to hold it there as long as he could. At first it slipped free immediately, but after daily practice he could hold larger and larger amounts until he fell asleep at night.

"I can't seem to hold it once I go to sleep."

Shelly snickered. "Colby used to have that same problem when he was little."

Colby just shot her a narrow stare and moved the conversation along. "That could be useful. I've never tried to store power before."

"Why would you need to, you can pull it freely as much and whenever you want?" Shelly asked.

Fizz answered that it was an extremely useful ability, if you are cut off or limited in access, you might need reserves. And sometimes a sudden burst of strength could be useful, though he refused to share examples. Fizz asked Jasper to begin helping the others learn this ability if able, by showing them the exercises they would need to strengthen their bodies to build a central spot within to store the power. Their core.

As Jasper went from each of his new friends to instruct them on the exercises they would need to perform regularly, he began to feel more acceptance. Gary listened to his instructions, but he still kept himself guarded and Jasper noticed. He would have to figure out how to prove himself loyal to Gary.

The kids all began testing their own talents without the phWatches. They found they each had little to no trouble calling their natural gifts since they could each pull directly from the Emassa now that Colby had exposed them to the source somehow. The only one having trouble was Colby.

"You still have some sort of block my boy," Fizz said. "I know you have worked on facing some internal struggles with your temper and emotions, but you haven't worked with your focus."

"I try Fizz, it's just not so simple."

Colby explained that as he would focus, he could see the source within his thoughts. He could grab the Emassa and will it to him, but as soon as he tried to focus it on a particular action, it pulled away and fought his hold. If he attempted to try less, it was the same result. No matter if he tried forcing the flow to his will or coaxing it to comply, he had the same loss of control. And now his head was beginning to throb behind his eyes.

"This is what comes of relying on your gadgets." Fizz frowned and pointed to Colby's watch. "In my youth, we trained and studied for longer than you could imagine, and we used no tools but our own will and strength."

"I'll keep trying."

Fizz softened his features and eased out of his slouch. "Perhaps try something simpler. You know the runes for a shield don't you?"

Colby nodded.

"Good, then focus on them in your mind and work on creating a shield without outside help."

Colby went back to his training, attempting to hide his feelings of inadequacy. He watched as the others managed to proceed well enough. Shelly was talking to some distortion in the air before her. Colby imagined it was a ghost, as he couldn't make it out well from this distance.

Darla was influencing rats to move around in tempo to a song she hummed. Dancing rats. Fizz was enthralled.

Rhea used a knife to cut herself and would heal the wound

effortlessly.

Gary levitated stones and other debris, then hurled them at Jasper, who used bursts of stored Emassa to knock them aside. Gary smiled as he hurled the objects.

Colby grimaced at the scenes playing out, more than a little disturbed.

In his own corner of the open warehouse floor, Colby began running through the runes in his head for creating a deflective shield of air around himself. He ran through their precise order over and over again until he was certain he had them clearly seated in the forefront of his thoughts. He reached out for the Emassa while trying to maintain his hold on the rune construct. It was difficult and his head began to ache, but he managed to slowly bring them together.

As they neared connection, the point where he could cast the spell, the veins on his temples throbbed and protruded. The pounding increased as rivers of sweat poured from his scalp and cascaded down his face. He squeezed his eyes shut against the stinging of the salty liquid flowing from his forehead. But he continued on, determined to succeed. A feeling of encouragement coursed through him as he felt a hand pressing his shoulder. Jasper.

As Jasper's hand made contact with Colby's shoulder, an instant rush of Emassa poured into him, igniting his spell. Punching out from his own core, an invisible force of air burst out around him sending Jasper flailing toward the wall twenty feet away. Colby watched in horror as his friend went flying through the air at great speed. But instantly, Colby felt as though time slowed and he pushed his hands out and reached for Jasper.

Purple tinted white ribbons of Emassa rushed from his fingers and wrapped around Jasper, halting his movement. Colby blinked and the ribbons flashed out of existence, releasing Jasper to fall a few feet straight down to the now debris cleared floor. Colby was thankful the girls brought their brooms.

Jasper's head hit the ground and met with a sickly smack. He moaned as his eyes fluttered and then went still. Jasper lay on the floor unmoving with a trickle of blood spreading into a pool beneath his skull.

Colby rushed to his side with the others close behind, but he reached Jasper first and checked his pulse. It was weak, but his friend was alive. Colby turned his attention to the blood pooling from the back of Jasper's head and quickly called a hashtag spell for healing. As soon as the spell began to construct, Colby felt something was wrong.

His wrist began to burn as pulses of energy emerged around his hand. Colby pulled his hand back to avoid hurting Jasper further and tried to dispell the construct, but it kept growing to the point that Colby's nose and ears began to bleed. Colby fell back screaming. Rhea and Darla ran to Jasper while Shelly and Gary tried to help Colby.

Fizz watched from a short distance. His lips curved into an imperceptible smile as the human Rhea quickly healed Jasper's wound and fed refreshing energy into him. When he was certain the boy would be fine, his attention turned to Colby writhing on the dirty warehouse floor. Shelly and Gary were unable to get close to him, the power growing out of control on Colby's watch as the others began to feel the heat rising from their own devices. Any moment now, Fizz thought.

Colby shouted and screeched unintelligibly as he thrashed around under the growing power surrounding him. His thoughts were a jumble of runes and symbols as the hashtag network unraveled inside his head. More and more pressure asserted itself within every corner of his mind until a single point of focus came to him. An image of his father played across his waning consciousness.

He watched his father gathering power and pushing toward him. He didn't understand what was happening. Why would his father be attacking him? Colby had no strength to defend himself. He wasn't even sure what he saw was real, all the while he held as much of the power within himself, afraid of releasing it upon his friends. Before he could ponder his thoughts any longer, the stream of Emassa from his father's likeness engulfed him.

A moment of clarity overtook Colby as the white energy buffered the agony of the swirling mass of blue and red magic surrounding him. At that moment, he knew where the menacing spell was coming from. His phWatch.

Colby summoned the strength through pure force of will and raised his right arm. With another forced movement, he slammed his phWatch down to the floor where it met the stone with a blinding flash, sending waves of energy out in all directions.

The rouge spell diminished and harmlessly dissipated as Colby pulled in a breath of relief. He sat up to see his friends and Fizz staring at him oddly. When the kids began to approach Colby, Fizz called them to a halt from nearing Colby.

"Stand back a moment." Fizz never took his eyes off Colby as he took a few steps closer. His eyebrows rose a fraction, enough for Colby to perceive. "What do you feel?"

"I feel fine," Colby said surprised himself that he wasn't in pain at least.

"That's not what I asked. What…not how."

Sensing the edge to Fizz's voice, Colby explored the meaning. He looked at the phWatch damaged and non-functional, but not destroyed. From the look on Fizz's cat-like face, Colby knew that wasn't what his question regarded. He delved into himself to check because he did sense something that was new. He searched within himself until he discovered a well of power. Emassa. He had created a core for storing a vast amount of Emassa within himself by holding back the spell that threatened his friends.

Colby gasped at the amount of power he held and looked and Fizz, wide-eyed yet proud. Fizz returned the smile.

"How did you know?" Colby asked.

Fizz twirled his right brow and turned, feigning interest similar to a cat that could care less for engaging with a human. "I can see it. You shine like a sun to those who can see as I do."

The others looked on with puzzled expressions, but Colby was more interested in checking on Jasper, who, still sitting on the filthy floor, smirked over at him.

"Are you ok?" Colby asked as he reach out a hand to help Jasper up from the ground.

Jasper took the offered hand and stood. "I feel fine. A little tired but I'll be good as new after a good meal." His stomach grumbled in time with Colby's.

They laughed together and clasped arms. Colby felt a slight tug of war between their cores. Jasper's was empty and it seemed somehow either he was inadvertently pulling on Colby's or Colby was pushing some toward Jasper. It felt oddly intimate. Again. Colby quickly pulled back and locked his power within. Jasper simply grinned.

Colby released Jasper's arm, confident he could stand on his own. Colby removed the busted phWatch from his wrist and placed it in his pocket. Another grumble from his stomach caused him to look at his father's watch he wore on the other wrist.

"I think that's time for lunch, and perhaps enough for today," Colby said. "Anyone want a lift back to my house?"

"We took public trans, cheesehead," Shelly said. "Beside, Darla packed a picnic."

"Um…I think it got a little messed up during the excitement." Darla pointed at the wrecked mess her packed lunches were in. The rats didn't seem to mind.

"I'll go get some food at the corner store down the street," Shelly said.

Colby smiled and popped from where he stood to the other side of the warehouse. "Not necessary. I think I have the hang of it now. Anyone want a go for a ride?"

No one said a word but shook their heads.

"I'd rather ride on the back of Darla's broom," Gary said.

"Fine," Colby said. "I'll just go get some food and be back in a few."

Without another word, Colby disappeared. Twenty minutes passed before he finally reappeared, scaring the crap out of Darla, who stood inches from where he materialized, carrying a large cooler bag and several plastic sacks filled with sandwiches and snacks.

They all sat around eating lunch and discussed more things to practice and what happened to Colby. He described what had happened, leaving out the part about seeing his father. He now had a large pocket within himself to gather and store Emassa, but his thoughts returned to the malfunction of his phWatch. He had no idea what had happened. The others' phWatches as well as Jasper's phone, still functioned with the hashtags stored in memory, but they no longer had an active connection to the hashtag server after Colby's watch was busted.

Colby needed to find out what happened and wondered if his computer somehow became infected after plugging in the thumb drive holding the data trace of the Shizumu from that MacroTECH laptop.

Chapter Nineteen

Colby made little progress in diagnosing the issues with his hashtag servers. There was no sign of a virus, but the few times he attempted reconnecting his repaired phWatch to the network the runes would jumble and begin to feedback. He quickly absorbed the excess power while severing the device's connection to the server.

Having the ability to store Emassa was indeed handy as Fizz had implied. Colby was getting better at controlling his teleports as well as creating a shield and sending out defensive bursts of power like those he accidentally sent at Jasper months earlier during their confrontation at school. There was still something Fizz was not saying, but Colby was not ready to press the point.

Now that they were able to at least use memory stored rune constructs from their phWatches or phones, the group could research and manually enter them as needed. It was arduous work, but they were at least building up a store of offensive, defensive, and practical spells. Work on the main server would have to wait.

After finishing analysis of the information from the thumb drive, the source was traced back to MacroTECH. No surprise. They now knew where to proceed next but had no idea how to break into the isolated network within the company. Shelly's new friend at work who worked in tech support had not been to work in weeks and Aria's latest news had them concerned. She was promoted.

Aria mentioned she would be working with the upper management pool of administrative assistants, but had more news to share at dinner.

Family dinner was a welcome return for Colby. It had been so long since he could remember sitting in the dining room, table properly set, with the entire family eating real food together. The only exception was the not having his dad present part. It was a start and a happy new beginning since his mother had cleared away the fog of drinking and denial. Shelly worked regular daytime hours in her new job. So they could all enjoy time as a family and eat together.

The table was set for five when Colby entered the dining room. He wasn't sure who was coming for dinner until he heard Gary in the kitchen talking to Nana. It seemed his parents were out of town again and Gary would be staying with the Stevens for awhile.

"Your parents sure are traveling a lot lately," Nana said. "That's no way to raise a child in my opinion." She looked to Gary apologetically. "We do enjoy you here with us, but don't you miss them when they are gone so much?"

Gary shrugged. "I haven't thought about it for a while." He turned to Colby standing in the doorway. "Hey dude, looks like we'll be bunking again for a while."

Colby smiled but felt odd. For some reason, he wasn't as pleased as he normally would have been to have Gary staying over. The two boys usually talked and played video games well into the night. They were like brothers, but for some reason, Colby was feeling put out by the latest imposition.

"Sure," Colby said. "It'll be great."

Gary tilted his head, sensing something off in his friend's response. "Something wrong?"

Colby caught himself. "Just the weird stuff with the hashtag server and now my mom getting promoted to and executive assistant."

"Really? Who is she working for?"

"She was supposed to find that out today, so I guess we'll hear about it soon when she get's home. But I wouldn't take a bet on who it is." Colby felt in his gut that it would be Mr. Bodine, but with all the bizarre happenings lately, he wouldn't be surprised if it were someone else entirely.

The boys finished setting the table and putting the dishes of food on the buffet when they heard Shelly and Aria enter through the kitchen door. Being as though the garage was in the back of the house, they hardly ever used the front door. And since they were small, the kids were always told to use the back because of the mud room. They were always covered in grime.

Colby looked at his mother expectantly, but she waved him off.

"When we eat." She looked at Gary. "Oh hello Gary, will you be joining us for dinner as well?" She asked, but there was no question in her tone.

"I'm staying over for a while since my parents are off again on some trip."

Aria tutted. "They travel so much, I can't remember the last time I had the joy of your mother's company for coffee. How is…your mom anyway?"

Colby caught the pause in his mother's question. Was she slipping again maybe, not being able to remember Mrs. Connor's name? Then again, Colby couldn't remember it either, but they were always Mrs.

And Mr. Connor. What were their names? Colby lost his thoughts as they made their way to the table and sat for dinner.

Before anyone would start eating, they all looked at Aria…waiting.

Aria smiled and looked at them. "Mr. Bodine."

"HA! I knew it. That wily old bas-"

"Mother…" Aria interrupted.

Nana cleared her throat and looked at the kids. "Please, these kids have a more colorful vocabulary than me I would bet. Anyway, he's behind all this then. This cinches it."

"Not necessarily," Shelly said between chewing. "That list had several people on it. Anyone of them could be working alone or together."

"Are you prepared to find out for certain mom?" Colby asked.

Aria swallowed. "Yes…just as soon as I get back."

"Tomorrow then?"

Aria shook her head side to side. "Not exactly, I mean back from my trip."

Aria explained that as part of her new job she would have to undergo a rigorous training program. This program not only taught her to anticipate the needs and requirements of her duties, but also required her to undergo many hours of extended training. Her training would include various tracks including legal issues, resourcing, vendor relations, media relations and more. She would be on a several week long retreat at one of the MacroTECH training facilities at some resort in Flagstaff Arizona.

She passed the brochure to Shelly, who began to thumb through its contents. A slow transition from curiosity to confusion then annoyance filtered across her face. She grumbled and handed the folded pamphlet over to Colby. He began to read through it and became aware of what had Shelly concerned.

"This is like a resort for letting loose, not learning anything." Colby showed the material to Nana, who grunted in agreement.

"Sodom and Gomorra," she said, dropping the pamphlet as though it burnt her fingers. "This is nothing but a ploy to get you out there and put you right back into the drunken daze you've lived under for years. Somehow that bastard found out your weakness and is intent on putting you back in the box so he might let Pandora out."

"I'll be fine, I read about the place. There may be a lot of…shall we say recreational options, but I am not in the same state I was so many months ago." She saw the doubt in her family's eyes and couldn't help but feel stung by their lack of faith in her. "I swear to you, I will be strong."

Feeling a bit at ease, but not entirely, Colby broke the silence that followed. "I wonder that this isn't a very convenient trip."

"What do you mean?" Aria asked.

"You are going away at the same time Gary's parents are away. Our club trip will be leaving as well and that leaves only Nana and Fizzlewink here to watch the house." He paused so they might understand his meaning. "Divide and conquer? Does nobody see this?"

Colby mentioned how it all seemed too coincidental. Everyone in different places. The house, with his father's study, left to an old woman with limited power and an obtuse and rarely present little blue Nefslama standing guard. Gary's parents are sent who knows where, and Aria being sent to a booze and party fest of a 'retreat'; it was all just too convenient.

"Someone wants us all separated and weakened. Who's going to protect the house?"

"I don't know," Aria said. "No one beside you can enter your father's study, we all know that. Your nannie is not so easily overpowered, especially not now that she is getting some effect from the flow of Emassa. You kids will be fine with Shelly and your professor chaperoning. What is there to gain?"

Colby pondered the question but had no real answer besides a feeling of dread. He wondered if maybe he could get the Dreggs to keep an eye on the house at least. They seemed intent on following the path that Colby's rise in knowledge and power was taking, it might be in their interest to keep outsiders away from his home. He made it a point to remember to contact Conrad and ask his help.

"I'll be fine," Nana said. "And you can take that magic blue dwarf with you. I have a pet carrier around here somewhere."

"What about MacroTECH?" Colby asked after dinner while they cleaned up. "Mr. Bodine is up to something and we all know it. There is something going on in that building associated with the Shizumu and I think he knows about it if he isn't behind it all. We need to get in there and gain access to the isolated network."

"You can get your chance in a couple days I expect," Aria said. "It's my understanding that your school has been invited to a surprise and rarely offered field-trip to the headquarters."

"What is he up to?" Colby asked.

"Keep your enemies at hand? Or something like that," Gary answered.

Nana agreed as she gulped a glass of wine. "Keep them close Gary my boy. Oh yes, he is a wily old…prick."

"I think bastard was better mother," Aria said.

Colby watched as his grandmother fidgeted at the table and grumbled under her breath. He wondered if she was upset at being left alone to look after the house. When he mentioned having the Dreggs look out for the house, from outside, of course, she only grunted her acquiescence. There was something else bothering her.

After dinner, Colby and Gary were in Colby's room looking at the progress of their trace on the Shizumu when they heard cursing and shouting from outside the window. Colby rushed over and threw open the window to see his grandma in the side yard yanking at her herbs and plants she had only just started planting. They had grown surprisingly fast and she seemed proud of them before. Now she yanked at them as though they were invasive weeds, choking out the other flowers and shrubs.

"Should we go down there?" Gary asked.

Colby, wide-eyed, turned to his friend. "Are you crazy? Look at her. She's acting like a nut-job. She's been acting weirder since getting exposure to the Emassa."

Colby remembered then, a conversation where Nana mentioned something about not liking herself and having some strange reaction when she had magic before. He knew in her younger days she had magic, but it had been blocked along with everyone else's access since he was a toddler. When his father cast whatever spell to protect him, it also kept his grandmother relatively sane it seemed.

He also knew from his habitual eavesdropping as a youngster, that his grandma remembered things from the night his father left. Images and words she sometimes let slip when she fought with Aria. If she was just a human with an ability, how was it she wasn't affected the same as the others. Why didn't she forget everything as well?

As he sat in the window wondering, Colby failed to notice the sudden quit that returned to the side yard. When he heard his name shouted from the yard, he jumped and nearly fell from the sill.

"Colby Jarrod Stevens," Nana shouted. "If you're gonna sit there nosing into my business, you can damn well get down here and help clean up this mess."

She pointed to the array of foliage and uprooted plants all around he feet. She stood there, hands on her over ample hips and stuck her head toward him. As she continued to shout at him to get downstairs, her chin waddle moved in time with her shifting head and wagging finger. He hadn't been busted for listening in on adult conversations in a long time.

In the yard, Colby and Gary helped replant some of the herbs and flowers that were not obliterated by Nana's tirade. She refused to believe them when told that it was indeed her that uprooted the plants. She professed that it was probably the little shits from the next house who had a tendency to play in other peoples' yards. Or it was that no good 'little blue monkey'.

"I've caught him in my plants before…doing his business. Why is it he can't just use a regular bathroom? Change back from a cat and pee standing up."

"I'm sure he wasn't diddling on your daisies Nana."

Nana sat on the bench beside the garden and put her head in her hands. She sighed and shook her head.

"Are you ok?" Colby asked. "You don't look good."

Nana waved off his hand. "I'm fine. I just keep having these episodes of deja vu, but they are disjointed and make me dizzy. I don't like having the touch of Emassa again."

Colby wondered if she wasn't suppressing something. An event that might have happened when she had magic as a younger woman. Something that made her glad to be rid of magic, that now resurfaced as her connection to magic returned.

"You boys go ahead inside and get ready for this field-trip announcement tomorrow."

"Are you gonna be ok?" Colby asked.

"Fine my little fart-blossom. I will be fine."

She gladly took a kiss on the cheek from the boys and sat there staring at the plants the boys did not return to the ground. They were torn apart and good thing. Looking at them she had one of her flashes of a fractured memory. It involved those plants and the noxious smell they emitted reinforced her revulsion of them. She flicked her hand at them and to her own surprise, they burst into flames and burnt to cinders.

Nana yanked her hand back and looked at it with horror in her eyes. She looked around and quickly got up from the bench. Tucking her hands in her housecoat pockets, she waddled back into the house passing by the yellow eyes peering out from the bushes without noticing them.

Chapter Twenty

True to his mother's word from dinner the night before, during the school's morning PA announcements the Dean said there would be a field trip on Friday to MacroTECH. The invite was for the members of certain clubs and they would receive permission slips to take home for their parent sign.

"Your parents aren't home to sign yours Gary. Do you think they'll accept if Nana signs it? She already has permission in the office to call you off or pick you up."

Gary winked. "I've been signing their names for years. Even if they were home, the school would probably think their real signatures were fake."

"Ya, nobody looks at these things that close anyway."

The rest of the week went by quickly as the kids met each day after school and practiced their natural gifts and those they had cached in the memory of their phWatches. Jasper finally had Colby modify the watch his father had given him that was made by MacroTECH. It wasn't much different from the ones Colby made, so reloading a modified operating systems and loading the #Magic app was not difficult.

Colby showed Jasper how it worked and helped him create a few basic constructs to store in the device. Once Jasper was comfortable, he began creating his own. The group practiced hard each afternoon and felt exhausted by the time they each went home for the night. Their work was paying off. However, each was able to feel more ability to store some Emassa and they began to coax out some basic spells naturally with little concentration.

When the day of the tour arrived on Friday, they were all beyond tired. Darla had barely applied her usual layer of makeup and wore a simple ponytail. Rhea looked much the same though she never wore makeup and usually wore her hair back anyway so the only indication of her tired state were the red puffy eyes and sour disposition. The boys barely combed their hair but at least they showered, brushed their teeth, and put on deodorant. The girls were thankful for the effort.

They all sat in silence on the bus as the rest of the kids invited handed over their permission slips and boarded. Before the bus could close the door and head off, the assistant dean stepped on and walked toward where Colby and the others were sitting.

"Mr. Connor, could you explain how your mother signed this slip while away on business?"

Gary stared back, too tired to think quickly. He began to mumble when the Assistant Dean reached out to grab him off the bus.

"You don't need to take him away sir," Darla said softly. "His mother scanned and e-mailed the slip back to Gary just this morning."

The man let go of Gary and stepped back slowly. He shook his head for a moment, but continued to stare at Darla who looked strained under the mental contact. He finally accepted the truth in Darla's words and left the bus. Once off, the bus driver closed the door and grinded the gears before jerking the bus into motion. The Assistant Dean stood on the parkway gazing after the bus for a few moments before heading back to the school.

"That was close," Gary said. "Thanks, Darla."

"OMG that took everything I had. I'm so tired I didn't have time to store much power this morning and pulling from the flow was hard."

"That was so cool," Jasper said. "You were so like…'these are not the droids you're looking for'."

They all shared a tired laugh before sitting back and resting quietly while their group headed toward the enemies lair downtown. Only Gary and Colby knew what the side plan was. They shared with the girls and Jasper that they needed to find out what the link was to the laptop they encountered at the fundraiser. But they weren't about to tell Jasper they thought his dad was behind it or even party to whatever was happening. Colby trusted him but still had an itch that there was something not right when he was around. Gary agreed.

Once they finally arrived at the downtown offices of MacroTECH, they all climbed off the bus feeling somewhat more rested, but not nearly at full strength. The five of them stood apart from the rest of the group. They stared up at the towering spires of the glass and steel building as it gleamed in the sunlight and stretched up into the thin clouds drifting past. It would have seemed beautiful if they were not keenly aware that there was work to be done inside, and they were outside the safety of their home or the warehouse where they practiced their magic.

They were quickly met by a staffer who guided everyone inside the immense lobby. Filled with potted trees, a miniature forest of bamboo, and fountains spitting water from the center of coy-filled ponds, the space felt more like an enclosed habitat at the zoo than the lobby of a building. The other thing the kids noticed was the uncomfortable feeling of nothingness that crept over them as they ventured deeper into the building. They were being cut off from the flow of Emassa.

"I don't like this," Darla said. "I barely had time to gather more, and now I can't touch the flow."

The others concurred and looked at Colby. "I have plenty if you need it. I didn't seem to lose any last night as I slept."

Jasper tilted his head as he accepted Colby's hand. He allowed the Emassa to flow into himself as Colby offered. "You'll have to tell me how you managed that."

"I just imagined a barrier around it, holding it in," he said. Colby spread some Emassa around to the others leaving himself more than enough for an emergency or two. He followed his friends as they took up the end of the line of students being led by their guide.

Gary sidled up to Colby, careful to not draw Jasper's attention. "Was that such a great idea, filling up Jasper's Emassa tank so to speak?"

Colby shrugged. "What's the harm? I have plenty and he can't store as much as I imagined compared to me."

"What I mean, is it seems a bit odd that his old man had him learning to store Emassa. Now we come to his building where the flow is mysteriously blocked…"

Colby slowed a bit, doubt creeping into his thoughts. It was too late now. Colby could probably take it back, but what if he were wrong. He didn't want to ruin the rekindled bond he was growing with Jasper if he was being played. He pulled Gary along by his sleeve and caught up with the others.

"Keep your eyes peeled." Colby tried not to laugh at how 'secret agent' he sounded.

They soon found themselves in the main cafeteria, though it more resembled a fine restaurant than an employee eatery. They all took seats as the guide told them they would first enjoy a hearty breakfast so they would be ready for the long tour around the facility. Colby and the others were glad for the food since they were too tired to eat anything before leaving for school that morning.

As the food was put out before them family style, all the kids dug in and filled their plates. While they ate, Colby noticed a familiar face approaching. Shelly walked up to the tables with the worst fake smile Colby had ever seen. He grinned and tried not to laugh. Now that she worked for MacroTECH and spied from the inside, she had to be something she wasn't…pleasant.

Shelly looked at Colby but held her broad and toothy smile. "Good morning students. My name is Shelly Stevens and I am the manager here at the MacroTECH employee lounge and dining facility. If there is anything you need before starting your formal tour, please don't hesitate to ask."

In spite of himself, Colby couldn't resist raising his hand. "Miss Stevens."

Shelly leveled her eyes at her little brother. Her mouth and smile sweetly said, "Yes, is there something I can get you?" Her eyes said, 'You're gonna get it you little shit.'

"Could we get some cappuccinos? Long hours of studying last night has left us beat."

Shelly knew all too well how tired they were. She was beyond dead on her feet as well since she trained alongside them. She smiled and nodded before returning moments later with the requested drinks. She set one down in front of each of Colby's close friends before leaning to his ear while setting his down.

"You're lucky I'm too tired to fight and it's too crowded to send sparks into your ass," she whispered.

"Love you too sis," Colby said with a wink.

She reached into her pocket and retrieved something before handing it off to Colby. "Take this. I lifted it off a flirty tech guy when I got in this morning. It'll be hours before he misses it."

Colby glanced at the restricted access badge before stuffing it in his pocket. "How will he not notice it's missing?"

Shelly smiled. "He still has his regular ID badge that gets him access to the only place he'll be for a while today. I slipped some liquid ExLax into his coffee after he pinched my ass." She winked and started to walk away. "Drink up little brother."

Colby was suddenly not in the mood for his coffee.

Finished eating, Colby wiped his mouth and began to stand when a pair of hands rested on his shoulders and pushed him back down. A strange sensation tingled then stopped as the hands met his shoulders.

"Good morning young adults," Mr. Bodine said, attempting to hide his contempt and superiority.

Colby felt his words more than heard them. He managed to wriggle free and push to the side as Mr. Bodine walked along the table and spoke.

"You will forgive my intruding on your meal I hope. I will not be able to join you on this tour due to my very busy schedule. I thought I would at least take a few moments to greet and welcome you to my home away from home."

"As if you ever left here to go to your real home," Jasper mumbled.

Mr. Bodine snapped his head toward Jasper and narrowed his eyes.

Colby, sitting next to Jasper, wondered how the man even heard Jasper at all. As though his thoughts sounded from a megaphone, Mr.

Bodine's eyes moved to center on Colby's.

"Ah, if it isn't the renowned Runes champion and academically superior Mr. Stevens. We are humbled to have you in our presence today. Perhaps you might observe something on your tour that might need improvement and share it with your guide." The sarcasm dripped from every syllable. "Perhaps you will be a good influence on my boy Jasper, after all."

Feeling the weight of his father's disapproval by way of humiliation, Jasper began to withdraw into his former self.

"You never know Mr. Bodine. He could be more like Colby sooner than you think," Gary said loud enough for the man to hear, eliciting a frown from father and son alike.

Jasper pushed away from Colby and got up from the table to sit away from the others.

Mr. Bodine's smile broadened as he walked away from the kids who now giggled and stared at Colby and Jasper.

Colby pushed at Gary. "What the hell was that?"

Gary shrugged like he didn't know what was going on.

Colby started toward Jasper but stopped when he turned the other way. Darla tapped his shoulder and shook her head.

"You stay, Rhea and I will keep Jasper company and talk to him while you and Gary find a way to sneak off and do what we really came here for."

They all made their way into a large auditorium and took seats in the first few rows except Colby and Gary, who sat further back. Soon they all settled their idle chatter when the lights began to dim and a curtain opened, revealing a large screen with the MacroTECH logo on it vividly lighting up the space before them. The room hushed as a movie began welcoming them to MacroTECH industries.

Colby and Gary saw this as their chance. With the room dark and attention split they could sneak out. As the film played, they watched the other kids in the room seem mesmerized by the images on the screen. Even the tour guide was entranced by the words and images that played across the screen showing the wonders and glory of everything MacroTECH. Without further hesitation, the two boys slipped out the side door off to find their way to the restricted server room.

***

After the film, Darla and Rhea kept close to Jasper, hoping to keep him from noticing the two missing members of their group. While they followed along with the others, they talked about what was bothering him.

"Why do you let your father's words get to you?" Darla asked.

Jasper looked at her like she was speaking a foreign language. "You have no idea what he's become. His word is more than just talk."

Darla felt the fear surge through him as Jasper thought of his dad. She sent soothing into him and watched as some of the tension left his shoulders. After a few minutes of walking in silence, Jasper was ready to talk more.

"You know Colby and I were once best friends long ago, but after my mother died and we moved away everything was different. My dad somehow changed overnight and I didn't understand. There are so many things…I just can't talk about them. All I know is that when he compares me to Colby, he isn't being nice. And I hate him for it."

"You don't blame Colby though do you?" Darla asked.

Jasper hesitated but looked at Darla. "No. I wish I could be more like him."

Darla smiled. "Then you should tell Colby that, and forget about what that…that man says. You know he isn't really your father at least not his words or feelings."

Jasper nodded. "I didn't want to admit it, but I've wondered since the day he introduced me to Emassa. All his previous drills on strength and endurance made sense. Then when he pushed Emassa into me a few months back, the confusion began to lift."

"You should share this with Colby," Rhea said. "He can help your father."

Jasper turned to look for Colby but didn't find him or Gary. "What are they up to?" he asked as panic covered his eyes. He realized they had moved off from the group and it sunk in. While everyone else was mesmerized by the film, Colby being somehow immune to Darla was likely so with the film's spell. "They're heading for a trap."

"What?" Darla asked. "How do you know?"

"I know how that thing puppet playing around with my real dad thinks. He didn't arrange for this tour without a reason. We were all dazed by that movie, Colby wouldn't be."

"What should we do?" Darla asked.

Jasper sent the girls to find Shelly and get out of the building while he tried to find Colby and Gary. He wondered how Gary was able to resist the effects of that movie.

***

Colby and Gary wandered around, ducking into doorways and around corners when they encountered security or other people who might catch them where they shouldn't be. Luckily, MacroTECH recruited young talent right out of college and didn't have a dress code so the boys were able to blend in, for the most part. Gary suggested, on more than one occasion, they should put illusions on themselves to look like one of the employees, but Colby refused to waste the Emassa they might need later.

As they snuck around yet another corner, they found the room they were looking for. They faced a wall of windows that showed a room beyond with raised floors and racks and racks of servers. Wires and flashing lights filled the darkness between the rows of machines. There was no one in the room.

"Now we see if this badge Shelly lifted will work," Colby said as he retrieved the employee ID from his pocket.

"Wait," Gary said. He pointed to a panel on the wall next to the box where Colby prepared to swipe the ID card. "That looks like a bio-security pad."

Colby pulled the badge back and scanned the hall behind them. "Now what?"

Gary smirked and snatched the badge from Colby's hand. "Let me do my thing."

Without looking around to check the coast was clear, Gary placed his own hand on the pad to align with the outlined hand of the security panel. He closed his eyes and focused prior to releasing Emassa from his center and letting it flow from his palm. After a few seconds, a light flashed on the card reader and Gary swiped. A light buzz filled the hallway, emanating from the door.

Colby looked around before grabbing the door handle and swinging it open. With a triumphant smile and silently mouthed whoot, Gary followed as the two boys entered the restricted area in search of a place to plug in their thumb drive.

Colby and Gary moved from the view of anyone directly outside the room. The windows that allowed for any passersby to see them lurking about only gave a direct view to a small portion of the room.

Row after row stretched before them. The limited light from the windows to the hall gave the illusion the server racks went on into the infinite darkness. Even the flashing of lights was swallowed up by the pitch at the far side of the room.

"What I wouldn't give to have a setup like this," Colby said.

Lost in his awe of the immense processing power of all these networked computers, Colby jumped at the tap on his shoulder.

"What are you doing in here?" the bulking security guard said.

Caught and unable to get his vocal cords, brain, and tongue to work as a unit, Colby gurgled incomprehensibly. Gary was nowhere in sight. As he began to back away from the guard, the buzzing of the door drew his attention.

"Sorry I was so long," Jasper said. "Are you ready to go?"

"Sure," Gary said emerging from the darkness between rows of servers. "This was awesome."

He grabbed Colby and pushed him toward Jasper, who nodded to the guard and led the way out of the room to freedom. Jasper gave each boy a look that told them to keep their mouths shut and play along until they were well away.

Once outside the building and reconnected to the flow of Emassa, the boys released their anxiety with nervous laughs and rushed breaths.

"That was so wicked," Gary said. "How did you know where we were anyway?"

Jasper told them about the movie and how they were somehow spelled by it. Once they exited and continued the tour, Darla explained where the two boys went. Jasper realized his father was likely behind it and that there would be trouble. Jasper used his own badge, being the son of the CEO, to get through the building and restricted area.

"Did you at least do what you went there for?"

Gary nodded.

"Good. Hopefully, the guard will not suspect anything. I know him and he's dumber than the jack-wads I used to hang with."

The girls soon found them and Shelly waved them over to her car. She quit her job after finding out what the girls told her, feeling it no longer safe.

"What do we do about mom, she left on that trip already?"

"Mom will have to take care of herself," Shelly said. "We leave for Mexico in the morning so there is nothing we can do besides send her a message of warning."

The kids joined the others on the bus back to school and Shelly drove off home.

"I really liked that job," Shelly said then turned the corner toward home.

Chapter Twenty-One

Riding to the airport in a limousine to catch a private jet, was beyond uncomfortable for someone like Colby, who until recently, lived not to draw attention to himself. Jasper insisted on picking everyone up that morning since they would be using his dad's company jet. He figured it was worth taking advantage while having the chance since whatever his dad was up to, it seemed in his best interest to keep the kids safe. They all knew it was a way to keep track and spy on their movements, but knowing your being watched makes it easier to deceive and keep up your guard.

Colby sat next to Jasper on the rear-facing seat after helping the girls take seats and settle in. After Gary had tossed his bag in the trunk, he jumped in and pushed himself onto the seat between Jasper and Colby. He interrupted Jasper before he could begin speaking with Colby.

"We were talking," Colby said.

Gary shrugged. "So talk."

Jasper looked at Colby and shook his head with a look of defeat.

Colby would have to find out what he wanted that was obviously not meant for Gary to take part. So they rode to the airport private plane and charters area in quit. At least from the boys end of the vehicle.

The girls were all chattering about the trip. Even Shelly was engaged - though less animated - in conversation with the younger Darla and Rhea. They were comparing their Indiana Joan's style clothes they packed and the excitement of going somewhere exotic. The boys just rolled their eyes and did their best to ignore them.

The private plane was ready for them to board when they arrived at the hanger. Besides the company logo on the tail, the plane appeared outwardly understated. Compared to the three-thousand dollar suit wearing ostentatious man who ran the company, the plane seemed… plain.

Jasper noticed Colby assessing the aircraft. "Dad bought this before he changed. I remember when he went to work wearing jeans and a rugby shirt."

The faraway look in his glistening eyes made Colby reach out and touch his shoulder. Jasper smiled as he looked into Colby's eyes. He fumbled over his words and quickly pulled away but called back to Colby.

"Don't worry, the inside has been upgraded."

Colby peered into the flight-deck as he entered and gave the pilot and co-pilot a quick scan, finding them completely human to his relief. The flight attendant passed his test as well when he shook her hand before heading into the passenger compartment. True to Jasper's statement, the inside of the plane was well appointed and luxurious. Everyone quickly claimed dibs on a favored seat in one of the several overly-sized leather reclining chairs or upon one of the two long sofas that ran the side of the plane just behind the wings.

Rigel was already onboard and reading a newspaper. He gave them a nod and smile, then went back to his reading.

Colby watched as the crew prepared the plane for departure and took notice of the commotion near the forward galley where the door was being closed. Before he could leave his seat to investigate, he heard a familiar voice talking to the attendant then the closing of the door. He looked over at Shelly, watching the creases form on her forehead as her lips twitched and puckered. Bruce came walking down the aisle and took a seat opposite her and narrowed his eyes on Rigel.

"Sorry I'm late dude. I had a bitch of a time getting past the guard at the gates." Bruce grinned at Rigel and looked at Shelly. "But I'm here now and we can get goin'."

"What are you doing here?" Shelly asked.

"The good Professor here called me late last night and asked me to join the trip." He nodded to Rigel. "It was a surprise, but I figured… what the heck."

Rigel nodded back. "I figured we could use another adult, and I remembered meeting Bruce at Halloween."

Colby watched the tension building as Shelly's shoulders bunched and she folded her arms. Looking away from Bruce and Rigel, she sat quietly and stared toward the front of the aircraft. The aura of Emassa was nearly visible as she fumed, Colby had to reach over and tap her arm.

"Careful, we wouldn't want any accidental misfire."

Shelly pulled back her anger fueled field of power and pushed it down. It was going to be a long quiet trip as Colby looked around to see the others silenced into watching Shelly, Rigel, and Bruce. They hoped the only turbulence during the flight would remain outside the aircraft and not pass between the love triad sitting up front.

Colby pulled out his father's journal and read through his notes and entries about the site the group was heading. He fell into a half trance state as he read and re-read the scribblings on each page, completely unaware of the soft glow emanating from the pages and the artifact firmly settled on the cover. Everyone else was busy with their own doings, except Rigel. Rigel watched Colby closely, staring intently at the journal and watch that Colby possessed.

Rigel pulled his attention away only after sensing a presence. His eyes dropped to below Colby's seat, where he met with the stare of two yellow glowing eyes. He heard the unmistakable grinding purr of Fizzlewink.

"What, may I ask is that thing doing here?"

Colby looked up at Rigel and shrugged. "By 'thing' I assume you mean my cat Fizzlewink? I couldn't leave him alone at home since Nana said she didn't want to take care of him and my mom's out of town."

Rigel was not convinced. "What is there to take care of? She could have put him out to fend for himself chasing other, smaller vermin and scrounging among the rubbish yards."

Clearly offended and not understanding Rigel's outward distaste for his cat, Colby pulled the carrier from under his seat and started off toward the back of the plane.

"Don't pay any attention to the cranky man Fizzy-Wizzy."

Fizzlewink let out a low-pitch growl and turned inside the carrier to display his backside to Rigel as Colby carried him away putting him down on a lounge where the other kids were sitting at a table.

"What's his problem?" Darla asked.

"I don't think he likes flying," Colby said.

Darla rolled her eyes toward Rigel. "I mean the Professor. He keeps staring this way. And the way he snapped about Fizz…"

"I don't know. Based on Fizz's reaction I think the feeling is one of mutual dislike. I think he'll be staying in the bag until we get to the hotel."

Colby brushed off further discussion on the matter and pulled a rolled-up chart from his bag. He spread it out on the table and put his notes on the table alongside. He pointed out the area of Chichén Itzá that his father made entries in his journal about.

There were three main places highlighted, Colby showed the others, based on how much larger they were in his sketches than the others. The pyramid of Kukulcán, the Sacred Cenote, and the main ball court were all prominent in his notes, but there was an obscure reference to celestial platform and Orion.

Gary brought out his tablet and brought up a map of Chichén Itzá and they compared the notes to what was on the satellite map. The first thing they noticed was that there was only the single large pyramid where Colby's father had drawn what appeared as two, one smaller than the other and nestled beneath the other. They wondered at first if there was perhaps a ruin of an older pyramid near the other or if perhaps it was once smaller and built overtop. Some research showed that there was indeed a temple inside the larger structure.

It was common practice to build over the top of temples or older structures for many reasons, least of which would be to obscure something from view in order to hide or attempt erasing it from history. They all wondered what the reason was and how it related to themselves and their trip. Because by now they had all begun to realize that there was no longer coincidence as they were all brought together for a reason. The only outsiders being Bruce and Rigel, but Colby was beginning to have doubts about Rigel's lack of involvement as he watched him talking to Bruce while occasionally looking over at him and the others.

Colby turned his attention back to working through the groups' plans of exploration. They knew that the significance of the pyramid steps during the equinox was important. Furthermore it was perhaps related somehow to the temple inside, but it was not clear by the unknown runes and symbols his father scribbled in the margins of his journal. Showing them to Fizzlewink had proved fruitless as he was also unable to decipher them. They were at least able to identify the celestial platform with an observatory built in the Mayan complex of antiquity. The first known structure of its kind.

The cenote was the large sinkhole and water reservoir, believed to act as a gateway to the afterlife and underworld. Bathing in its mineral rich waters was thought to be healing and impart powers. Another connection to the Emassa they all thought, but again the full scope of these places and their relationships to each other and the celestial events was perplexing. Colby's eye kept wandering back to the constellation of Orion.

"I can't help but think there is something we're missing that's looking us right in the face," Colby said.

He pulled out a piece of tracing paper and drew the stars of Orion then connected them to form the outline of the celestial man, the hunter. He lay the paper over the map of Chichén Itzá and turned it in several different directions trying to line up the stars with points on the map. Nothing seemed to align, but Colby felt more than before there was something important still missing.

"What are their names?" Jasper asked.

Everyone looked at him somewhat annoyed or confused. Gary was mostly annoyed. But Colby thought Jasper might be on to something.

"Gary, google Orion and find a map with the names of the stars."

Gary begrudgingly complied and moved the tablet over to Colby, who began to copy the names onto his sketch. He started with the head, Meissa. Then he added the shoulder star names, Betelgeuse, and Bellatrix. The belt stars names, Alnitak, Alnilam, and Mintaka, he added next. When he saw the names of the stars of the feet of

Orion, he paused.

Colby didn't need to look behind to know where the itching feeling of a stare on the back of his head was coming from. Colby looked at his friends for a moment before steadying his breath and writing the last two names of the major stars in the Orion constellation. Saiph and Rigel.

"Whoa, things just got a whole lotta weird," Jasper said.

Colby laughed. "You mean they weren't already?"

"Well you know…I kinda already was getting used to the magic stuff. Now we're off on some crazy expedition based on your dad's notes in an old book, one that I've noticed Rigel keeps looking at. And now this stuff with the stars, it's just all a lot more than we were expecting isn't it?"

"I know what you mean," Darla said. "Why is this involving all of us anyway. Is it written in the stars? Seems kinda cliché."

They all let out a light nervous laugh and then remained silent for several moments.

"So what does this stuff with Orion mean?" Shelly asked. She now looked at Rigel through different eyes. "And why did you hesitate on the one called Saiph?"

Colby thought back to his father's message. "You remember reading dad's note to me? He mentioned keeping the journal for Saiph. I thought it strange and maybe he meant to keep it safe, but now I'm certain he meant what he wrote literally."

Shelly and the others looked at Colby, hoping he would provide more detail, but he wasn't ready to expand on his thoughts. They were incomplete.

"I'm sure we'll find out soon enough, but we need to be careful about what we tell him." Colby pointed to the star named Rigel and looked to the others for an agreement. They all concurred and Fizzlewink purred.

Chapter Twenty-Two

Arriving in Cancun, they made their way through customs and out to a waiting shuttle. They would be staying near Chichén Itzá to make the most of their time by not having long travel to and from accommodations to the park. Once they pulled in front of the hotel that Rigel booked, they checked-in. Everyone went to their respective rooms to rest and freshen up for a late dinner before heading to the Mayan site for a private overnight tour. They needed to be on-site when the equinox began on the opposite side of the world. The solar eclipse would occur early in the morning there so whatever connection it had to the Yucatan, they had to be at Chichén Itzá to witness it.

By the time they met to leave for dinner, Colby's mind was spinning with ideas and images of his father and that he may have meant for him to come to this place. He left Fizzlewink, who said he would manage on his own and followed the others into a large passenger van that would take them to the restaurant for dinner and where they would meet their guide.

When they arrived just outside the park, Colby felt a shiver ripple over his skin. Not an unpleasant feeling, but one that indicated something both magical and unsettled was nearby. A quick glance at the others confirmed that they felt it also. Before he could speak to them, the voice of a stranger redirected their attention. Coming down the few steps from the dining platform was an older man, near elderly in outward appearance, but his movements gave away the vitality of a much younger person. He looked familiar somehow.

The man's clear blue eyes and warm white-toothed smile centered on Colby.

"Welcome to my home…of sorts. We have been waiting for you."

Colby was disturbed by the meaning of the man's words. Was he waiting for them to have dinner and the tour, or was there something more clandestine simmering beneath his greeting? Colby accepted the man's outstretched hand and in the instant their hands met, Colby knew that his sense was definitely leaning toward the latter.

A barely perceptible tug-of-war played out into their hands as the Emassa surged and retreated between their skin. It wasn't anything visual, Colby could tell by the unchanged expressions of his friends, but this man had power and a great deal of it. And he was familiar.

Colby was entranced in a way, not wanting to let go of this mystery, but Shelly stepped up to great the man as did the others. When they all began walking toward the banquet spread out for them on long elaborately decorated tables, Rigel made a more extensive introduction.

"This is an old colleague of mine, Dr. Meissa. He has studied these ruins for longer than anyone else and holds information you will not find in books or the internet."

The mention of his sir name caused an exchange of glances between the kids. They recognized that as the name of one of the stars in the Orion constellation. Most definitely no longer a coincidence. Colby watched the man as the night progressed.

Servers dressed in elaborate native costume of the ancient Mayan people began dancing around the table as they carried various trays of foods and drinks. They moved effortlessly around one another, twisting and spinning, flowing in and out of the main body as they presented the trays, laying them upon the table. Soon the room was filled with music and voices singing songs that regaled the ancients. Though they voiced the words in Mayan tongue, Colby, and the others could feel the power in their words. He soon dropped his attention from Meissa and watched the progression of the entertainment.

Song and dance, wrapped together effortlessly as the beating of drums joined with the percussion of primitive instruments and whistling of flutes. The Emassa responded as if called by ceremony and filled the air before settling on everything around them including the food and drink offered. As the presentation reached its apex, Dr. Meissa stood and spread his arms out in a welcoming gesture. When he lowered them down toward the table, spilling over with abundance, the night went silent.

"Blessings on this bounty and our honored guests as we partake in what the flow provides." Dr. Meissa winked at Colby, who had his eyes locked on the man.

"Jenkins," Colby whispered. A slight gathering of the creases under Meissa's eyes told Colby the man heard and recognized the name raising his suspicion.

While they ate dinner and enjoyed more entertainment, Colby disregarded the servers swirling around them with trays on their heads. Dancing and twirling as the trays spun without spilling their contents. As amazing as their displays of dexterity and control were, Colby would have a conversation with Jenkins or Dr. Pace Meissa or whatever his true name is.

As the dinner was winding down, Colby saw Meissa get up from the table and step off the platform toward the entrance to the park. Wanting a few private words with the man, he hurried from the table and followed. When he reached the man, he waved Colby over without looking to indicate he knew someone followed.

"Welcome young star child. You undoubtedly have many questions." Meissa looked at Colby and then toward the night sky.

The moon had yet to rise, but the vast starry night provided an illumination that Colby had never experienced in the light polluted skies of Chicago. Here in the wilderness, away from the congestion of street lights, billboards, apartment and office buildings all lighting the cities, the eyes could adjust to the natural lights of the stars. His words were stolen from his tongue as he swelled with the serenity of the unfettered sky.

"Do you feel the power out there Colby?" Meissa asked.

Colby searched himself and reached out for the flow. He didn't know why he hadn't noticed it before, but there was a strange flux in the Emassa around them. He could feel areas stronger than others and dead spots where there seemed to be no flow at all.

"It feels broken Mr. Meissa or is it Jenkins," Colby said.

The man laughed. "Broken is as good a description as any, but not quite accurate. And no, I am not this Jenkins fellow I heard you thinking about. Pace Meissa is my name in this place and time. I am your humble guide Call me Pace."

"So you are guiding me? Toward what…Pace."

Pace placed a hand on Colby's shoulder. "Do you believe in destiny… fate?"

Colby stiffened. "No." His answer was fueled by a need to change whatever led his father to disappear. He wanted nothing more than to find him and forget everything else that has happened. But his voice sounding the answer was weak.

"You want nothing more than to find your father, I understand that my boy. And it will happen…but you must embrace your destiny to accomplish your goal."

Colby could not accept that blindly. "What is my destiny?"

Pace laughed a bit of humor with an edge of worry again. "That is not the real question. Your fate is something more directly answered because your destiny is not as fixed as your fate."

Colby stared into Pace's eyes. They were clear and bright as a man who may have lived only a few decades, but behind them was wisdom that defied all sense of time. This man has witnessed much, Colby thought.

"I don't understand."

Pace moved further toward the entrance to the ancient city. "Your fate and destiny are connected, like a sphere. They exist together within the sphere, on the surface or somewhere within. You can take that sphere, shape and mold it all you like, but eventually the two parts will join."

Colby began to understand. "I can't change this thing can I?"

"No, my dear boy. No matter how long it takes and numerous lives you may live, you can twist your destiny all you like, but you can never escape your fate."

"So what is my fate?"

Pace exhaled a long sigh and looked up to the endless field of stars, focusing on the ones just beginning to rise over the horizon. The Orion constellation. "You will do or not do what we were unable. Control the flow."

Before Colby could ask more, the others approached from the direction of the dining platform. He looked at Pace, who gave him a look that spoke of more to come when the time was right.

Pace turned to the rest of their group. "The time is perfect for our tour to begin. This night will reveal the path of the ancients and the power of the Equinox and super moon."

They entered the park from a special gate that was on the far side of the main visitor entrance. Though night tours were allowed, they were by special permission and only allowed if guided by a trained archeologist that worked for the park. There were a few other tours happening the same night, but there was little chance of running across the others in the vast ruins as they all entered separately and took different paths through the ancient city.

The walk took them first through the Northeast Colonnade, past the ancient steam baths and down toward the market square where they would find the few merchants allowed to sell their wares during the evening tours. These people survived off of selling their goods to tourists. Items made of wood or stone and often times plaster for the mass produced items being presented as authentic hand made works of art. They may have been locally made, but the majority were created in a factory and trucked over to the many souvenir shops where most of these merchants were employed.

There was a time to shop and haggle, much to the delight of Darla and Rhea, who dragged Shelly along from stall to stall. Colby could see that Shelly wasn't altogether upset with being pulled around by the two younger girls. It gave her a chance to escape the smothering presence of Bruce who followed her around as though he were her bodyguard. Though Colby felt, he did so as though she were his possession. Creepy.

Looking at the many tables, benches, and blankets on the ground, Colby wondered at the vast array of trinkets and paintings, jewelry, and statues. These things were for the most part display items of no significance. His eyes caught something, however, something with a familiar symbol at its center and runic carvings along the outer edges that were completely out of place in a Mayan ruin. Colby lifted the thin disc and examined the piece. It had a power in it, but something unfamiliar. He looked at Pace but saw him clear across the market talking to Rigel.

"You like mister?" the youngster said standing behind the bench of goods.

Colby had not noticed the child there earlier. And failed to see the slight glow and cat-like eyes. "What is this?"

"Oh that special talisman. Power to trap evil and bring good sleep."

Colby looked at the disc skeptically, but still he felt some sort of power in the object. Uncertain of what to do, he haggled a price for the piece and stuffed the now wrapped object in his bag alongside his dad's journal and his tablet. He hurried to catch up with Pace and Rigel as the others finished their shopping and followed his steps. They fell in behind Colby as he veered off from Rigel and Pace then lost sight of them as the kids entered a forest of stones.

Without hesitation, Colby led the way between the hundreds of stone columns. Grateful for doing his research, Colby knew this was the group of a thousand columns, the warriors of the temple they were likely headed toward. His assumption was confirmed as the steps came into view. One by one the six of them arrived and waited at the foot of the Temple of Warriors.

"What are we waiting for?" Jasper asked. "Let's go up."

"They don't let people just climb these ruins anymore because of the careless damage they do," Rhea said.

"We'll be careful then," Colby said. "Besides I think we are meant to do this. Can you feel that." Colby reached an open palmed hand toward the stairway before them. "The flux in Emassa is strong here now that we have arrived."

Not waiting for a response, Colby took the first few steps and turned to the others. He waved them on and once they began to ascend, he led the way to the top. He waited for the others and once they arrived, they all moved as a unified group past several towering columns to stand behind an altar and looked out on the ruins before them. The grounds below then gave an unobscured view of the center of the ruins complex. The Pyramid of Kukulcán, the Platform of the Eagles, the Great Ball Court, and the Platform of Cones were all lit by the stars. They all pulsed with fluxing Emassa, as a beacon might guide ships from jagged shores. Standing in the center of the ruins, Rigel and Pace stared up at the group on the altar and pointed at something above them.

Colby turned and looked up to witness the shield of Orion hanging over them. It felt significant somehow, but he didn't yet grasp why. When he turned back, he felt impelled to step forward and rest a hand on the Chac Mool Altar before he lost his footing. The pulse of energy that entered him nearly threw him off his feet, but he was caught by the strong and steady hands of his friend, Jasper.

"Hey what was that?" Jasper said. He helped Colby regain his balance but didn't let go until he was sure his friend was able to stand on his own.

"I'm good," Colby said. "Just a jolt like a static charge, but way bigger."

Gary stood at the altar touching it. "I don't feel anything." He frowned at Jasper still holding Colby's arm.

Colby looked back at Gary, glowering toward himself and Jasper. Colby cleared his throat to get Gary's attention. Gary forced a smile on his face and waved Colby and the others over.

"Come on, let's go down and see what we can before sunrise."

Colby tried to call after him, but Gary was already halfway down the front of the temple and headed toward the pyramid. Colby knew they had less time than that before the solar eclipse happened halfway around the world. He felt more than knew for certain that he needed to be somewhere among these ruins when that celestial event took place. Perhaps Pace would help though Colby wasn't sure he wouldn't get a riddle for an answer…if he received any help at all.

Colby sent the girls to Gary and took Jasper with him to find Pace. He wasn't difficult to locate, he was standing near the entrance to the Great Ball Court, alone. Rigel was no longer with him. Colby walked up to Pace, who stood silently waiting.

"Where is the Professor?" Colby asked.

Pace tilted his head back toward the ball court. "He has company, I would not dare to intrude."

Colby wanted to go question Rigel. He knew the man was part of this and wanted answers, but something in Pace's presence told him that confronting Rigel was not a wise plan.

"What is his role? I know you and he are connected, each having a name associated with the stars of Orion."

"We play a part, as guides you might suppose. But each guide may lead you on a different path. You must choose your own I think."

"And what path would you lead me?"

Pace smiled. "My first name, Pace, it means peacekeeper. I do not lead you anywhere young star child. I watch and occasionally hint at a suggested path, but ultimately I mind all the paths and am concerned only with the destination."

A riddle, Colby was afraid of that before he asked the question. He didn't know this man well, but well enough to know that was the best answer he would get. As he moved closer to the serpent head topped wall that marked the entrance to the ball court, Pace stopped him with a gesture of his hand.

"There is a wonderful acoustic value to this court. One need only stand at the edges to hear a conversation held at its center. That is if one wished to remain hidden, with the advantage of knowing what was spoken." With that, Pace left the boys and headed toward the pyramid. "I'll see you when it is time again, star child."

"Why does he keep calling you that?"

Colby shushed Jasper and crept to the edge of the wall, peering around the corner to see Rigel walking toward the center of the court with someone he could not make out. When he slowed his breathing so he stopped hearing his own breaths, he could make out what was being said as though standing directly behind the two men.

"This has to work this time, everything is different with these children," the man said.

"We've thought so in the past and it didn't work out so well for those children did it," Rigel said. "Patience, if we make a misstep we could ruin all our work. The boy's father may have caused a problem with his disappearance, but if I can get a look at his journal I may be able to track him down."

"We don't need Saiph for this to work. We don't want the original plan."

"The boy will not be pliable if he doesn't find his father; we need his cooperation. The others can be forced to help, but not the Stevens boy. He is growing too strong. We can not decide our next steps until after the spirit talker has communed with the ancients at the sacred pool during the equinox. Only then will we know how long the flow will grow in this place before the flux returns."

Colby's sweat covered hand lost its grip on the stone wall and it slipped. His hand hit the hard packed earth at the base of the wall. He caught himself but let out a whimper when his hand met with a sharp stone embedded in the ground. He backed up behind the wall when the voices stopped. Taking a deep breath he signaled for Jasper to lead the way north along the wall so they could hide behind the Platform of Eagles and its ruins.

Rigel reached the wall and looked behind it to find no one there. He looked around seeing a group at the pyramid, but Colby and the boy Jasper were not among them. He turned and walked back to find his visitor gone. When he began his walk toward the pyramid, he thought he saw forms moving along the wooded ridge back toward the Temple of Warriors. Another group of tourists walked out of the woods and headed toward the other ruins.

Chapter Twenty-Three

Colby and Jasper ran past the far end of the ball court. Instead of running to hide behind the Platform of Eagles, they continued around the north side of the ball court and entered from that side. When they reached the entrance and looked inside, the court was empty. Both Rigel and his visitor had left. Jasper convinced Colby they should continue through and exit behind Rigel and follow quietly behind. He wouldn't be expecting that.

True to Jasper's plan, Rigel never once slowed or turned as the two boys followed behind him. Of course, that was likely due to the help of Colby's invisibility shield he had stored in his phWatch. Luckily the ground was mostly grassy and smooth so they made little noise to give away their position. Had Rigel turned around, however, the boys hoped he would not see past the spell?

Once they reached the pyramid, the boys split off and raced around the side to take another set of steps to the top. When they reached the upper platform, Colby dropped the spell and they moved around to the west side and began heading toward the steps down where the others were standing and talking to Rigel.

"Impressive," Pace said from behind them.

Only startled a bit, Colby turned and smiled. "The Sacred Cenote, it is our next stop." Colby waited for confirmation but received only a slight nod. He figured that out from what he overheard Rigel and the mystery man talking about in the ball court.

"If that is where you wish to go, I am but your humble guide." Pace led the way down the steps.

As they reached the bottom, Colby's skin prickled from the cold stare of Rigel. "Hey professor, where have you been?"

"Exploring," he answered after a few moments. "Where have you two boys just come from?"

Colby pointed to the top of the pyramid and then wiped the sweat from his brow. "Up there, it takes a bit out of you climbing that thing."

Not waiting for more pointed questions Colby looked at Pace, who tilted his head north and began to walk. Everyone fell into step behind him as he spoke about the many historical facts surrounding the region and the ruins they walked past.

Looking at his father's watch, Colby guessed they had plenty of time to reach the Sacred Cenote before the equinox started. He told the others he would let them know what was next when they got there. Colby was still wondering about Rigel and his intentions. He supposed he couldn't be all bad if he wanted Colby to find his father, but that could also be out of a selfish desire to complete some goal other than the one Pace must have. Pace seemed content to let Colby find his own path with only the slight push here or there. One thing for certain, the key to finding his father lay hidden in the locked pages of his father's journal and he would do what was required of himself to reveal that path.

The walk through the trees brought them to a small temple. It was simple and looked more shelter for a picnic than what was once a temple structure in a sacred place. It marked the stairway into the earth that lead down to the underground reservoir of fresh water that flowed below the entire complex. The waters pooled here and one smaller and less accessible pool to the south. This larger one is more significant for the obvious fact it is nearly completely hidden, except for the relatively small hole at the top of the grand cavern that let in air and light.

The man carved stairway led them deep into the ground. They could feel the moisture as they breathed and exhaled mist, signifying the change in temperature and rise in humidity as they descended. Along the steep and narrow stairs, the sheer wall gave way to carved alcoves where idols sat ready and waiting for offerings. Once they came to the first landing, the vast pool stretched out below them. A reflection of the stars peeking through the small hole in the ceiling showed the ingress of Orion into the full of view.

Pace lit a torch that was fixed to the wall and continued the trek downward toward a long walkway out into the pool where a large circular platform awaited. The further down they stepped, the more their eyes adjusted. The single torch from higher up the stairway reflected off the millions of minerals and crystals in the cavern walls. The reflections added to the stars from above to fill the room with an inner-earth planetarium that rival the Adler in Chicago. Long strands of tree roots stretched themselves from the roof opening, reaching for the waters below. Two additional bright lights set near the edge of the broken roof were peering into the cavern below. Each was split in the center like a cat's eyes.

Colby exhaled when they reached the bottom, not realizing he had been holding his breath in reaction to the beauty and peace he felt in this chamber.

"Care for a swim?" Pace said. "The eclipse will be upon us shortly, and I for one would enjoy feeling the energy of eternal life that is believed to flow within these waters."

Shelly reached her hand into the water at the edge and drew it back, tucking it under her arm.

"Are you crazy? That water is freezing cold."

Colby took Shelly to the side and summarized to her the conversation he and Jasper overheard in the ball court. There was a significance in the timing and the place as well as Shelly's ghost whispering talents. She agreed to do as he asked so long as he and the other kids joined her in the frigid water.

The boys stripped down to their underwear and stepped into the water and back out again. The girls laughed and made their way to the center platform. They pulled off their shirts to reveal bathing suits underneath. Darla winked at Colby. Of course, she came prepared, all the girls did. They must have seen the pictures of people swimming in these waters from the websites they researched before the trip.

As the girls eased themselves into the water. Colby looked at the other two boys and winked. As one, they ran down the walkway to the center circle and jumped high, tucking their legs into their arms.

"Canon Ball!" was followed by the shrills echoing off the walls as the girls were splashed.

The boys broke the surface and had barely time to catch a shocked breath when each girl chose a target to dunk back below the chilly surface. Splashing and laughing followed for a short time before they all settled down and returned to the serenity of the cavern. They floated around the pool, gazing up at the night sky both natural and created by the illusion of reflections on the walls. They bumped into each other from time to time but remained silent, for the most part.

Colby paddled his way toward Shelly to see if she was ready.

"That better be you warming the water around you with Emassa little brother."

Colby chuckled and winked. "Of course, what else would it be?" He smiled at the scowl he received. "Are you ready for this?"

"I suppose. Just stick close in case I start to sink or something."

"I gotcha sis."

The others stayed near as well, but keeping an eye on Rigel, who seemed just as happy to stay on dry land. He had begged off, saying he didn't have anything appropriate to swim in around the ladies. Darla announced that must mean he went commando, much to Rigel's embarrassment. Jasper kept an eye on him just the same, in case he got too close to Colby's backpack. They all now knew how much he wanted to get his hands on Jarrod's journal and why.

Everyone felt the moment when the eclipse and equinox began. The chamber filled with the flow more powerful than ever felt before. Echoes of sharp intaking of breaths thundered around the stillness of the space as they all absorbed the power. There could be no denying that each and every soul in that cenote was attuned to the magic though Rigel attempted covering himself by coughing and feigning ignorance.

Shelly took a few deep breaths and closed her eyes while opening her mind. The echoes of breathing quieted down as the room took on an ethereal glow that emanated from the depths of the watery entrance to the underworld. The breathing was soon joined by whispers and chattering as wisps of smoky energy lifted from the surface of the pool.

Opening her eyes, Shelly's vision was flooded with a whirling cloud of disembodied phantasms while here ears fought to make sense from hundreds of voices shouting to steal her attention. When she moved her eyes to glance at her companions, all eyes were on her except Colby's. He was sharing her vision from his contact while holding her steady in the water.

"What should I ask them," Shelly said.

Colby thought for a moment, he was unsure as well. He knew they needed to know what would happen with the equinox and the eclipse happening together. He also had to figure out what would help open the next section of his father's journal.

"Ask them what causes the flux in power at Chichén Itzá."

Before Shelly could ask, a specter floated near Colby and began to take a more defined form. His head swelled into shape from the mists showing an ancient looking man with sun-weathered and wrinkled skin. A band of intricately carved and hammered gold circled his head. A crown with jewels that signified this man as a one-time leader or king among these ancient people. He stared into Colby's soul.

"You are a star child. You have come to reclaim the magic and serve the will of the gods."

"I don't understand, reclaim it how?"

The ancient spirit opened his mouth and released a howling rasp that might have been a laugh. He drifted away and was replaced by another ghost. A priestess of some kind, but she looked less Mayan and more European in heritage.

"The great shield is failing again, either it must be powered by sacrifice or shattered by those who can control the flow. The snake spirit shall descend when the flow is even. It is a time when the power will be most balanced and the light joins the shadow."

As Colby spoke to the spirits using Shelly as a conduit, the others just watched seeing Colby speaking at what seemed to them as empty space. The only ones who could see the spectral visitation were Shelly and her brother, but they could all sense a presence.

Another ghost flew in and pushed the other aside. "You must bring the power child and return our ancestors who journeyed north. They hold the secret and guard the path. You are the key to-"

The apparitions all evaporated with a sudden clap of thunder that shook the chamber. The waters began to bubble and churn as the light grew angry and red. As bubbles rose from the depths, all buoyancy was lost and the kids flailed in the water while they fought to keep their heads above water. They paddled and thrashed in the water trying to make for the shore.

As the kids made their way to the rocky edge, a screech sounded over the preceding echoes of thunder. Tumbling down from the cavern's natural skylight came a bluish colored cat, flailing for purchase in the empty air. The animal hit the water and gurgled as the bubbling liquid filled its mouth. Without thinking, Colby dove back into the water to save the companion he recognized as Fizzlewink.

From the safety of the shore, the others shouted for Colby to get out of the water, but he did not hear them. His ears were full of water and the gurgling yowls of his friend being pulled below the water's surface. Colby dove below the water and opened his eyes in search of Fizzlewink, only to close them tight in reaction to an offensive sting that assaulted him. He rose back to the surface searching and saw Fizzlewink pop back up for a moment. He was still far from the cat and couldn't reach him before the waters pulled him down again, likely for the last time. He wished he had more time as his instincts told him to form his spell of teleportation. The moment the two thoughts merged something new happened. Colby thrashed and found the water semi-solid.

When his hand hit the sloshing liquid, it pushed up slowly and stopped. Colby looked around and saw everything frozen. Time had stopped. He looked back around and noticed a drip of water falling in front of him. It moved so slowly it left an illusionary trail. Time had only slowed to nearly a stop, but close enough he finally realized. Colby pushed himself forward in the resisting and viscous water until he was within reach of Fizzlewink.

He grabbed the flailing feline, who remained frozen in time as Colby cradled him to his chest. He turned toward shore and began raising out of the water as he pushed forward. By the time he was within a few feet of the safety of the shore, time had returned to normal speed and he sunk to his knees in the water. He made the rest of the way and laid the non-responsive cat on the ground.

"Rhea, can you-"

She was already reaching out while she ran for him. She laid her hands on Fizzlewink and pushed Emassa through her hands into the cat. Water flowed from his open jaws, but he did not breath. Rhea tried again but still her power stopped before it would enter the body lying still beneath her hands.

"The cat is dead," Rigel said.

Colby swung his head around and raised an Emassa filled palm toward Rigel.

"Enough of your games 'Professor'. He is not just a cat and you know it. We all know who your are."

"I very much doubt that," Rigel said. He tried his best to sound smug, but he didn't want to test Colby's temper any further.

Pace put a soothing hand on Colby's shoulder and left it there as Colby lowered his arm and turned back to Fizzlewink. Tears flowed freely from his eyes as he sobbed over the motionless animal form of the little blue man who had become a fixture in his new life. The others were also caught by grief and failed to notice the cat transform back into the undersized wrinkly old man they became to love.

Fizzlewink's eyes fluttered and opened. He took a deeply needed long breath of air and coughed. Shocked giggles erupted in his ears as he was swept up into Colby's arms.

"I thought we lost you."

Fizzlewink pushed back from Colby's embrace. "That would be a fine mess."

After more hugs and several moments of relieved crying laughs, Colby finally helped Fizzlewink to his feet.

"Rhea tried to save your life. I thought it didn't work."

"It did not work," Fizzlewink said. "You can not give life to something that already has nine to begin with."

Everyone looked at him with confusion clouding their minds.

Fizzlewink sighed. "I was in cat form. Where do you think the tale of cat's having nine lives comes from?" He brushed himself off and without ceremony, trotted toward the stairs, growling at Rigel on his way past.

Colby started toward Rigel, who turned and followed Fizz and the others up the stairs toward the surface and away from the gateway to the afterlife. They had enough of death and the dead visitations for one night.

Colby picked up his bag, checking to see that his father's journal was safely inside. He noticed the strange disk souvenir he purchased earlier had a strange glow, but soon put it out of his mind when Pace came up beside him.

"What happened when you went after the changeling?"

"The what," Colby asked.

"Fizzlewink, your changeling friend."

"Oh, he's a Nefslama."

Colby explained what happened when he was trying to reach Fizz and then wished for more time and also thought about transporting him to safety. When he explained how time slowed to nearly a full stop, Pace gasped.

"Few of my kind could ever come so close to a full stop of time. This is very unexpected."

"How so?" Colby asked. "Is that a problem?"

Pace looked at Colby and then back at the pool. "There have been a few strange things this evening. Things that should never have happened. Your controlling time is an enigma I will have to ponder."

Colby took his words as gospel. He knew the man had more answers and information than he was ready to share, so he decided to focus on his own tasks. First would be to visit the Mayan observatory after the next sunset. The full equinox started and something would hopefully be revealed as it ended.

"What happened with the pool? Did Fizzlewink have anything to do with it?"

Pace laughed. "No, that is not something his kind could do alone. Someone else is about and interfering. Your changeling friend is not a Nefslama, by the way. Not a full blood anyway."

Colby was not sure how to take that news. He wondered if Fizz even knew because he sounded so convinced of what he was. There was so much more to what was going on than Colby realized.

Stories change over the eons. Truth wraps itself in myth and legend until there is no definitive line between what is real and what is fantasy. The truths that are believed by one could be the lies spread by another for their own benefit. Man's history was mottled. That included everything that he was taught from school, his parents, even the Bible. It was all written by men and they present uninformed, biased points of view. The truth was likely so blinding that none would dare chance to see it for what it was. Colby knew one thing for certain, He needed to seek the truth for himself.

Colby followed Pace up the stairs and slowed his pace as he muddled through his scattered thoughts. Everything was changing so quickly. His young heart felt heavy. His youthful body seemed aged. The levity of the burden upon him was beginning to push in on his soul.

A final clinging apparition followed Colby up the steps as he exited. Though he could no longer see them, he felt the presence of an ancient soul seeking him out. He turned his head at the sound of desperate whispers just beyond the normal realm of human comprehension. Lucky, Colby is not entirely human.

"You must seek the path from the stars when all is equal and K'in has bedded. Return to the celestial temple to search out direction. Time will be a tool, not an anchor for the star child triple blessed."

He recognized something in that voice, but it seemed broken somehow. Colby turned back up toward the surface and saw Pace waiting for him.

"Pace, what is K'in?"

"The sun, star child."

"And 'when K'in has bedded?'"

"That would be sunset in the modern tongue." Pace smiled at Colby and motioned for him to return to the surface.

Chapter Twenty-Four

The group stayed in the park to await the sunrise at Fizzlewink's insistence. He proclaimed his wellness and said the arrival of the serpent was more important than his rest. Colby tried to protest but was stopped when he sensed the flow of Emassa permeating the land as they approached the main plaza. They hurried their pace toward the Pyramid of Kukulcán.

Rigel was first to reach the steps leading up as he pushed his way past park staff trying to prevent his approach. He began to move toward the side when Pace called out for his halt.

"Stop Rigel, it is not for you to take the altar."

Rigel, not being one to be dissuaded by anyone for any reason, halted in spite of himself. He stepped back and waited as the others approached and were allowed to pass at the nod of Pace to the staffers keeping the crowds back.

People were gathered for the spectacle of watching the sun rise over Chichén Itzá this time of year. It happened only twice per year, when the angle was perfectly aligned with the sun. The Stairs of the pyramid would cast a shadow that crept along the serpent carved sides, signifying the ascent or descent of the serpent god.

Pace held the others back and pulled Colby near. "It is your place to take up the Jaguar Altar. More I will not say. Hurry child take the stairs and sit upon the stone."

Pace motioned to a doorway that opened on the side of the grand staircase. Inside Colby found a hidden stairway that led up to the structure. It was the temple beneath the pyramid.

Colby didn't hesitate. Something drove him forward as he entered the dark and cobweb covered passage. He took a first deep breath inside the dank stairway, coughing into the stale air. He slowed his breathing as he paused for a moment and gazed upward at the platform awaiting him.

He stilled his trepidation and proceeded up the narrow stairs, bending low to avoid the lowering ceiling. He could see the seams where the already ancient stone of the covering pyramid met the even older construction of the temple he now climbed. The barrier between the ancient and older epochal shined. It stood out not only from the coloring that differentiated their age of creation, but also the flow of energies from the Emassa that began to gather and shift between the two structures. There was a symmetry between them that acted as the flow of current to a power source. A powerful battery charging for some momentous purpose.

Colby soon found himself standing before an altar of stone, carved from a single source and formed into the shape of a beast. A jaguar. He held out a trepidatious hand toward the carving and felt the tug of two opposite forces pulling him closer. Despite his internal struggle against the unknown, something stronger and primal drove him forward and into a seated position. He soon realized he couldn't have removed himself from that altar if he tried. It wanted him there.

The darkness of the space around him began to retreat from a white-purple light that expanded from the base of the altar. A familiar sense of presence began to fill the room as the light engulfed the surrounding walls and obscured the cramped space. Colby no longer felt the walls pushing in on him as the white-purple light now took up all that surrounded him and expanded out into an infinite place of peace and stillness.

Colby looked down at the Jaguar Altar to find it replaced by a white alabaster bench, delicately inlaid with intricate runes. He stared at the symbols and stroked his finger over them with care and a light touch. They glowed in response to his energy that flowed freely now over his skin. A deep purple, yet thin and translucent. He knew his father was there the instant he smelled a faint spicy fragrance.

Colby stood and turned around to face the apparition, expecting to witness another spelled scene such as the one from his father's study. This time there was no pre-recorded scene. No three-dimensional act playing back something his father wanted him to see. This time, the image of Jarrod Stevens stood before his son, looking into his eyes as tears welled in his own.

"My boy," Jarrod said.

Colby let out a gurgled laugh that was caught between a shout and a sob. He moved to his father but halted at the raised hand from Jarrod.

"You must not near me or the spell will break." Jarrod shook his head in defiance of his own words, struggling to keep from scooping his son up into his arms. "We have little time, this spell will not last long so listen close and try to remember even though most of this encounter you will likely forget."

Colby held his tongue against the uncountable questions that fell from his thoughts and surged into his mouth. He held his feet in place, determined to show his father the strength he was building.

"I am waiting for you to free me, in a place only you can reach. You hold the key to a vast power that none has held since before my people fled to this world. You must discover what you are capable of before you will have what you need to free me and take control of the Emassa that threatens to destroy everything. My book, now yours, will lead you to self-discovery, but it is only a map. You must use what you have to gain more than you could ever hope to attain.

"Beware of those who offer an easy path, for they seek only to enrich themselves at the expense of the lessor. Your friends and family are a resource and a comfort, there is always safety there, but look deep into the trust you give because betrayal is often disguised by eagerness and well intention."

Jarrod began to fade. Colby reached toward him but held back as his father warned.

"Papa, I'm scared."

Jarrod shook his head. "You would be a fool not to fear. Hold onto that and let it make you strong yet cautious. I love you."

"You can't go yet. There is more I need to know. What is this all for dad?"

Colby sat back down, watching his father's presence begin to melt away. So many questions for which he needed answers. A direction. A reason. He needed some guidance beside falling into everything by accident and destiny. Colby shook his head as a thick fog enveloped his mind. Already the moments of this vision were dissolving in his mental grasp. He was forgetting.

His father faded to near nothingness as Colby sat frozen in place, sobbing.

"Remember," Jarrod said as his voice faded with his being. "The easy path, it never leads to fulfillment and will therefore never satisfy your soul. Believe with your heart, above all."

Colby blinked as a bright flash broke his trance state. He rubbed his eyes at the spots before his vision, waiting for them to readjust to the shadow-filled chamber. He pulled his hands away from his face and wondered at the moisture streaming off his cheeks.

He tried to remember what had happened moments ago, but it faded faster the more he chased the images through his mind. A dream he would remember for an instant upon waking but became fragmented and lost in the blink of the eye. He was able to hold onto one lasting image and three powerful words. His father saying 'I love you'.

His heart was filled and aching with a throb of loss and gain. Something had happened to him in this empty chamber, something he could not remember but felt somehow he would never forget. Colby pushed himself up from the altar and headed for the stairs. He looked back for a moment and sighed as he felt a loss greater than he ever felt and could not understand why.

As he emerged from the hidden door, he raised his head to the rising sun and allowed it to dry the tears on his face. He felt the others draw near though his eyes were closed. He felt their energies, each distinct and special in its own way. He allowed himself a quiet moment to reach out with his own extra sense of Emassa and feel those energies.

Through the light brush against each he could perceive something but could not yet make out what he felt. Trust maybe, love, friendship, and loyalty. He also felt pain and confusion, envy and hatred. Emotions flooded him as he tried to pull back from the contact. The pressure on his mind increased until he buckled and fell to his knees.

This was something new. He could sense magic, even see the demonic presence of the Shizumu festering within a human host. Now when he opened himself up to the magic and reached out, he could touch another's aura, their soul. He could sense it, know it, maybe even take it. Part of that realization shocked him. The thought of taking someone's magic seemed abhorrent. Sure he could borrow magic, and even share it willingly, but forcing to take the magic seemed like a violation…even rape.

Yet when he looked more closely at the magic, he could see the differences in them. Each person around him had a different feel, like a signature. He couldn't tell who was who with his eyes closed, but he could guess.

The blue tint to most of the magic, he felt through this new vision was recognizable as that of the Nefslama heritage they all had somewhere in their family line. Five of them stood out against the natural energy he also saw in their surroundings. When he moved his sense to the others, they seemed much different. They retreated instantly at his gazed, as though hiding. For a moment, he thought he saw something but it was all new and he couldn't be sure. So he returned his gaze to the first five.

They shone in his new vision at different intensities, Colby wondered if that related to how much Emassa they had stored in their core. He felt that these were his friends and sister. He couldn't be sure yet which was which among them, he needed to put their face with the signature to know for certain.

One stood out brighter than the others, carrying more magic perhaps. Colby felt instantly that it was Jasper. He realized this as true when he searched the magic more deeply. A part of him wanted to go further into that well of energy and that frightened Colby. He couldn't do that without permission. Colby forced his eyes open to find the wave of energy fall and his friends rushing to help him to his feet.

Jasper grabbed Colby and held him up.

"Are you ok? What just happened?"

"I was looking into the Emassa. I could see it in everything and everyone." He turned to look at Pace and Rigel, then to the cat sitting and staring at him. "Almost everyone."

Pace smiled and patted Colby on the shoulder. "Some of us hide our magic better than others. You will learn this in time, but not today.

You look exhausted for someone who was only gone a few minutes."

More questions about his well-being and what happened as well as what he encountered in the temple came at him in quick succession. Colby mumbled he was ok but tired and needed some water. He allowed himself to be led away from the pyramid and off to an open area where Darla laid out a large blanket and basket of food. The girls had thought ahead to have a picnic ready for breakfast since they were spending the night in the park. Colby was grateful for his friends.

"It was still and quiet. The room started to light up and there was a flash." Colby took a heavy drink from a canteen of water. "That's all I can remember." He shook his head. "At least…"

"Take your time, perhaps it will come back without forcing the memories." Pace looked back at the pyramid, now casting a deep shadow over the area they sat. "It is strong magic that was placed in that temple. Someone who had a natural affinity with time and memory magic."

"My father," Colby said. "I know it was his spell. I could sense it and part of that involved knowing his magic."

"Yes, you have developed a memory for the magic and can sense what magic others have left behind. That is a useful gift indeed."

Pace looked at Colby, thoughtful, he turned to scowl at Rigel, who sat nearby squinting at Colby. Doubt played across his face. Pace knew Rigel was planning something, and if he guessed correctly, it would not work out for him, but he kept this information to himself and smiled.

"I believe it is well past time we get you lot back to the hotel to clean up and rest."

They all agreed and Colby, though wishing now more than ever to push forward, felt every fiber of his being fighting to keep him awake.

One thing was for certain. He needed to get into the ruins of the observatory. There were several references to celestial temples and the platform of the star watchers. There was little doubt what that place was.

The group made their way back to the hotel just outside the park and headed to their rooms without ceremony. Colby tapped a text on his phone and sent it to the group leaving Rigel and Pace out of his plans. They would return to the park after sunset to explore the observatory, without the adults. Of course, that left Fizzlewink out as well, considering it would be just too weird having a cat wear a watch or carry a phone.

Chapter Twenty-Five

Colby waited until ten that night, when everyone was rested and Rigel, Fizz, and Pace were either asleep or otherwise occupied. The other kids began arriving as instructed in his earlier text message. Darla, Rhea, and Jasper fidgeted silently while they waited for everyone else to arrive. Colby was cryptic in his message, so no one knew what he was planning.

When finally the last of the six kids entered Colby's room, he closed the door and told them to gather close. Without giving time to object, Colby lifted a backpack, it's seams bulging, over his shoulder and transported them all into the park near the back of the Temple of Warriors.

He chose this spot because he could remember the area and knew it was large enough for them all to fit without his magic doing any damage, but also because it was hidden from the main trails. There was park security that roamed the ruins during the night, as well as evening tours, so Colby wanted to minimize the chances of being seen 'popping' into the park from out of nowhere.

While the initial surprise wore off, Colby explained where they were and what he had in mind. He felt more than he knew that there was something connected with the ancient observatory he needed to discover. Writings in the journal and cryptic messages eluded to this fact, but Colby was impelled to seek out the connection even without the clues. The moment he first saw the building the previous morning, he was drawn to an energy flux within the structure.

Even with a map, the ruins complex is easy to find oneself lost in during the day. It was now well after sunset and the moonless sky provided only the light from the blanket of stars covering them from above. Using a hashtag spell stored in his phone, Colby produced a fist-sized sphere of light to illuminate the area just enough to see a few feet. He didn't want to draw attention from any but the people he transported with him into the ruins.

They decided the best way to reach the observatory unseen, was to skirt the tree lines of the surrounding jungle. This provided both an ability to see where other people may be congregating and cover to hide in if discovered. In a worse case, they could split up and try to blend in with one of the few tours they heard walking past. Before they made it from behind the temple, a snap, flash, and smell of ozone alerted them to another presence transporting behind them. Colby felt the familiar aura of Fizzlewink before he even turned around.

"Fizz, what are you doing here? And how did you follow us."

Fizzlewink trotted up to Colby as he looked this way and that. Perhaps he was afraid of being followed, or perhaps he didn't like the jungle and ruins at night. Colby neither cared to ask nor wanted to ask. His main concern was that his attempt to sneak away had failed.

"Boy, until you learn to mask your use of Emassa, anyone can follow you."

Fizz held a blank expression Colby could not read. Whether he was irritated or bemused, it was hard to tell, but he certainly didn't look like he was going to leave Colby and the others alone.

"This place is not safe at night even when the flow is tainted. Now that it has a few days of unrestrained Emassa coursing through the waters below ground, there is no telling what that will attract."

Colby smirked. "So what, you plan on being our guard-cat?"

The slightest twitch of Fizzlewink's lower eyelids was the only indication of his annoyance. "I can become more than a mere house-cat boy."

Fizzlewink snapped his pointy-nailed fingers and transformed into a large black wildcat. A jaguar. Though he was black as the surrounding shadows, there remained a slight blueish hue and his same yellow eyes. He stalked up next to Colby and head-butted his leg before moving forward toward the observatory.

With Fizzlewink leading the way, the others followed behind, slinking between trees and stepping as soft as possible to remain quiet. Though they could have invoked invisibility shields, it would not have muffled any noise and would just as likely attract the wrong kind of attention. For this reason, they also released all but a minimal amount of Emassa from their internal stores. Anything lurking in the darkness might be able to sense their magic. And they all felt that there was indeed something out there.

More than once they stopped along the path through the trees. Two tour groups had already passed and now whatever they sensed out in the shadow-filled jungle, appeared to be stalking them. It was a sense of being watched that grew more intense the deeper they proceeded toward the observatory. But just as they finally reached their destination, the sensation eased and all but ceased. Feeling safe enough to do so, they all congregated on the west side of the ruins. They began looking for an entrance into the large domed structure atop the main building without rounding to the open yet exposed entrance on the east side.

The obvious doorways were either gated and locked or completely obstructed by fallen debris. Colby climbed up to the roof of the main structure before walking over to the dome and trying to look for another door. There was none so he had to risk moving around to the doorway at the front.

He motioned everyone to follow him up and around, this time they felt no concern about using invisibility. If there were people in the knoll out front, they would be far too concerned with the large black jaguar that headed around the other side to provide a distraction.

As he feared, Colby spotted a group of perhaps a dozen or more tourists looking his direction and taking photographs of the ruins. Without being prompted, a deep and menacing growl came from the south end of the structure, drawing gasps and muffled screams. Attention focused elsewhere, the tourists did not see or hear the movement of six figures as they crossed the threshold of the domed structure and lost hold on their spells.

Something in the building broke through their invisibility magic, but they could still touch the flow of Emassa. Colby could feel the others gathering as much power as they could store. He began a steady draw as well. Thought the Emassa was strong in the area for the present time, it was still shaky in this ruined building for some unknown reason and took concentration to maintain a hold on the lines of power. He continued his efforts to store that power as the six of them walked along the interior and headed around the sections of walls and toward the central chamber.

The walls were covered from floor to ceiling with intricate symbols, idols, and runes. Though they were well placed within the symbology of ancient Mayan stone craft, the runes were unmistakeable when knowing what to look for. The runes, as Colby walked past, glowed with a purple-white light just powerful enough to gain notice, but faded soon after he passed.

Once in the center of the room, Colby set a light sphere in the air above a pedestal located directly in the middle of the space. It rose to just below his waist and held a slight indentation in the center where something narrow might slide in; something thin and round, like a disk or a wheel.

Colby swung his backpack around and set it down at his feet. He shifted things around until he found the disk that he purchased at the market the day before. He wasn't sure why he bought it because it looked far from authentic Mayan artwork. Now that he looked closer, he could see the faint etchings that left hair-thin openings through the opposite side of the disk. Though he could not make out what they were, his instincts told him to place the disk in the slot on the pedestal. As soon as contact was made, a vibration emanated from the base of the cylindrical stone and spread outward toward the inner walls. A sheen of energy raced from the floor to ceiling in each gap of the walls, enclosing the chamber.

Rhea gasped and reached out to touch the force field that now held them in the room. It pulsated with power but did not hurt or send any surge of repulsion. Neither did it allow her hand to penetrate the barrier. As she pushed again, her hand went through as the wall collapsed. She turned to see Colby had removed the disk from the slot in the stone.

"Just checking," Colby said.

He replaced the disk and the energy wall was once again erected. Colby felt confident that this barrier was likely intended not to keep them held within, but to keep others out. Now he just had to figure out why and what his next step entailed. He looked at the artifact as he circled the central point of the room.

"Where did you say you got this thing?" Gary said. "It seems fishy to me."

"Like I said, some little kid offered to sell it, and I just felt I should buy it. When I looked for the kid, he or she was gone."

"He or She?" Shelly said. "Really cheese-head, you can't tell the difference by now?"

"Funny…NOT. I really wasn't paying attention, besides I was more interested in what happened to my change, seeing that the little snot ran off without giving me any."

Gary looked closer at the disk. "Or perhaps, they had done what they were supposed to by delivering this to you and then took off."

As they continued to discuss the possibilities, Jasper walked along the walls and began studying the runes hidden among the carvings. Every few feet he stopped to give closer consideration to what he was seeing before moving on to the next significant set. It wasn't until he finally noticed how quiet the room got, when he turned to find everyone staring at him.

"What?"

"You were mumbling. And it sounded kinda strange."

Jasper wasn't aware he was making any noise, at least not so anyone would hear. "I was just naming the runes etched into these glyphs on the walls. They're really well placed as far as hiding them, but they make no sense."

Colby walked up beside him and asked Jasper to point some out.

"Well, like these two here," he said and pointed to two runes about a hand apart. "You would never place these two beside each other in a spell. This one with the swirl and staff, it represents drawing from a well or pool. This other that looks like a broken stickman within a broken circle, it represents releasing something from oneself."

The blank expressions of his friends told Jasper they weren't getting it. He went on to show the other surrounding runes that each represented conflicting actions, materials, and conjunctions of runic magic.

"These would never be legal moves in Runes that we've been taught.

Not unless you wanted to throw the match. To place, these together would be committing suicide."

Silence followed until Shelly spoke out.

"Ok, that's just creepy. Maybe you're taking them too literal."

"I don't know Shelly," Colby said. "Jasper is by far the best at assembling runes."

Shelly shrugged and moved over toward the pedestal and kicked it out of frustration. It moved and light flickered for a moment in the room.

"What was that?" Colby said.

Shelly told them that the cylinder moved when she kicked it. Colby joined her and looked down to see a small gap at the base of the pedestal where the dirt shifted. He placed his hands on each side and twisted. It barely moved so he asked Jasper for help and together they were able to spin it forty-five degrees so that the disk was facing the east window and the light of the stars shone on its surface. The stars of Orion.

Light passed from the surface of the disk and into the thin etchings around the top. That light passed through and cast scattered images on the wall behind them, but they were somehow jumbled and made no sense. Colby tried to spin the disk to see if it would perhaps align the images but cut his finger in the process on the sharp edge.

Blood dripped from his finger as he lifted it to his mouth to ease the sting. He spit out the dirt from his filthy hands and used water from a canteen to rinse the cut. Rhea healed it quickly since it wasn't deep. As they focused on the cut, they were barely aware of the images dancing across the wall beginning to coalesce. Shelly noticed the blood that dropped from Colby's finger, being absorbed by the disk.

"Not suicide, sacrifice," Shelly said. "Give it more blood."

Colby looked at Shelly with wide eyes and gaping mouth. "Are you serious?"

Shelly explained how Mayan culture was wrapped up in blood sacrifices as many other ancient societies. That coupled with Jasper's reading of the runes on the wall began to make sense. He needed a sacrifice from himself to feed the magic in the disk. He stepped up to the artifact, and gliding his finger along the sharp edge, dripped more blood onto its surface. The offering was immediately soaked up by the thirsty artifact and the magic propelled from its circular face.

Across the wall was written a single line of runes, but they were unlike anything any of them had ever seen. Colby opened his journal to a blank page and copied the runes down in case they had to refer to them later. As he finished the last symbol, the magic blinked out followed by an ear-piercing shrill as a red glowing figure slammed against the wall of energy sealing the chamber. A seeker.

Gary squealed when he saw the menacing thing, pulsating with angry red light. He remembered all too well what it felt like to be touched by one of those things. He also remembered what it meant if there was one around. They were being tracked down.

"Someone sent that thing to find us."

Colby concurred. He knew that they could absorb the magic they used from hashtag spells. He was somewhat relieved that the magic from the disk was stronger and proving more difficult to break. The power was waning though as the kids watched as two more of the energy seeking creatures appeared at other entry points and began pounding on the shield. The walls flickered.

"We need to get out of here," Gary said.

Colby ran around the room pushing people together toward the pedestal. He told them to all hold hands as he placed one of his own on Jasper's shoulder and the other on the disk. He concentrated on the hotel room and only hoped Fizz was able to sense his escape and soon follow from wherever he currently hid. Colby squeezed his eyes shut and pushed Emassa into his teleport spell.

He strained under the effort. The magic of the disk or the structure itself was hindering his magic. He looked to Jasper, who nodded his approval, knowing what Colby needed. He required more power. Separately, Colby and Jasper could store more power inside themselves than the others combined, Colby more so than Jasper. Together they could power an immense spell when cut off from the Emassa. Somehow this shield from the disk, coupled with the strangeness of the structure that dispelled their invisibility upon entering, were together crippling his effort to pull more power from the flows. Colby had to rely on what was available.

Colby tapped into Jasper's energy and joined it with his own. He immediately felt a wave of euphoria flood his every cell. He had never felt anything like it, the joining of one's magic center with another's was intoxicating. As much as he wanted to enjoy the moment and from the look Jasper was giving him he enjoyed it just as much, the faltering shield around the chamber nagged for immediate attention.

Refocusing the blissful magic, Colby shoved it into his spell. It was still not enough, he needed more to overcome the structure's dampening of Emassa. He asked the others for their help and they gladly provided what he needed. The extra boost from his five companions pushed through the barriers against his spell and in a blinding flash of purple light, the chamber emptied and the magic force field evaporated. The seekers entered the chamber and wailed at the loss of their quarry.

As much energy as Colby required to get out of the chamber, he didn't have enough to get them safely to the hotel. He had only enough to get them a few hundred yards away from the observatory and landed them on an open trail surrounded by jungle. There was no light, the stars were obscured by the cover of the trees growing over the path and sweeping down on them. The howling of the seekers reminded them they had no time to catch their breath as they forced themselves up and tried to replenish their depleted reserves of magical fuel. Another wail of anger, this time closer, pushed them into a run away from the observatory, but they were unsure of what direction.

As they ran through the trees down the overgrown trail, Colby heard a familiar growl ahead and saw Fizzlewink the jaguar at the trailhead and he had company. Pace.

"Quickly," Pace said, his voice shouting at a whispers volume. "They are closing. We need to get out of the park and back to the hotel."

Colby panted as he reached Pace and Fizzlewink. "I'm spent. We all are, I haven't the power to transport and can't gather enough that quickly to move everyone."

"Time for me to break one of my own rules," Pace said.

Pace raised his hand and purple haze flowed from his palm. It swirled around the entire group and engulfed them. The deep glowing cloud of purple energy twisted into a vortex and swept everyone up in an instant and carried them back to the hotel property border. As soon as they crossed over into the grounds of the resort, the cloud vanished and they found themselves standing on the manicured lawns behind their hotel.

They followed the lead of Pace, who motioned for them to all walk the rest of the way. They turned at the wailing of three seekers standing just behind the trees at the border, unable to pass an invisible barrier.

Pace smiled. "They have no power here. This is a protected place." He looked at the sunken eyes and weary faces of the six youngsters and smiled deeper. "Now off to bed, we'll talk more in the morning."

Colby was already passed out on the lush grass.

Chapter Twenty-Six

Colby felt an emptiness upon waking that he had never felt before. It was a deep-seated hunger, not unlike a desperate need to eat, but more ingrained in his chest than his stomach. He realized he was completely void of Emassa. Ever since he began storing the power required to fuel his magic, he took every opportunity to 'top off his tank'. His body was becoming so used to it that he sensed it now required the flows as much as he needed food to nourish himself. He reached out instinctively to feed his requirement only to find the Emassa blocked.

He jumped from his bed, too quickly, and nearly tumbled into the wall as the dizziness took him. Colby slumped to the floor beside the bed and tried to clear his head. A tittering in his ears alerted him to Fizzlewink's presence.

"Foolish."

"Morning Fizz."

"Thoughtless."

"Fine thanks, and you."

"Reckless."

"Oh yes, I would love some breakfast."

"Inconsiderate."

Colby sighed. "Give it a rest."

Fizzlewink grunted and hopped down off the chair by the window. He walked over to a tray by the door and carried it over to Colby, dumping it without ceremony on the floor in front of him.

"Eat, and for heaven's sake take a shower. We'll be in the back courtyard when you and the other's are ready."

Colby began shoveling food into his mouth. "Who's we?"

"Pace, myself, and that fraud professor of yours."

Colby could hear the distaste in Fizz's voice for Rigel, but he could almost feel the sting when he spat out the man's name. He got up and headed to the bathroom as he finished the last of his bacon and toast. His stomach stopped rumbling in displeasure, but he was hungry yet for something else. Though he was rested, the emptiness of his core where he stored his Emassa caused him to remain exhausted in a completely internal way. His innards still felt asleep somehow.

After his shower and getting dressed, Colby picked up his things and noticed his journal, once belonging to his father, was lying open on the desk. It was turned to the page where he copied the runes projected on the wall in the observatory. He didn't remember leaving it open when he went to bed. He didn't remember going to bed either.

Colby closed and locked the leather bound tome and placed it in his backpack before leaving his room. He made his way through the hotel, admiring the colorful murals of ancient scenes painted on the walls. When he stopped to look at one closer, he discovered, hidden in the paintings, familiar runes of protection delicately and deliberately placed around the depictions of ancient Mayan activities. They were everywhere he looked now that he was aware of what to search out. Impressive.

When he made his way to the back courtyard, he found the others already gathered and waiting for him. None of them seemed as inwardly depleted as himself. He wondered at how that could be. Without being able to touch the flows and use his abilities he couldn't be certain, but he suspected they all had refilled their core with Emassa.

"You look like moldy cheese," Shelly said. She smiled with only a hint of mischief in the crinkle of her nose. She moved aside to make room for him on the couch where she sat with Bruce.

Where had he been, Colby wondered. He had seen very little of Bruce since they arrived. Then again, Colby was well occupied with other things, but he expected that Bruce would have been trailing behind Shelly like a guard dog. When he asked, all Bruce said was that he had some shopping and other things to do in Cancun. He said his good mornings and left to go get the van ready that they would be using today.

"Are we going somewhere?" Colby asked.

Pace smiled and handed a bluish crystal stone to Colby. As soon as Colby touched it, a surge of Emassa siphoned out of the rock and into his body. He felt his head rush like he was drinking a milkshake too fast. Much like brain-freeze, but in the base of his head and down his spine to his chest. Colby squeezed every last drop out of the stone as it began to crumble under the pressure of his hands. When the rock was completely dry, it broke apart and fell through his fingers as he sat back.

"Better?" Pace asked and laughed. "After discovering your three shadows last evening, I felt it necessary for the first time in quite a long while to activate the protection spells around this area. Unfortunately, they already breached the main complex but the other outlying areas are well guarded against those vile things."

"You know what they are then?" Gary asked.

"Oh I should think so. I helped create them."

Pace raised his hand against the protests and questions.

"It was a very long time ago, and unfortunately they have been twisted into something other than intended. When they were first brought into this world, their only purpose was to locate and identify those gifted with an affinity to magic. Being seen was never part of the process, let alone to engage or hunt those they identified."

Pace shook his head and sighed.

"As is often the case with stories and histories over the millennia, things get twisted to the story teller's point of view. This is also the case with what the original use for the seekers where. Someone has manipulated the spells to call them forth and changed their primary objectives."

"So someone called them, does that mean this person also controls them?" Colby asked.

"Oh yes, and that someone needs relative proximity to do so unless they have multiple masters."

"More than one person could have control over those things?" Gary asked.

"More likely joint control. A group of individuals could have joined the magic to call them forth, thereby increasing the control over them and the range at which they could venture from their masters. You see they have no magic of their own. They require a steady feed of power from whoever called them forth."

"But these things seem able to feed off of our hashtag magic. It happened on Halloween to Gary."

Pace explained that was a different use of the magic, one that connected their spells directly to the flow of Emassa and did not come directly from their own core power. By not linking with their spells, they could easily be broken, absorbed, or taken control of by another with the skill to do so. The seekers could absorb the magic as a source of energy for themselves because it was not tied to an individual.

"So where are we going anyway?" Colby asked. "Bruce said he was getting the van."

"To the place you identified in your journal," Rigel said. He stood off to the side of the patio, brooding.

"You read my book?" Colby said. "How?"

Rigel smirked. "You left it unlocked my boy. You really should take better care if you insist on not accepting my help."

Colby immediately reached for his wrist and was relieved to find his father's watch where it belonged. Hearing that he passed out on the lawn of the hotel before making it inside, Colby was more embarrassed to hear that Rigel carried him up and put him in his bed. He realized that was when Rigel had his chance to take his father's journal, but he didn't. He read what he was able based on the section that Colby had failed to lock, but he hadn't stolen it or his father's watch. Colby nodded to Rigel with a reserved thank you and an understanding passed between them.

"Alright, so where is this place? We couldn't read the runes."

"Of course not boy," Fizz said. "They aren't the same symbols used for spells. They are runes for language."

"What cat-latin or something?" Gary laughed at his own joke along with the others, except Fizzlewink.

"No wise guy, Nefslamian."

Fizzlewink explained, with Pace's permission, that the runes they encountered were a verbal map or directions to a city outside the area, but nearby. A city called Uxmal, where they would require the knowledge of an ancient sorceress. The runes said they needed to seek the House of the Witch near the Pyramid of the Magician.

***

They arrived at the city of Uxmal ruins in about two and a half hours. They encountered less and less traffic as they approached the area. The city lies in a deeper part of the jungle covered Yucatan that was not pillaged as badly by the conquering Spanish. There was indeed very few tourists and not many locals about either. Being warned of the area being unprotected by the spells near Chichén Itzá, everyone was glad they could maintain a connection to the flows of Emassa. That is until they discovered there were little to no areas that contained more than a trickle of connection to the power this far out.

Pace explained that because of the proximity to the Gulf of Mexico, the underground rivers became often polluted with salt water, which had a negative effect on the flow of magic. The moist ocean air that blew in from the west didn't help either. He assured them that they would be far enough away from the seekers that they should be safe. Nobody else knew where they were headed, so it was unlikely they could be located easily. Colby, like the others, had taken advantage of the time they spent in the van, connecting to flows of energy as they passed along the heavily jungled roads.

Upon arrival, they exited the van and it dawned on Colby that they would have to figure out what to tell Bruce. During the drive, he was surrounded by a sound dampening spell by Fizz, so he was unaware of their conversations.

After talking to Shelly, she convinced him that she could keep Bruce distracted by having Rigel lead her on a tour of the ruins. Colby was worried that he might need his sister there since it seemed the six of the youngest in their group were somehow connected. Shelly told him that if something came up to text her. Colby would soon realize that the benefits of being out where people seldom ventured, also meant there would be a problem with mobile signals.

Pace left the others to explore and look for what they came to find. Returning to his rules of non-involvement, he thought it best that he find a place to observe rather than interfering more that he already was. That left Colby and his classmates venturing out toward where Pace suggested they seek out the House of the Witch, with Fizzlewink the cat trotting close beside.

There may have been few to no other people about, but why risk them spotting a little blue man. A cat could be explained away like a stray looking for a handout.

They were amazed at how more preserved this area was compared to Chichén Itzá. Where the first place of their exploration was overrun and falling apart, which in respect to how old the site was that would be expected, but this site seemed like a newly build city in comparison.

The painted walls and glyphs were vibrant and in good condition. The carvings were far more artistic and intricate than those found in the other ruins. What Colby found most amazing was how easily he spotted the inlaid runes everywhere he looked. Jasper was proud of him pointing them out first.

Again they faced runes they could not interpret. Jasper took a notepad out and took charcoal rubs where he could. Unlike their previous location, here in Uxmal there were few roped off areas and they could traverse any path they came across. Colby allowed himself to be instinctually guided along one such path when he felt a tug on his magic.

At the end of the winding path, they encountered a moderately sized structure that besides being well preserved, radiated with an unmistakable energy. Unmistakable to Colby, that is to say because it was encased in a special field of energy that warped time and had a familiar family signature. As they approached, Colby noticed Fizzlewink take off around the building and off to the other ruins. He didn't understand that little man half the time so Colby paid his actions little attention.

Colby headed toward the building and stood at the barrier of time. He passed through without using magic and found nothing extraordinary on the other side. It was a ruin of an ancient building, nothing more. He walked back out to the others and decided to use the hashtag spell he saved from the time he entered his father's study. After pushing the Emassa, fueled spell free of his hand, a portal opened. Swirls of purple and red mists spun around the event horizon while the center opened up to reveal a well kept and recently built appearing version of the same building. Smiling at the result, Colby headed through urging the others to follow.

On the inside of the barrier, the outside world still looked aged and deserted. That was how this time bubble seemed to work, somewhat different from the one surrounding his father's study which slowed time to a near standstill.

"This spell somehow seems to displace time altogether differently than the study at home."

"Not exactly star child," came an elderly yet somehow familiar voice.

There was that name again Colby thought as he turned and face the source of the voice. A middle-aged and attractive woman stood in the middle doorway to the structure. She looked at the five kids standing there before her with an appraising eye.

"There should be six of you. Not five, never five." She turned and walked back into the building.

The kids followed behind her, bumping into each other in their haste. They entered a large room, filled with dozens of aromas emanating from the many vats of liquids boiling over hot coals. There was no fire they noticed. The coals glowed with heat but not from a natural source. The mixture of smells became overwhelming and they all began coughing.

The woman frowned at the noise the kids were making and waved her hand. The room filled with a gentle cool breeze that pushed the noxious smoke from the boiling potions out the nearby window. She turned back toward the kids and sat down on a stool.

"Where is the sixth?"

Colby looked at her through squinted eyes. "Are you the Witch of Uxmal?"

The woman laughed and wriggled her finger. "Is that what they are calling me in your time?" She looked back at the kids. "I was a Goddess to some, soothsayer to others, and perhaps a witch to the rest I suppose."

Rhea stepped forward, holding a pamphlet she picked up when they entered the park. "It says here that you were the mother of nature or some fertility goddess."

The woman nodded and smiled. "Closer to the mark." She looked closer at Rhea. "You are the healer?"

Rhea nodded and stepped back, humbled by the presence of a goddess.

The goddess looked at each of the children in turn, calling them out for what they were naturally gifted with. She looked at Gary and called him out as the manipulator of mass and energy. Darla she winked at and called the temptress and muse, one who could compel actions and the will of others. She raised an eyebrow at Jasper, who stood next to Colby, hand on his shoulder.

"You are the vessel of strength and valor. A warrior and faithful friend." She tilted her head and smiled. "You've been tested recently…and passed."

She set her eyes on Colby. "You are the key and the lock. The means to and end or the path to a new beginning." She sighed and turned away. "Where is the sixth? You never answered my question."

Colby cleared his throat. "My sister is out distracting a non-magic user from discovering our purpose here."

The goddess chuckled. "You brought a mundane here with you? Interesting…"

"Excuse me, but how is it you speak English so well?" Darla asked.

"I have a connection to the outside my dear, I have always been both inside and outside, forever caught in flux and displaced."

"I don't get it?" Darla whispered to Rhea.

"Let's just say, that should I step outside this bubble now, I would soon fade, replacing what was with what is." She got up from her stool and sniffed the air. She pushed past the kids and stood facing a six foot by three foot pink crystal that was embedded in the wall behind them.

"Speaking of one who would call me a witch," she said to no one, in particular. She turned to Colby. "How is it your return should bring with it the dwarf mage? He never accompanies the star children."

Colby immediately knew she was referring to Fizzlewink, but he focused more on the words she used calling out his 'return'.

"What do you mean return here?"

The goddess huffed and moved around the room. "Six always come, six always fail. It is an endless cycle of futility. Never five…this is odd. But the presence of the dwarf mage is new."

She moved around her room, ignoring the kids, for the most part. When Colby moved to block her path, she turned to him.

"Come back when there are six."

She waved her arm and the kids all felt themselves pushed by invisible hands out the door and back through the portal. It closed as soon as Colby exited.

"Best get Shelly here," Gary said.

Colby pulled out his phone to text her and noticed he had no signal. All jungle and no cell towers. They agreed they needed to go find her.

Chapter Twenty-Seven

Trekking back they way they came, the five kids ended up on another path that led them to a towering rectangular pyramid. It had a single steep stairway that led up the front to a small structure on top with a single door. As interesting as the old ruin appeared, and again in better condition than the Pyramid of Kukulcán, seeing Fizzlewink standing at the base of the steps transforming from cat to man stole their attention.

They stood at the entrance to the clearing before the pyramid, which clearly had some spell covering it from the glow they could all see every time Fizzlewink approached the stairs. He started again for the stairs, only to get thrown back and landing on his butt. The frazzled blue man stood and began chanting, followed by the illumination of runes around his hands. He threw the spell at the barrier to no avail. He finally noticed the kids watching him when he heard muffled laughter.

Turning to the kids heading his direction he grumbled. "Did you get anything useful out of the old witch?"

"We have to find Shelly and go back. All six of us need to go into that time bubble I think before she'll help us."

"Figures," Fizzlewink said.

Colby looked at the frustration on his face and knowing that he was the dwarf mage the goddess referred to, he placed a deeper connection between the two.

"She called you the dwarf mage."

Fizzlewink snorted. "Indeed."

Rhea started reading from her pamphlet allowed for the others to hear. It read of a dwarf mage, hatched from an egg by the Goddess herself and that he built her this city where life was renewed and a new people flourished. Sometime later, the inhabitants disappeared and the city was left abandoned except for the dwarf mage who, it was said, could be seen wandering the ruins searching for his lost people. His sadness turning the pigments of his skin blue from the grief.

Fizzlewink stood in a huff. "Hatched indeed…my people did not disappear, they were slaughtered. I could do nothing to save them from the power of the ones who killed them out of petty jealousy and a need for revenge."

"So your story about your arrival here, your city disappearing and all the history you taught us. That was all a lie?" Colby was tempering his anger with the empathy he managed to feel for Fizzlewink's tragic past, but he was simmering with a feeling of betrayal.

"Half truths. Look around…the city I knew disappeared centuries ago. All I have left is locked away in that pyramid. I so hoped she would have given you the way to get me back in."

Fizzlewink explained how the Nefslama, the original ones who came to this realm, began to experiment with magic and through some practice were able to split their magic. They did this to avoid some cosmic moral compass that prevented them from succeeding in certain spells and rituals that were both dangerous and considered evil. This is how the Shizumu truly came to be. They were the side of a Nefslama that could do anything and everything they wanted without restraint. A separate consciousness.

The Shizumu eventually sought out and destroyed their own better half for fear of being rejoined and restrained. They didn't stop there. They sent beast to hunt down and destroyed any whole Nefslama they found, including the children. The Dreggs. Those few who managed to survive, hid themselves away until they found the means to restrain the Shizumu.

Colby was shocked to find out the reason Fizzlewink held such seething hatred for the Dreggs. It made sense now and he felt horrified for speaking out for them. He was still confused though at why they had not attacked Fizzlewink or him and his friends. There must be something more, but as he tried to think more about it something else intruded on his train of thought. How the Shizumu were restrained.

"The shield of Orion," Colby realized.

Fizzlewink was impressed. "Yes. The six remaining elders and six remaining children combined their magic to create the shield but at a great cost. The spell did something unexpected. It absorbed the children and it was their energy that became the shield that blocks out the full power of Emassa. It surrounds the planet, but it is failing."

"What happened to the adults?" Darla asked.

Fizzlewink shrugged. "I have only kept track of four of the six."

"Pace?" Colby said.

"Yes, and Rigel."

"You knew all of this and didn't say anything? What was your plan, keep us in the dark until what…you could break back into your house in the jungle?" Purple licks of energy whipped around Colby's hands.

"I hoped that none of this would happen. When Rigel showed up and then Pace contacted me, I knew I had no choice but to aid them in pushing you on this path."

Colby stood in silent shock as the gravity of the situation began to settle in his mind. They were tools to the Nefslama. A means to keep themselves safe from their own evil sides. Now he understood the reason Rigel was always so full of questions and showed up out of the blue. He was being manipulated from the beginning. Thinking back, he realized there was something else.

"Who are the other two pure Nefslama you know?"

"The witch, but she is not what she once was. That spell of hers has her scattered through time and is little help."

"And the other?" Colby feared he already knew the answer and anger mixed with hurt seated deep in his heart. "Tell me."

"Jarrod Stevens, your father. His true name is Saiph."

Colby erupted, blowing everyone off their feet. Emassa flowed off of him as a dam burst and pushed everything out of him. Grief filled cries of anguish shook the trees, sending birds to the skies in retreat. The birds halted in mid-flight as time stopped. Not the imperceptibly slow movement that Colby managed in the cavern of the Sacred Cenote, but a full stop.

Colby gasped for air and looked around at the faces of his friends, frozen in a frightened shock as his pent-up emotions exploded in all directions. They were stuck in the middle of trying to reach out to him, even in his display of raw power they wanted to help. Jasper, most of all, must understand, Colby though as he stepped up to his friend. He reached out with his index finger and plucked a tear that escaped his friend's eye and had stopped on its journey down Jasper's face. There was magic in that tear, in spite of the saltiness.

As he continued to look around, trying to put aside his feelings, he felt at peace and wondered what it would be like to stay like this, frozen in time. He could stay here, feeling nothingness and everything at once. The light from the sun was pure and sat in the sky among the stars. He could see everything clearly now that the atoms in the atmosphere could not scatter and refract. When he focused, he could see the tiny universe within each and every fiber of reality that surrounded him and wondered what it would feel like to crush one.

He could, he felt, destroy anything and everything using this power. He could be the one manipulating and seeking his own goals. Colby Stevens could rule everything and answer to nobody. He sighed. That wasn't who he was. Regardless of what cards he was being dealt, Colby would play the game. He did realize though, that he could change the rules. Not cheat per say, but he could learn to win with enough time. And he now realized he had all the time he needed.

Colby walked back to where he first burst out in a fit of rage. He looked down to find the worn leather journal laying on the ground. Another lock was open. He knelt down and perused the pages, taking in everything they offered and his heart lightened. He found something to replace the grief and heartache of knowing his father set him on this quest for another purpose. To manipulate his fate and that of his friends.

Colby closed the book and looking out to notice Shelly and Rigel stopped mid-stride coming from the jungle, he locked the book and put it away. Looking around, he realized how much Emassa he expended in his outburst, but it too was frozen in his spell. He decided to try something new.

He began pulling on the Emassa around him, calling it back inside. It was difficult, but as he eased up on forcing it and began to simply coax the power back, it flowed more easily back to him. His time spell began to reverse and things started moving again. As the last of his power came back, a final pop of energy snapped in on him and time was back. Colby sat on the ground with his pack in his lap, looking at the others and smiling.

"Ok…WTF just happened," Jasper said. He reached out as he approached Colby and pulled his friend to his feet.

"Just a minor outburst." Colby shrugged. "Shelly's coming, we should head back to see a witch about a shield."

"Seriously?" Darla said. "Didn't you hear what the blue furball said about this shield business. It didn't end so well for those first kids and they were full-blown Nefslama."

Shelly walked up at that moment to hear the end of Darla's sentence. When Darla gave the condensed version of what they found out, Shelly was ticked. She spun around at Rigel and smacked him across the face.

Rigel took the slap and said nothing while Shelly screamed at him for several minutes and used a more colorful vocabulary then Colby realized she had. Once she took a breath Rigel held up a hand.

"It isn't entirely as it seems. I have never liked the methods we used since the first blunder that took our children from us. I admit for a time when we attempted to fix our mistake over and over, I was lost in my own grief at losing my own child to the spell. I somehow hoped that if we could fix what went wrong and get our little ones back, the means would justify the end. I came to realize my delusion and have done nothing but try to find another way. That is why I wanted your father's journal.

"I believed he might have found another way. You must believe me when I say that there is no way I would allow that old spell to be tried again. Our children are gone and there is no bringing them back. The only thing left to them is the energy that feeds the shield and even that has become diluted over time with the energy of the children that followed. Even if we were to put more energy into the shield now, it would eventually fail again.

"Your modern science has already discovered it and call it a third toroidal field. It isn't long before they find some way to try and tap its power. The Russians already have Tesla towers that pose a threat. If your father found another way, it's in that book of his."

Colby slung his backpack over his shoulder and out of Rigel's view.

"He has a theory, but I won't share it until I have the entire book unlocked. There are still a few locks left and we have other things to worry about at the moment."

"Like what?" Gary said.

"Well for one, we have to figure out who is sending seekers after us and why. We can assume it is Shizumu, but not how many and what their plans for us are. I think that since they haven't killed us yet, they want something. We just have to figure out what without them capturing us and forcing it out of us."

Shelly was more composed, but she still glared daggers at Rigel. She agreed they needed to keep him close for now, along with the dwarf mage, Fizzlewink. She reluctantly took up the rear as they all trekked back toward the House of the Witch.

Shelly caught up to Colby, noticing he was somehow different after she and Rigel rejoined him and the others.

"What has happened to you?"

Colby explained to Shelly what he experienced including the feelings of betrayal and hurt that propelled his magic to something new. He already had some affinity to the time spell around his father's study as well as the one at the House of the Witch. His outburst did something new to him and he began to get a clearer picture of what was to come. Though he didn't go into detail about the new information in the most recently reveal a section of the journal, he assured Shelly that their father did not betray them.

"I think that this is all part of the test," Colby said. "If I hadn't felt those emotions and had the sudden release of power, I don't think the lock would have opened."

"You pulled the entire spell back? What like you reversed it?"

"Not exactly. I sort of rewound select moments in time and space. I reabsorbed the magic."

"Well you seem different. A good kind of different," she said.

"I feel different. It's like I've hit the Control ALT and Delete buttons on my internal computer."

"So you rebooted yourself?"

"I guess so."

They walked along and caught up with the others. Colby smiled at the frustrated look on Fizz's face as he tired of answering Jasper's questions.

"So if you were hatched, why aren't you a duck?" Jasper asked.

Colby laughed. As smart as Jasper was in some ways, he was still sort of thick when it came to others. He was poking a bear, or at least a little cat-like blue man who could become a bear.

Fizzlewink explained that it was a metaphor. The Goddess created his kind by combining her own Nefslama blood with the essence of animal nature. Fizzlewink was mostly Nefslama, but the part that allowed him to transform into any animal came from that bond. Unlike the hashtag spells Colby and the others could use to change into an illusion of an animal, Fizzlewink actually becomes the animal.

"I still think you were hatched from a big blue egg," Jasper said. He was purposely teasing Fizzlewink.

"It is just a story that changed over time just like the great flood and Noah. That story has been told in so many ways and is part of nearly every religion that has existed since man made up stories to explain the unexplainable."

"And why are you blue?"

"An accident bore from a misunderstanding. I don't want to talk about that."

"You mean the story of the flood and Noah's ark isn't true?" Darla asked.

"All great myths are based on a shred of truth, but over time they change with the telling. The problem with much of your human religions is they started out as verbal history and like any great story, changed with each telling. By the time they were recorded in stone and then eventually books, many things again changed due to mistranslations and man's ignorance."

"You mean like how misogynistic the modern religions are and have been for centuries?" Shelly said. "Men writing what they want to keep women in their place. Like we are property and some fragile thing that needs a protector."

Colby looked at Rigel with a shrug of apology. He was Shelly's current target and when she climbed up on her soapbox, he found it best to find somewhere else to be. He wanted to stay out of this argument, but he realized they were missing someone.

"Speaking of protectors, where's Bruce?"

"We got separated when he stopped to water a tree," Shelly said. "He can't have gone too far, I have the keys to the van."

When they made their way back to the house, they found Bruce. He was in the company of a dozen seekers and Mr. Bodine.

253

Chapter Twenty-Eight

"Glad you could join us Mr. Steven's. I was worried I'd have to send a few associates out to retrieve you?" Mr. Bodine was standing near the barrier that shielded the home of the Goddess.

Bruce stood near the entrance, flanked by a seeker on each side. He looked at Shelly and then Colby, but gave no clue as to what he was thinking. He had no magic as far as Colby could tell, so the seekers were of no real threat to him. He wondered what the guy was thinking about all this.

"Are you ok Bruce?" Colby asked.

Bruce nodded but said nothing and his expression changed little.

"Oh he's just fine. As a matter of fact, I think he has something for me?" Mr. Bodine turned to Bruce and held out his hand.

Bruce tossed over a chunk of pink crystal. It looked to be of the same quartz crystal that was inside the witch's house. He looked back at Colby and the others and smirked.

"Bruce, what is this all about?" Shelly said.

Bruce's expression hardened.

"You magic brats and your stupid school. Always so holier than thou when you are nothing but demons and witches. I found out what that place was about years ago when they rejected my application. I broke in one night to find a ritual happening in the basement. When I told my mother, she didn't believe me and sent me to a hospital.

"When I got out I played stupid, but I knew what was going on in there and vowed to one day watch the place burn to the ground. When Mr. Bodine came to offer me a way to help put an end to your kind, I took him up on it. You see I've been spying for him this whole time. Once I saw what the cheese-poof there did to that bus on his birthday, I shared what I learned. How do you think you even got that job at MacroTECH, your sweet disposition?"

Shelly, in her anger, sent a blast of energy from a spell in her watch. It shot forward only to be absorbed by one of the seekers beside him. She tried again and again hoping to sneak a blast past them, but it was useless. Bruce laughed at her, making her that much angrier.

"Save your strength Shelly, we have other things to focus on." Colby watched as the crystal in Mr. Bodine's hand began to glow. He moved it toward the outside of the time barrier surrounding the house and it began to fluctuate.

As time flickered inside the bubble, Colby could see flashes of images within. He saw the Goddess exit her home and move toward where Mr. Bodine was standing. As the power from the pink shard broken from the present day mass inside the building grew more intense, the time bubble wavered under the stress. Mr. Bodine gave a silent command to the seekers who moved toward the barrier and reached out to touch the field of energy.

They were able to begin absorbing the power. All but the two who stood guard over Bruce were taking the energy of the Goddess's spell and breaking her barrier of protection. She stood inside, now partially visible as time and space reset in the area. Her face was filled with anger instead of surprise or shock.

When the last of the spell fell apart, the Goddess reached out and snatched the crystal from Mr. Bodine's hand. She took the power it gained from destroying her spell and pulled it within herself. She turned her anger at the seekers that were edging their way toward her. She was a beacon of power and they were starving for it. These twisted beings were resurrected with misguided intent and she was not going to allow that.

The first one to reach her thrust out its arms in an attempt to draw the Goddess into an energy-depleting embrace. It didn't stand a chance. The magic that they craved was being used against them. One by one, the seekers descended on her with single-minded purpose, to steal her magic and make it theirs. The magic from the crystal, however, the magic she took inside herself, was different. It was a magic she crafted over the millennia left to herself inside that time sealed house.

She had regrets and guilt. It festered and maddened her over time and she eventually had to find a way to release it. She had been storing it in her crystal. Time was relative and mysterious. While inside the bubble, things didn't seem to change. She used the crystal embedded in the wall as a scrying stone, but that was in a moment of time frozen and forgotten to the rest of the world. In the continuing stream of time and space that existed beyond her spell, the crystal remained unused in the house and was growing with the negative energies she had fed it in the interlaced time stream.

The power became so strong that even the locals and tourists began to stop visiting the ruins of her home. Being a Shizumu, devoid of all goodness, the creature possessing Mr. Bodine would not have sensed the power in the stone Bruce threw at him. And Bruce, so filled with hate, was drawn to the large rock as a bee is to pollen. Her time to strike was now.

As the seekers fought for the best position from which to drain her power, they all made contact and she let go of the power from the stone. It burst free from her and pushed through the seekers, dissolving them. They thrashed and shrilled in agony as the bonds of magic and reality split them apart. When at last the light and power waned, the seekers collapsed in on themselves. Each one was replaced by a deep red ruby that fell to the ground where they once hovered.

Fizzlewink ran to the Goddess and helped her sit up. He held her head against his chest and rocked her as she visibly aged in a matter of moments. Her breathing became ragged and she whispered something to Fizzlewink. He got up and helped her to lean against the side of a large stone.

"Colby, she wishes to see you before she…"

Colby ran to her side and asked her what he could do to help. He tried giving her some of his stored magic. She refused.

"I am fractured, star child. You have already changed things by twisting your destiny in a new direction." She looked to see the others joining Colby. She waved them closer.

"All six are here. The star children always come to me you see. Always six, never five." She looked at Shelly and smiled. "You are very much like me I think. I see fire in you, spirit guide. I think we would lock horns if I were a few millennia younger." She coughed as she tried to laugh and smile.

She reached down to her chest where she wore a simple stone pendant in the shape of a tear drop. It was no bigger than Colby's thumb. She pulled it over her head and held in between both hands.

"I am fractured. You must take this part of me and return it to my current self. The part of me in this fabric of time."

"Where do I find you?"

She smiled and shook her head. "You will find me, have no doubt. I will not know who I am until you put me back together." She took a deep breath and began to shatter. Light poured out through the fissures forming along her entire body. The pendant soaked up the light as the body crumbled to dust.

"I am fractured," was heard on the breeze that blew the dust and carried her away.

For many moments, the kids all sat there in silence. Having just witness the death of an actual Goddess was mind blowing to say the least as Jasper had described it. Their contemplation was interrupted by the howling and screaming coming from where Mr. Bodine had been sent flying minutes before. They turned to see Fizzlewink attacking the man who seemed at a complete loss and in disarray.

"Fizz, get back," Colby said as he ran over.

Colby stopped before Mr. Bodine and looked at him closely. He could not see any trace of the Shizumu inside. It had escaped. He turned to look at the house and found that Bruce was gone as well. Turning back again to Mr. Bodine, he found that the man had fainted and was laying back on the ground. He was covered in scratches and was beginning to bruise where he was hit by Fizzlewink.

Colby called Rhea over to heal what she could and led a reluctant Fizzlewink away from the object of his anger. Once he was well enough away from the others, Colby sat down with Fizz and asked him what was he thinking.

"I was lashing out. I never stopped to think the Shizumu would have left him. That thing is responsible for what happened here. And now she is gone. The only one who could get me back into my home."

Colby wasn't sure what was so important about his pyramid. Sure it was his home, but it was old and dusty. Whatever he left there was long gone. Colby sensed no time distortion in the spell that sealed it from anyone with magic from entering.

"She is not gone, you know. She has an incarnation or something in the here and now. We just have to find her."

Fizzlewink looked up and then away toward his pyramid. The top of it could be seen peeking above the trees even from a seated position on the ground. "If we find her. And even if we do, there is no telling if she'll know how to get me back inside."

"Fizz," Colby said. "What is so damn important about that pyramid. What is inside that you need so badly you would lead me, my family, my friends…on such a dangerous path?"

It took only moment for Fizz to answer. "My wife."

Colby found out from Fizz that his wife was placed under an enchantment that kept her locked away inside that pyramid in an eternal sleep. In order to gain his cooperation millennia ago, the Goddess cast the spell and would only release it when Orion's shield was restored or the Shizumu were destroyed. Now Colby understood why Fizzlewink called her a witch. He probably started that story himself.

Fizz was also hurting over the loss of the Goddess as well. She was for all intents and purposes his mother. She created him and his kind, a hybrid race of Nefslama. Her hope of recreating the race dashed to dust when the Shizumu sent the Dreggs to wipe all but Fizz and his wife from the planet. They couldn't get to his wife and Fizz was elsewhere in the world hoping to find the next star children.

Now the next six children required to be sacrificed for the sake of a shield that surrounded the Earth and keep the magic at bay were finally assembled. Only they weren't going to go through with the plan as prescribed.

With heavy hearts over the passing of the Goddess and her knowledge, they picked up Mr. Bodine and helped him out to the van and were heading back to the hotel to checkout and then go home.

***

Pace sat alone at the top of a pyramid in the center of Uxmal. He watched everything that transpired and couldn't help but feel hope. Six star children accompanied by the Nefslama original Rigel, and a shape-shifting dwarf-mage were all headed off on a new path in their combined destinies. The shield would get weaker still, that much he had no doubt. Perhaps there was another way. Perhaps his own words would prove wrong. It seemed that the young Colby Stevens was determined to change his fate, after all.

He needed to inform the others…

Hashtag Magic

Blue Screen of Death

Control+ALT+Delete

Web of Trolls (Winter 2015)

Chronicles of Aurderia

The Balance

River of Souls

Queen of Shadow

Follow on Facebook and Twitter:

http://fb.com/Author-JStevenYoung

@jstevenyoung

Website: http://jstevenyoung.com